*"With all the people in the city going about their daily
lives, who would have thought that with just one look,
you were about to turn my world upside down?"*

If someone told me ten years ago that I'd be
spending my working day in a nine to six shop at
my age, I would have laughed and walked away with
my head held high. Well, doesn't life come around
and smack you with smugness?

Yes, I am indeed stuck in that very job. How the
hell did I let this happen? Where did I go so wrong,
in what was meant to be a walk in the park towards
a high-end career? Every day I feel like walking into
a group meeting where we all share our feelings
about how we managed to fuck up what was meant
to be easy.

I'm a thirty-two-year-old whose ambition it
once was to become a successful artist. I was going
to create elegance for a living, and see my life's
work being displayed in the Tate Modern.

"I was going to be proud, goddammit."

Yet here I am talking to you, a sales desk, thinking I'm in a group discussion about life!

My God, now I'm talking to myself.

Chapter 1

S top watching the time! It's not going to make the end of the day come any faster.

It felt as though Megan Ashton was watching a clock with no batteries while waiting for her shift to end. It was almost the end of the working week, as her friends who were in office jobs kept telling her, and it was rare to be blessed with a weekend off in her career. A glorious five o'clock finish and not having to go back until Monday. Days like that didn't come around too often. She decided she would have an early dinner that night, then a hot relaxed bubble bath with a bottle of chilled wine or beer, depending on her mood and what the supermarket was offering as a deal. Then she would take the free time to research evening courses at her local college, where she studied Art and Design.

She was good at her job. Over the years she'd learnt many styles of selling techniques that could easily show up the sales teams of large corporate companies. That, however, did not mean she wanted it to be a lifelong career. She had ambitions, she just had to find the right path to walk down to make them happen.

One more minute. Come on, clock, show me that magical big hand on the twelve. YES, there it is. Goodnight, I am done for the day!

How it would be a pleasure to shout that out loud.

Instead she asked her boss, Laura, if there was anything else she needed, before making a beeline for the door. She was too kind to people sometimes, and it made her feel like her kindness was constantly taken for granted. They didn't acknowledge her hard work. She always tried to make a difference, but most of the time her efforts were overlooked and she felt that her skills could be more useful elsewhere. It

one night FOREVER

AMY C. BECKINSALE

ONE NIGHT FOREVER

Amy C. Beckinsale

RhetAskew  Publishing

United States of America

*To everyone who thought
I was a day dreamer...
thank you.*

Turns out you were right.

*Being a visionary is a blessing,
and I love where my dreams
have taken me.*

was just the way she was, eager to please on the outside, while the inner Megan screamed.

She grabbed her parka and matching Zara bag, then checked her phone before she left the staff room. She wanted to see if anything exciting had come through. Just the typical likes on Facebook and birthday reminders for friends she hadn't seen since school. Followed by some not-so-typical borderline harassment. She knew that having Lucy and Emma so desperate to get hold of her could never be a call that was regarding a simplistic issue. Oh and seven missed calls, two voice mails, and texts.

Waving goodbye to her work colleagues, she headed out the door before she could be collared by her manager again. The evening closed in as she walked back to her flat; its gentle glow soothed her skin and bathed her in warmth that she'd remember for a long time.

Her phone began to vibrate in her pocket. It had been going crazy for the past couple hours. She answered the phone and didn't even have time to say hello.

Emma was in Megan's ear before she even got a chance to think. "Finally she picks up!"

"And good afternoon to you too, Em." Megan replied. "I take it by the popularity of my phone, you and Lucy have been trying to get hold of me?"

"Lucy's been trying too? Well, it is important."

"What's up, Em? Men? Work?"

"Work, but better, so much better." She took a pause, gathering her thoughts. "Remember I was up for a promotion that got delayed last year? Well, I've only bloody gone and got it! I've just this minute come out of the meeting!"

Emma worked for a big computer company in the centre of London. Programs, software, security, apps—you name it, they probably do it. She'd studied hard, worked her ass off, and it was finally paying off, even if Megan was a bit jealous.

"That's brilliant, Emma, congratulations. You've worked so hard, you deserve it." Megan tried to reply in a way that hid the sound of disappointment in her voice. She'd had interviews for larger companies before, but had never been successful. This news was a bit of a kick in the teeth.

"Megan, I know that sound. You will get there."

"One day, Em, if I can keep using that phrase? I'm happy for you, really I am."

"Thank you."

Megan stifled a sigh and instead focussed on her feet. One in front of the other, one step at a time. That was how life went. She just wished that her feet didn't get tangled up every five steps.

She released the breath and turned her attention back to the matter at hand. "Any idea why Lucy was trying to reach me?"

"We've decided to celebrate, in style. We're going out in the city for dinner, followed by a night none of us will forget for a long time. And don't you even think about worrying about the costs because we're going to cover them. Just get on a train as early as you can and meet us at Waterloo," Emma demanded.

Turning around on the spot in the middle of town as if someone had just tapped her on the shoulder, Megan blurted out the words faster than she wanted to. "I can't expect you to foot the bill, Em, seriously. And as wonderful as it sounds, I've got plans to–"

"No! I'm not hearing those words that are escaping your mouth. Help, some strange voice is speaking through my friend! Please, someone help her!"

Megan knew that Emma was shouting at a passersby, probably in the middle of Canary Wharf's shopping centre where she worked, knowing full well that she was getting through to her via sheer self-embarrassment.

"Ok! Ok, I'll come if it shuts you up. Just stop managing to embarrass me from two and whatever hours away."

"Fantastic, I shall now behave myself. But you can bet your slippery ass that I won't be saying the same thing tomorrow." There was a brief moment of silence. "Seriously, Meg, I'm really happy you're coming up, I miss you so much. A good night out is exactly what's needed."

"You're probably right, and I miss you girls too. It's not the same without you here. I'll book a train for first thing tomorrow morning, and text when I leave."

"Good girl, can't wait to see you. I'll call Lucy and give her the good news. Say hi to Ben for me?"

"Of course, bye."

Emma hung up. The sound in her voice left Megan with a sense that she hadn't told her everything. Those girls were up to something. Absolutely, without a doubt, up to something.

During the rest of her slow walk home, all sorts of things were going through her mind. What should she pack? Should she bring anything in particular? Should she be doing this? No. She should be researching, not going off to party in a city that she really can't afford to go to. Why the last minute planning?

Oh, quit stressing. This is going to be fun, and probably just what you need.

After giving herself a telling off, she opened the front door and was greeted by her flat-mate, Ben.

"Took your time getting home. I'm bloody starving. Thought we were having an early dinner. Went ahead and ordered our usual from the Chinese, but with extra sweet and sour sauce. Last time was a joke."

"Sorry, Ben. Had a call from Emma. She wants me to go up to London for the weekend. Pretty last minute, but you know Em." Megan kicked her shoes off, dropped her bag on the spot, and slid her feet into her worn-out slippers. "She says hi, by the way."

"Hi, Em." Ben handed Megan a beer. "And I guess the reason behind us having to eat late is that she had to persuade you? Seriously, Megan, you need to be looser. You've got to go with the flow sometimes."

"I'm not a fucking hippy, Ben."

"You're going by train, right? I hate taking the coach."

Jeez... what was it with everyone riding around on her back today?

Megan only just stopped herself from shaking her head. "I've already agreed to go."

"Megan, that's what I'm here for. Now, let's see what you've got while we wait for dinner to arrive."

They headed to her room so Ben could rummage through the wardrobe to find appropriate outfits. Megan didn't know what she would do without Ben Garrison. He was another of her close friends, someone she'd met while working alongside him at the same clothing store in town. They'd instantly clicked, and after a few months decided to get a flat to share.

Emma and Lucy had moved out of the flat she'd shared with them, dashing off to find flashy jobs in flashy London.

Ben was Megan's only hope.

Chapter 2

S itting at the head of the conference room table, Aidan listened in silence to his colleagues argue between themselves over the contract deals his software company was involved in. He was listening, yes. But most of all, he was trying not to laugh due to the exhaustion he had succumbed to.

He'd had meeting after meeting that day, and it had been a long few months building up new connections and contracts between financial giants, but today the pressure seemed too much for his team. He would let them all put their points across, then in the smooth and slick manner he was known for, dismiss them and put the instructions of how the deals would take place into order. For now, he was enjoying the banter. It lightened his mood.

He'd begun his journey while studying at university, working for companies around the city at a young age. Learning, growing, and quickly working his way up ladders to higher positions. Eventually, the day came in which he realised he couldn't push his own career any further while working for someone else. With the knowledge he'd amassed and relationships he'd made, Aidan started his own company—and it wasn't long before his company was one of the largest computer software companies in the UK.

There weren't many CEOs his age, but it was hard work and determination that had gotten him to where he was today—one of the top businessmen in the country at thirty-five, and slowly beginning to grow even further, making deals with companies in America. Okay, cash wasn't so much of an issue. It never had been. And he wasn't ignorant as to how that had played a role in his success.

His parents, James and Marie Costello, were high earners. They had died in a tragic accident when he was a boy, leaving a healthy sum of cash in his name. Both his parents had successful careers which put them at the top of their own professions and when they died, he inherited everything. His grandparents took him in, became his guardians, and were temporarily in control of the funds before they also passed away from old age. Some of the money was used to send him to one of the top universities to study his craft. The rest went into an account that he was allowed access to when he graduated.

People knew he had money, but he didn't flaunt it to the extreme like he'd seen others do. He'd grown up learning the truth. If you wanted something in life, you had to work hard for it. His parents taught him that. He decided to name his company in their memory, as thanks for their support and for setting him on the path to success. JMC Ltd. It still felt good to think of.

As entertaining as the morning had been, it was time to fill his boots. There was business to do.

"Everyone, please stop arguing and let me get straight to the point," Aidan said, as he rose from his leather chair. The action caught the attention of the entire room. "Here it is. With all the companies investing, legal areas will be handled by Owen and his choice of lawyers. I, along with a team, will take on the investment and contracts, also focussing on the deal with the guys in the States. We good? Or do we have to spend more time arguing over stuff we already know?"

A silence fell over the room. They were like a group of school children who had just been told off by their teacher.

Owen Turner, Aidan's second in command and closest friend, nodded in acknowledgement. He understood the command from the other end of the grand table. As Aidan walked to the window to look out over the London skyline,

Owen addressed the rest of the room. "Okay people, you heard the boss. Let's end this meeting and formulate a plan first thing Monday morning, eight a.m. sharp in this room. Thank you for your time."

Once everyone had left, Owen joined Aidan at the window. For a brief moment, they both stared out into the overwhelming sea of modern-day architecture. The autumn sunset made the city glow in imperfect orange hues that reflected off the endless glass panels and only grew stronger. It was as if the city was painting a self-portrait out of sunlight—a wonderful sight to behold from the top floor of their office block.

Aidan smiled to himself as he felt Owen settle beside him. They'd met one another whilst working for the same company, Cooper and Son's Electrics, on Liverpool Street, and had grown close. Aidan made a vow that if he managed to build his own empire, he would bring Owen with him as his vice. A promise he did not break.

"Why do I have this sinking feeling you are about to offer some of your wisdom onto me, Owen?" Aidan asked in a sarcastic tone. He knew when a brotherly talk was on the cards. It was always lecture time when Owen put his hands in his pockets

"Aid, come on, I've worked with you for, what is it, fifteen years now. I can see when you need to take a break. These past months—years—you've been to numerous meetings at God knows how many companies across the UK; some even in America. When, may I ask, was the last time you saw your own home? And I'm not talking about your city apartment." He sighed, and looked down when Aidan didn't meet his eye. He kept watching the skyline. "I'm worried about you, Aid, so is Clare. You haven't stopped. Please, just take the weekend off and try to just try to relax. At least so you are fresh for Monday?"

If only you knew how hard it was for me to try and relax, Owen.

But Owen wouldn't listen and he knew it. It's what he liked about him. He would always support him in his decisions, and was one of the only people who could see though the barriers he usually put up to protect himself. It's what made him a loyal friend. For now, Aidan was going to listen to his advice and take the weekend to regroup and relax.

Whilst running his hand through his already displaced golden brown hair, he responded with what he felt his friend wanted to hear, but with some guidelines. "If I agree to, as you call it, relax for the weekend, you have to agree to come out for some drinks tomorrow night. That's only fair. And don't try and use that old excuse of having to get home to the wife. Because from what I've heard, Clare's been nagging you to go out and have fun." Aidan smiled when Owen's face fell. "Looks like you're all out of excuses, buddy."

"Who the bloody hell have you... Oh, Lois?"

Aidan grinned at his friend like an all-knowing beacon of knowledge.

"I should have never introduced those two. Got no hope of keeping secrets from you." He was quickly hushed by Aidan throwing his arm around him in a brotherly manner.

"So it's settled. I relax; you come out for some well-needed drinks. I'll meet you for some food first, then we'll head into London for some fun? Drag your brother out too, he's always known how to crack me up." Aidan grabbed his suit jacket from his chair, threw it on, and headed for the door. He grinned as he turned back. "Owen, for goodness sake man. Just go home and relax. It's been a crazy day."

With that, he made his way out, leaving Owen to stand on his own in the rareness that was conference room silence. A small smile spread over his face as he shook his head back and forth.

Asshole.

***

After driving back to his home town of Farnham, Aidan couldn't imagine living anywhere more peaceful. Why would he want to sell his home and stay in the city when his barn conversion was so comforting? Why would he leave when the neighbours he'd grown up around were so welcoming and cared for him dearly? He decided that he would try and stay in Farnham every weekend, and whenever work wasn't too crazy, he could commute back and forth. That was what the apartment in London was originally meant to be for. When business deals took off and he got super busy, like it had done in the past, he'd stay in the city. But when he got some downtime, he'd return to his barn conversion. Yeah... that plan hadn't lasted long.

Pulling into his gravel drive, he stopped the car to admire the house that his headlamps lit up. He'd worked hard for this house, and hoped to one day return to find it full of family life. The building was a mixture of the original wood from the barn and glass panels to allow natural light to fill its rooms. Inside, he'd kept the original beams so the ceilings were high, giving the rooms an open feeling. The fireplaces were made up of natural stone, which mixed beautifully with the wooden flooring.

The house had everything he needed. An office that looked out over the countryside, a living room, a dining room, and a vast kitchen (where he secretly enjoyed to cook when he had the chance) which had its own living room attached. It boasted five ensuite bedrooms for guests, a personal gym, a conservatory, and a games room (where he'd shared many lads' nights with Owen, Tom, and his oldest friend Nick). If all that wasn't enough, there was also a large garden with a pool. But the thing he loved most was the natural wood in every corner of the place—it mixed beautifully with modern furniture. It was why he'd chosen to design his apartment in a similar fashion. Home from home.

Walking through the front door, he pulled his mobile out of his jacket and dialled Owen's number.

"Owen Turner."

Aidan couldn't resist. "I've never understood that. Why do you announce yourself when the person who's calling knows it's you in the first place?"

"To be honest, I haven't the faintest idea. I guess it's a habit I've picked up over the years." There was a short pause as Owen thought things through. "What's up, Aid? If this is about work I'll drive over there, lock all means of contact in a safe, and throw it in the pool."

"Like to see you try. Just let me get some popcorn first. I'd need to get settled on a sun lounger to watch," he said through laughter. "No, it's not about work. I was calling to arrange tomorrow's meeting times. Your brother's coming, right?"

"That's a stupid question. At the mere mention of a night out Tom started planning venues, transport, and anything else you would need. So yeah, he's coming." Owen sounded tired just from the mention of his brother.

Tom was a bit of a party animal. Letting him attend a night out was like letting a tiger out of a cage for its dinner. He was only a few years younger than Owen and Aidan, and was one of the best designers at the architectural company he worked for in the city. Aidan had asked him to design the new JMC building for their upcoming move to Canary wharf, but Tom's bosses wanted to assign a more experienced architect for the job.

Their minds were changed when Aidan waltzed into their office block unannounced, demanding the designs that he knew Tom had already drawn up. Once word got around that the stunningly modern building had been designed by Thomas Turner—the young up-and- coming architect—his name became known, and pretty soon, people were in constant contact asking him to design buildings up and down the country.

"Fantastic! Should we say that after my 'relaxation', we meet outside the office and go from there?"

Owen knew Aidan was taking the piss. It was what their friendship was like—always trying to get one over on each other. Owen's wife, Clare, said they were more like a married couple than her and Owen. But she couldn't imagine the pair living without each other.

"Seven okay?" Owen suggested.

"Perfect. Do I need to wear a white rose so you can find me?"

"Shut up, I think I know where the building is! Anyway, since we'll be using one of the cars, you can look out for me." Owen hung up so he had the last word.

Aidan knew without a single doubt that he'd be turning to Clare, saying he'd finally won an argument.

Aidan lowered his phone and opened his apps to order a takeout. While he waited, he changed into comfortable joggers and a hoodie, then grabbed a beer from the kitchen.

Collapsing into his luscious sofa, he opened the movie channel and enjoyed the peacefulness of his own home. He figured he'd better enjoy it while it lasted. Their big night out was less than twenty-four hours away.

Chapter 3

S ettled into her seat on the train to Waterloo, wrapped up in one of her scarves to keep warm, Megan lost herself in one of her favourite books. She was trying to keep herself distracted from pondering on what else her friends could be up to. Although, it was proving difficult with the noise of crying children, who'd been woken up early by their parents for a daytrip to London. No doubt to view the Palace or Westminster Abbey. At least she didn't have to put up with the tedious train journey back until tomorrow afternoon. Engrossed in her book, she hadn't heard the coffee trolley coming until the waiter asked if there was anything she wanted.

"Sorry, coffee please."

"No problem, dear. Milk and sugar?"

"Just milk, thank you."

As she took her first sip of coffee, which was far from pleasant, she checked her messages. Emma and Lucy had both texted her the night before with instructions of their dress code for the night ahead. They all agreed to go along with the proposed code, though Megan soon wished she hadn't. Ben had helped her attempt to find the perfect outfit, but her wardrobe simply didn't supply the goods. Even Ben, for the first time since the day they'd met, couldn't supply an answer. Either she'd have to borrow something or splash out on a new outfit. It was that black and white.

A night out in her home town consisted of skinny jeans, a nice top, and some stilettos—simplicity at its best. Though simple as it was, Megan knew she made it look pretty damn good. So why the need for dresses and fancy shoes? What was wrong with the good old jeans and a pretty top? She shook her head at the thought. Luckily, she didn't have to bring much else with her. Everything she'd need, the girls already had: hair equipment, makeup; shoes. It meant she just had to bring her essentials, which she was grateful for. The thought of having to a pull a large bag around the London underground was extremely off-putting. She'd rather attend the night out butt-naked than face that fate.

God, what was she doing? How was she supposed to read this book with a head filled with thoughts and a pair of ear canals filled with endless whining? This was hopeless.

She pulled out her phone, and opening a new message, began sending a group text to the girls.

I'M ON THE TRAIN, LADIES, SURROUNDED BY CRYING CHILDREN! PACKED ALL I COULD THINK OF FROM YOUR LISTS YOU SENT ME LAST NIGHT. BUT ONE PROBLEM... I HAVEN'T GOT A DECENT ENOUGH DRESS FOR THIS EVENING. HELP! M Xxx

Relaxing back, she waited for a response to her cry for help. Within moments, her mobile started to ring. From the glances she received from a few tired-eyed mothers, she thought that maybe she should have put her phone on silent. Oh well, it wasn't her fault they'd only just managed to get their screaming children to sleep now, was it?

She put the phone to her ear. "Lucy! Hi, how are you this morning?" Megan whispered.

"Hey Meg, I'm good. How far away are you?" Lucy Stone, Megan's friend who she'd met in school when her parents moved to Somerset, sounded like she had just woken from a deep sleep.

"I'd say a couple hours? Did my text wake you?"

"It's okay, I needed to get moving. We have a big day ahead of us and I can't wait to meet you at the station. Now, tell me about this dress situation."

Lucy worked with some of the biggest designers in the fashion industry and helped dress the stars, organise fashion shows, and set up large-scale shoots. If anyone knew how to solve this little outfit problem, it was her. Megan began telling Lucy her issue in a panicked rush, which once again got the attention of the already irritated parents.

"Whoa! Calm yourself, Megan. This is just a minor blip that can be sorted easily."

"Really?"

"Really, really! I know your size and shape, so I'll simply find you the perfect dress and have it here waiting for you."

"You know you're my personal life saver, right Lucy? I don't know what I'd do without you. I owe you. First drinks are on me, ok?"

"Just get your backside to London. See you in a couple of hours."

***

The train pulled up to Waterloo's platform three at around nine-thirty. Megan texted Ben to let him know she'd arrived safely and that the girls would be waiting for her. He always made her promise to inform him of her arrival whenever she travelled anywhere. He'd worry about her otherwise.

A feeling of excitement came over her. She hadn't seen Emma or Lucy for quite some time. It had been a few months since their last meeting, and even though they called and texted each other every other day, there was nothing like a good old in-person reunion. People used to think they were more like sisters than best friends. They decided they'd go along with it and as the years passed, they felt more and more like family.

Megan waited for other passengers to leave the train first before picking up her bag and book. Stepping onto the platform, she glanced around, taking in the architecture of Waterloo station as she presented her ticket at the gate. She looked from left to right, trying to find her friends through the busy crowds and decided to stand under the large clock that hung high above and looked up at it. If they were looking for her, at least she was in central, most obvious spot of the entire station. She heard someone call her name, and instantly recognised the voice.

She practically sprinted towards the direction of her best friend's voice, all three laughing as they hugged, not caring that people were watching their over-the-top greetings. Megan stood back to look at her friends.

"And here I was thinking the city would have made you look rundown and tired, but you two are looking just as fabulous as when you left home."

"Always the charmer!" Emma nudged her with her hip. "You, look at you! I am loving your new hair by the way. Au natural suits you."

Megan had recently treated herself to a new mid-length hair style after years of living the long-hair life. She was known for her blonde locks, but chose to go back to her natural brunette shade. It was a change that had made her feel fabulous since the second she'd walked out of the salon.

"A well needed change, Em, and one that makes me feel that the cost of it was worth every penny."

"You'll be battling the guys off with your heels at this rate. It's going to look stunning with the dress I have in mind for you." Lucy held her hands up as if she were about to describe a painting. "As stunning as a golden Goddess."

"As long as it's not too, you know, provocative. You know I'm not comfortable wearing that sort of thing. I know what you two are like."

Emma threw her arms around Megan, leaning her head on her shoulder. "Oh, you need not worry, my dear, this dress, from what I've heard, will make you look the classiest woman in the room."

Megan rolled her eyes. "That's what worries me. I'm not the most confident person in the world."

"Get some alcohol down you and you will be. I remember what you were like at Ant's birthday party last year," Lucy teased.

Ant, Lucy's ex-boyfriend, was the guy they all thought she would end up marrying. But when Lucy came home one morning to find him in a compromising position with her neighbour's wife, she broke up with him on the spot and moved in with Emma across town.

"Right, I don't know about you two, but the coffee I had on the train was disgusting. I need a fresh one, fast," Megan said.

"I know this lovely little place across town, and no, it's not a Starbucks." Emma always had a coffee in her hand when she was on the move, a tradition that went all the way back to when she was in college.

"Coffee, salon, lunch, dress, and dinner. Onward!" Lucy reeled off some kind of structure for the day, leaving Megan and Emma laughing.

"You can try and PA me Lucy, but it isn't going to work." Megan struggled to reply through fits of the giggles.

This weekend may be exactly what Megan needed. Seeing that the girls were happy to see her instilled her with a sense of purpose and belonging. It was nice to feel as though she meant something to someone. She was with her family, and they loved every part of her.

***

It was evening time now—their big night out was closing in fast. Megan stood in front of the full length mirror in the bathroom of Emma and Lucy's flat in Hammersmith, looking herself up and down.

They'd had a great day so far, having lunch in a little restaurant hidden in Covent Garden and then moving onto a salon to get their nails done. Their final stop was Lucy's work, where they were presented with the largest wardrobe of designer outfits they had ever seen. That was where Megan got her dress. It certainly was stunning, though the cut didn't leave much to the imagination. It was a golden, long-sleeved sequinned dress with an open back and a hem length that needed questioning. One stumble and she could be showing London a bit too much of the West Country.

"Lucy," Megan shouted. "Lucy!"

"What?" Lucy called back. She ran in with her curlers in hand, thinking there was a problem. "What's the matter?"

"I can't wear this. It's, well..." Megan gestured to her legs. "I'm not exactly in my twenties anymore."

"Oh please, you look amazing in it. Yeah, it's shorter than I let on. The model who wore it was a tad shorter than you." Lucy turned her head to the door. "Emma!"

Emma joined the gathering.

"Whoa, Em! Clothes perhaps?" Megan laughed.

Emma sighed, and picked up a towel. "Not like you haven't seen me naked before, Meg. We did live together once." She wrapped the towel around her and sat on the edge of the bath. "What were we shouting about anyway?"

"Tell Megan that the dress looks good on her."

Emma looked over to Megan, who was looking less than comfortable. "It really does, Meg. Wait, I have the best shoes that will match." Emma ran off, returning with a gorgeous pair of open-toed heeled boots.

Megan put them on and looked in the mirror once more. In an instant, she felt way more confident. It was bizarre, since the only change was a pair of shoes, but Megan wasn't going to stand around questioning the confidence boost. Damn Emma. She'd always known that heels were her kryptonite.

"Okay, okay, I'll wear it. I'll just have to take care of these little beauties for you. You know, to keep them safe."

"See? I knew I made the right choice." Lucy smiled mischievously. "Now, can we please get the drinks flowing? Someone put the tunes on." She began dancing around the room. "Emma? Get dressed?"

While Lucy attempted to use up her energy before the night had even begun, Megan continued to put the finishing touches to her makeup while Emma did as she was told, presenting them with dress after dress, until she finally made her choice. A mid-length red body con number she had only worn the once at a family wedding.

After one last check in the mirror, Megan grabbed her clutch bag. "Come on then, ladies. Let the night of our lives begin."

As she watched Megan walk out of the room, Emma leant closer to Lucy and whispered, "If only she knew what we have to surprise her with."

Chapter 4

"Oh sweetie, you found me. I was worried you wouldn't notice."

Aidan leant against the side of one of his black company cars with what could only be described as a bouquet of white roses and a bunch of balloons with Owen's name printed on the side. Owen couldn't believe his eyes as he and Tom walked up to the JMC building.

"Holy hell, no shame tonight then?"

Tom looked like he was close to passing out through laughing at his embarrassed brother. "Bro, that's what you get for being cocky and saying that you won a phone call."

"Never gonna win, Owen, never gonna win. Why do you think I'm the CEO and deal with the contract negotiations?" Aidan teased.

"Fuck off, the pair of you." Owen laughed. "Can we just get going and admit that throughout the years, you've always managed to get one over on me?"

"You'll get to my level, Owen. One day."

Aidan gave him his balloon and as some women passed by, he offered the white roses to them, which had them swooning and trying their absolute best to join the guys on their night out as they got in the car.

"Sorry ladies," Tom said. "This is a lads' night, which means it's no place for sophisticated ladies such as yourselves."

"Get in the bloody car, Tom," Owen shouted from the open side window, shaking his head.

Tom climbed into the car and shook his head at Owen. "Way to ruin it, bro." He turned his attention to Aidan. "How are you so smooth with the women? One look and they fall all over you."

Aidan smiled. "It comes with the territory."

"What's the plan then?" Tom closed the window. "Any particular place in mind?"

Owen sighed. "Did we read the group text at all? Jesus, you're useless. Grab some food, then head to Camden–"

"Nope," Aidan interrupted, "change of plan." Owen looked at him dumbfounded.

"There's a new place in Leicester Square I thought we'd check out. Rang ahead earlier to let them know to expect us."

Owen sighed. "Changing plans again?" He rubbed his temples. "Anything else you wanna own up to?"

"Not right now" Aidan sank back into the middle seat. "Let's forget about all that tonight." He raised his hands into the air and let an arm fall around each of their necks. "Tonight is for the boys.

Chapter 5

S itting in an Asian restaurant in the heart of Soho, Megan admired the modern decoration around her. There was nothing like what she was seeing back home, and it took her breath away. It was like a theatre crew had rocked up and lit the room with stage lighting, and to make it more magical, the table they sat at glowed with a vibrant sea green. She looked under the table to see if she could figure out how it was lit.

Emma slugged the rest of her drink and, setting the glass down, turned the conversation to the topic of work. "So, Megan, how's the shop?"

Megan sat up. "Do we have to talk about it now? We're having a nice time." Neither Emma nor Lucy said anything. "But since you asked, and are obviously waiting for a response, I'm trying to line up as many interviews as I can. I want to finally move on from what was meant to be a stepping stone to something better."

"Ah, glad you brought the stepping stone up."

Emma was definitely up to something, just as Megan had predicted.

"Here's the thing, Meg," she began, while folding her napkin, "my promotion... it isn't the promotion I told you about. That news on the phone was, well... well, it was a bit of a fib. And I'm sorry about that."

Megan felt herself deflate even more, as her friend continued to talk about her fabulous new position. What had she fibbed about? Was there a promotion at all? The questions raced through her entire body.

"The new role I'm in isn't just a step up in the department."

Megan looked between the girls, and saw that Lucy was almost about to burst with excitement. "What is it, Em? Spit it out. Looks like Lucy's about to wet herself."

"Megan, I've been promoted to head of the department." A squeak escaped Lucy, making both girls look at her.

"That's amazing, Em!"

"Yeah, yeah! What I am getting at is that I am in control of who I employ for my department, and there is an opening in the sales of software and design."

Megan sat perfectly still. Her heart began to race. Was Emma actually saying what she thought she was saying?

"Oh my God, Meg!" Lucy practically screamed, grabbing her hand. "Emma's offering you the job in her department!"

"What?" Megan stared at her, shell-shocked.

Emma started to grin and raise her eyebrows which meant: yes, that was exactly what was being offered. Megan felt all the colour leave her face. Her breathing quickened and as she tried hard to say something back, her eyes began to fill with tears. Emma continued, taking her other hand, catching the eyes of others. They must have thought she was about to propose to her girlfriend.

"Megan Victoria Ashton" Emma got down on one knee. "Please say you'll be my new sales advisor?"

Tears were flowing down her face. This was insane; amazing, but insane. "I–I... don't you, uh... I mean."

"Spit it out, Meg," Lucy teased.

"Do you, like, don't you, um... need to interview me? I don't know much about software design," Megan stuttered.

"Come on. I've seen you in action in the store. You can sell things to people when they don't even want them." Emma smiled. "Besides, we'd all be together again. Think of the positives."

"We would, wouldn't we?"

"And you'd be beginning on that new path to a great career, without the need to study all over again," Lucy added.

Megan nervously nodded and began to smile.

"So, can we say that all these tears means: 'Yes please, Emma. I'll take the position'?"

Megan stared at Emma, then met Lucy's excited eyes. She found it hard to get the words out, even though she knew what she wanted to say. She took a deep breath, pulling Emma up into a big hug and shouted at the top of her lungs, "Yes!"

The audience of restaurant customers began cheering, joining their celebration.

"Yes, I would love to. Thank you, thank you so much. You have no idea what this means. Actually, you probably do.

Thank you!"

***

London had come alive by the time they had finished dessert and coffee, and left the restaurant. People filled the streets—dressed to impress—and the excitement was over-whelming. Groups of girls tottered around in ridiculously high heels that they couldn't walk in, and people gathered outside the many theatres of the West End, waiting to take their seats for evening performances. There were tourists taking pictures of the magnificent views that the lights of Piccadilly offered; late night workers were heading full speed for the underground to get home.

Emma, Lucy, and Megan walked the short distance to the club they had been pointed towards. Their conversation turned to where Megan would stay and how long it would take to get up to London. She would need to cancel her part of the lease in the flat, break the news to Ben. The list she was creating kept growing and was quickly spiralling out of control, but Emma and Lucy were prepared and had the answers for all the questions she was throwing at them.

It was decided that she would move in with them, and that they would look for a bigger flat. Megan would go back to Somerset on Sunday afternoon to break the news to Ben, hand her notice in on Monday, then begin the packing and organising to move to London in a month's time. Lucy said that she and Emma would come down to Somerset to help her pack and transport her belongings using a friend's van. Just the thought of them driving a van cracked her up into fits of laughter.

"We can beep at all the fit guys as we pass them. Think of it as payback for all times they made us feel uncomfortable." Emma laughed louder than usual to counter the noise growing around them.

Megan burst into laughter. "Oh my gosh that reminds me of when we went to Alton Towers in college and—"

"We were on that log flume ride with those guys that wouldn't stop trying to flirt with us?" Emma took over. "They were all like 'Hey sweetness, if you get scared you can hold my hand', but they practically shat themselves when we went down the steepest slide."

Lucy stood with her hands on her hips, watching Emma and Megan bent over in a fit of giggles.

"What's wrong, Lu?" Megan asked her. "Don't you remember? It was hilarious."

"The only thing I remember about that, Meg, is that I had to spend the rest of the day with fuzzy hair, when neither of you would give me at least five minutes with a hair dryer."

Emma pointed at her. "Fluff ball! We called you fluff ball."

"For at least two months!" Lucy tried to remain mad at them, but couldn't help it when a snigger escaped her.

Passing the famous Odeon in Leicester Square, the girls rounded a couple more corners to reach the club where they would spend the evening celebrating. Walking up to the line, Emma caught the eye of the doorman. She smiled and winked in his direction. He smiled sweetly at her and escorted them into the venue.

Once inside, Lucy stopped her, grabbing her arm. "Wanna tell us how we've just managed to get into one of the busiest clubs in the city that easily? Have you seen the queue of envious glares we're getting right now?"

Emma ignored them. Trying to avoid the question she knew was coming. "Emma?" Lucy teased her, as they entered the pristine elevator, which carried them to the top floor.

"Just luck of the draw?"

"Rubbish, Em." Megan smiled. "I saw that look you gave the doorman. Did you sleep with him?"

"No!" The doors opened to their floor. Emma walked out first, and turned to gesture for them to follow but was greeted with two faces, both pulling the same expression, waiting for the answer. "Ok, maybe just a little bit."

"Little bit?" Lucy laughed. "How can you sleep with someone just a little bit?"

"You know, just a spur of the moment little bit."

"You had a one night stand with him, didn't you?" Megan asked.

"We're living in modern times now, Meg. You never know who you're going to meet on a night out." Emma linked arms with her two friends, in an attempt to stop their questions. "And no, before you ask, I'm not planning on doing it again."

Lucy and Megan looked at one another, before bursting into laughter.

"You know I hate you both sometimes, right?

Chapter 6

A idan asked their driver to pull up at the club's entrance. Light shone up the side of the building, illuminating the red drapes that hung from the roof. Red carpets lined the front entrance and large lanterns hung at either side of the doors, with church candles giving the feeling of a medieval gathering. From the look of the venue's bouncers, it wasn't just any old club that you could pop into at random. It could get to maximum capacity within an hour of opening, so you had to either get there early, know someone who could get you in, or be someone people knew. Luckily for Aidan, he could check off two of the three.

It was at the top of the party scene in the city and didn't open its door easily. It consisted of four different levels—one in the basement—and each one had a different theme. Aidan had called ahead before meeting Owen and Tom at the office and the owner of the club, Drew, couldn't have been more thrilled that Aidan Costello had chosen his venue for their night out. Drew suggested (because it was busy) that it was probably wise for them to go in via the side door when they arrived. He would reserve an area on the top floor for them, so they could spend the night undisturbed.

Whenever Aidan and Owen went out, someone would want to get a picture or the press would stop them to try and get information about the deals the company was working on. It was a celebrity status that they had learned to deal with. It definitely wouldn't bother them tonight. This was a lads' night out; they were here to wind down and forget about the business deals for the weekend. It was just what was needed and nothing was going to stop that from happening.

Once outside the car, the noise of the streets really hit them—the crowds were out in force tonight. They were greeted by the club owner and escorted to the private area. A balcony that overlooked one of the dance floors; it led to an outside area above the main entrance.

Aidan extended his hand to the club owner. "Thanks, Drew, this is great."

"You are more than welcome, Mr. Costello. Anything you need, just ask our staff. Have a good night, and thanks again for choosing to spend the evening with us."

Owen looked over at Aidan and raised an eyebrow. "No doubt we'll be seeing him again?" He sat down to look at the drinks menu.

Aidan crashed sideways into one of the large luxurious sofas and put his feet up on the arm. Gazing to his left, to admire the venue, he was almost blinded when a strobe lights shone in his eyes. Swearing under his breath, he peered through the railing of the balcony. The club was already full. LED panels lighting up the floor, giving the venue a feel of Saturday Night Fever. He was sure it wouldn't be long until he saw a John Travolta wannabe.

"Making yourself feel at home there, Aid?"

"Mm," was all Tom got out of him. Aidan rested his head back and sighed. "So, it's the last to sit who has to get the drinks in then, is it?"

"No, I'm up. I've made it my personal mission to get your brother smashed again tonight, Tom."

"A drunk Owen? No way. Haven't seen you smashed since your stag, bro. It's been a while."

Owen's stag had gone down in the history book of lads' nights out, if there ever was such a book. They had managed to spend the whole day, evening, night, and the early hours of the following morning, drinking and daring each other to maximum risk. They'd even made the morning papers the following day. Owen, unfortunately, but quite rightly, was given the most embarrassing dares—much to his fiancée's amusement. But the following day, when Tom made it back to the hotel, her mood changed like the wind. Owen was nowhere to be found.

She called Aidan, demanding to know where her fiancé was and when she was to expect him back. He tried to calm her down, saying that he'd left him with one of the limos at some airport, but that was all he could disclose. This was followed by Clare giving Aidan the biggest lecture he'd heard since his grandmother had told him off as a kid. He tried so hard not to laugh while Clare shouted at him, but failed terribly. He was usually so in control, but when you're still drunk that skill goes right out the window.

Owen had turned up a few hours later wearing a French maid costume, looking less than impressed. He gave Clare a look that explained he'd been screwed over by his friends.

"Where were you? Aidan said something about an airport?" Clare demanded, looking him up and down.

"Airport? Yes, there was indeed an airport. Those twats left me there with the company jet running—fuck knows how much that cost. Anyway, the captain asked Aid if this was the little beauty he was told about."

Clare was trying not to laugh. She tried to keep a serious look on her face.

"Then, as I'd turned to ask Aidan what the hell was going on, they had all ran off. I had no idea where I was, and it wasn't until I had to walk through the terminal—in a bloody maid's costume—that I saw they'd been kind enough to leave me one of the company cars."

Clare couldn't control it, she burst out laughing. "Oh they got you. They got you good, babe!"

Owen shuddered as he recalled the events of his stag do. Those arseholes sure knew how to have fun. He was just pissed because it always had to be at his expense. He shook his head. "Yeah, no bloody costumes tonight, Costello."

"Yes, dear." Aidan laughed. "Not having you moaning like a bitch like last time." Stopping at the top of the stairs, he checked the orders before visiting the bar. "Usual?"

"Like you need to ask," Tom said.

Battling through the crowds and ignoring Tom's sarcastic comment, he spotted a group of three women coming onto their floor. All of them wore different styles of cocktail party dresses and looked like they were geared up for one hell of a night. One of them in particular caught his attention. She was dressed in a backless, long-sleeved metallic gold dress. Her chocolate hair was styled into waves that emphasised her green eyes. Aidan pushed through the final row of impeding clubbers and rested his arms on the bar.

He lost his train of thought as he watched her laugh with her friends and felt himself smile. When she glanced over and caught his eye, his whole world felt as though it had slowed down for the duration of the encounter. She gave him the slightest smile, then returned to the conversation she was having with her friends.

The barman coughed in an attempt to make him aware that he was waiting for an order. It broke Aidan's attention. Or lack of.

"Yeah, okay!" He turned and snapped at the barman, unaware at first that he was using his business tone. He quickly addressed the situation. "Sorry, sorry. I didn't mean for that to come out that way." He smiled, looking over to her again. He noticed that she and her friends were trying to decide what drinks to order, and he suddenly had an idea.

"Not a problem, Sir. What can I get you?"

"Three beers and a tray of, I don't know... any of the spirits that you think are nice. And one more thing. Come closer? Those ladies there, in particular the one in gold," he said while he pointed to the three women, "anything they order tonight, put it on my bill." He gave the barman his card to make up the tab for the evening.

"Certainly," the barman took his card, "Mr. Costello." He was stunned as to whom he was serving, and that the request being made was from such a high-profile name.

Aidan watched him, waiting for him to return to the ground. "Ready to chat again? What's your name?"

"Kev. Kevin Hunter. Sorry sir, I didn't recognise you."

"Not in a suit." Aidan laughed. "First off, Kev, none of this sir nonsense, okay? I get called sir or Mr. Costello every day, and I'm out of the office trying to have some fun here. Secondly, I want you to be the one who looks after those ladies tonight." Aidan slipped Kevin a fifty pound note. "We good?"

"Yes, Sir!"

Aidan tilted his head to the left and rolled his eyes.

"Er, Aidan... sorry." Kevin kept his eyes on Aidan and twisted his face.

"What is it?"

"If they were to question who's buying the drinks?"

"Just say the guy on the balcony and point up there." He gestured towards where they were spending their night. "I'll take care of the rest. Keep this between you and me, Kev. I have a habit of remembering people who do a good job for me."

Aidan made his way back to Owen and Tom, but not before managing to catch the eye of woman in the golden dress once more. She looked like she wasn't breathing. He smiled and carried on walking and could sense Owen watching him from above. He looked up and saw Owen and Tom hanging over the railing like a pair of wild vultures. From the look on their faces, Aidan knew they were wondering what the hell he was up to now.

Chapter 7

Holy crap, he is gorgeous, and of all the people out in the city tonight, he is looking at me. And not in a 'hi, what are you looking at' kinda way, but a 'yeah, I'm not even gonna make an attempt to hide the fact that I'm looking at you' kinda way.

The bright blue of his eyes caught her unaware and she found it hard to look away. Not that she wanted to look away. She could have lost herself in those eyes all night. The room's lighting didn't help, but she could see that he had brown hair. Maybe a bit golden? He wore dark jeans, a black leather jacket with a hoodie underneath, and a white t-shirt. This guy knew how to dress, and he wore it well. Each item of clothing looked like the designer had made it especially for him. He beamed confidence and looked like he was in complete control of whatever conversation he was having with the barman.

Megan was quickly brought back to Earth by Lucy tapping her arm. "Are you going to decide what to drink? Or are you away with the crazy fairies again?"

"Yeah, of course, sorry. Drinks. What were we talking about?"

Emma gave her a knowing look. "Explain? Who, where, and what did he look like?"

"Gorgeous. Seriously, is this where the world's been hiding the decent men? He was just by the bar." Megan pointed in the direction of where she'd seen him. "Shit, he's gone. No! There he is."

He was now facing the other way, so they could only see his back.

"A fine looking back of the head," Lucy mocked.

"Oh shut up, he may turn around in a minute."

He didn't. He was too engrossed in the conversation he was having. Megan sighed in disappointment and returned to looking at the cocktail selection, but she kept looking around to try and spot him again. While Emma and Lucy were looking at the menu, she noticed him leaving the bar. He glanced her way and smiled again. His smile had to be the most beautiful thing she'd seen. She found it hard to breathe. She decided at that moment not to tell the girls she had seen him again. It was like their meeting was a private moment, and she wanted to keep it that way.

There were times she had been out with her friends and thought a guy was interested, only for him to end the night with Emma or Lucy. A definite confidence killer, but it wasn't their fault. They were both stunning women, and it was no surprise guys found them irresistible. Emma had long, dark brown hair with an hourglass figure that made every dress she put on hug her curves beautifully. She also had dark mysterious brown eyes that matched her hair, and full lips some people would pay for.

Lucy was at the other end. Chin-length platinum hair that matched her light complexion; a fairer version of Megan some people said. She had hazel eyes and a figure that would make people run for the gym. Why she wasn't a model Megan could never tell.

These were some of the reasons she felt that this time, she would keep this mystery

man to herself. They'd wanted her to come to London to celebrate a promotion and Emma had offered a new job. Her life was finally moving in a new direction, so why not have a little fun in the process, and walk on a more daring path? She may not see him again, but the thought of how she felt when he looked at her was something she would never forget.

She tried to watch him as he left, but he'd disappeared into the crowd. There was no sign of him, like he had vanished.

Where'd he go?

She took a step towards the direction she knew he had headed in and bumped into the back of a dancer. Apologising, she took one more look around the venue, glancing up at the balcony that stood high above, with its neon lights edging the railings. She wanted nothing more than to gaze upon him one more time.

She brought her attention back to the matter at hand. Drinks. She wasn't going to give up, but she knew the girls would start nagging about wine. She tapped the bar. "Okay ladies, I'm getting the first round." Her spirit was on a high. Her evening had just taken a turn and gotten that little bit more exciting.

"Are you sure, Meg?"

"Yes, I'm sure. It's only fair. You've offered me a job, Em. And Lucy, I did promise you on the train." Megan waved her hand in a random direction. "Go find us somewhere where we can, you know, stand? We're here to celebrate and that's what we are damn well going to do!"

"Oh, someone's excitable. Anything to do with the 'gorgeous guy' you spotted?"

Surely Lucy can't read my mind, can she?

"I just want a fun night with my girls. Is that too much to ask? Now go find somewhere. I'll get our usual, since we're incapable of deciding on cocktails." When they didn't move, she added, "Go! Bugger off!" She continued leaning on the bar.

"Good evening, my name's Kev and I'll be taking care of your orders tonight. What can I get you?"

"Hi, Kev. Can I please get a large rosé, a Jack and Coke... oh, make that a Diet Coke. And for me, I'll have a..." Since she was so indecisive, she decided to opt for her favourite. If in doubt. "Budweiser, please."

"Certainly, coming right up." Kev left to fetch her order, leaving Megan to give the club a onceover to see if she could see where the girls were. She imagined they would have gone outside, to an area where Lucy could smoke. Just off the edge of the fluorescent dance floor, she spotted them, near the DJ booth. They had found a small table and were standing guard, giving them a clear view of the entire club.

Kev returned with her order. "Anything else, madam?"

"Madam? Classy! I think that will do us for now, thanks. How much?" Megan asked, while she tried to locate her purse.

Kev held a hand up to stop her. "It's taken care of."

"What? I'm sorry, pardon? Have you?" She pointed at the drinks. "Are you allowed to do that?"

"Not from me. I'm afraid that's against our employment rules. These and all your drinks this evening are being covered by another of our customers."

"Really? Do people do that here?" Megan leaned on the bar. "Am I allowed to ask who?"

Kev thought that question was coming. He was completely intrigued as to how Aidan was going to play this, and couldn't wait to see if it worked. He pointed up to the balcony. Aidan was standing there waiting, just as he'd known he'd be.

"The gentlemen on the balcony, madam, but that's all I know. I am here if and when you need anything."

Megan slowly turned around to look where he was pointing, trying to be subtle. She looked up and recognised him instantly. She was unable to react at first, but eventually formed a smile.

He tipped his head and returned her smile, and then walked back to what she assumed was his seating area.

Facing Kev again, she felt a stupid smile growing on her face. "Well thank you, Kev. I think we'll be seeing you again shortly in that case."

Megan couldn't believe it.

What sort of guy—especially a guy as gorgeous as him—offers to pay for our drinks? We haven't even spoken yet.

Back at the table, Megan could barely contain herself. She was bouncing in her shoes, her eyes looking all around the room. At first, when she told Emma and Lucy that another customer wanted to pay for their drinks, they seemed a bit uneasy. But when she told them they had a private waiter to call upon when they needed him, they'd soon relaxed.

"Well, if someone wants to foot our bill, let's rinse it for what it's worth."

"Sure, I'm up for that, Lucy." Emma took a sip of her first free drink. "Just be careful. We don't want to end up going home with some crazy stalker."

Megan burst into laughter. She decided it was time to hit the dance floor and let the party begin. She set her drink down and grabbed the girls, dragging them onto the floor. She was happy to be getting to the boogying, but she didn't let on that the real reason she wanted to dance was to keep an eye on the balcony above them.

Chapter 8

The club was in full swing. The dance floors were full and drinks were flowing. The lights illuminated the room and the DJ played a mixture of different styles of music, catering to everyone's taste. Megan had quizzed Lucy on the party location while they waited for Emma to get dressed and it was everything Lucy had described. A bohemian style, mixed with the retro styles of the seventies. A modern retro paradise for any party animal who wished to escape the pressures of life. It was a venue Megan had never witnessed with her own eyes and she couldn't help be reminded of the nightclub from Boogie Nights.

Megan, Emma, and Lucy had been dancing in the middle of the floor most of the night, and were taking it in turns to order more drinks from Kev, who was taking good care of their needs while updating Aidan whenever he took drinks up for him.

At one point during a slower song, a man tried his best to make a move on Megan, coming up behind her and holding her waist. She politely dismissed him and the girls thought she was crazy. They clearly didn't know that Megan was hoping a different guy would show up again. She kept glancing up to where she last saw him in a hope he would be watching her too. She couldn't stop thinking about that mystery man. Who was he? Where was he? And when would she be able to find the chance to be close to him?

**

Aidan tried to stifle his smile but failed miserably. He found it amusing that the golden dress was captivating to others as well as him. If it caught his attention, it was no surprise others were finding it mesmerising. From the sofa, he watched her elegantly dance with her friends, ignoring everything Owen and Tom were saying. If they were to quiz him on what the conversations were about that night, he would have failed miserably. Quiz him on how she moved across the dance floor, and he'd ace the test.

The place was packed by now, and because of that, the guys had started walking down to collect their drinks. Kev was pinned down with extra duties and Aidan didn't want to bestow him with the added burden of being their personal stair-climbing servant. Aidan insisted that when he had his break, he should join them on the balcony to discuss his career prospects. When Aidan saw potential in someone, he would invite them into the office so he could sum up what they wanted out of life and see if he was able to offer them anything. It's what made people like and respect him.

In Kev, he could see that he was extremely loyal to a job, punctual, and hard working. If he could find out where he wanted to take his career, he was sure he could help him to take the steps into whatever direction he wanted—as a thanks for his help this evening. He would probably employ him himself, put him in a customer service role and let him work up the ladder. But he wouldn't say that to him here.

***

The time was flying by and neither party wanted the evening to end. Aidan had successfully managed to get Owen beautifully drunk, to the point where his wife would probably be calling him, demanding an explanation. Again. Clare's rants always were amusing.

Owen and Tom decided they could murder a pizza and began to stumble their way back downstairs.

Megan spotted their movement and sensed that they were getting ready to leave. Panic struck her hard, and she thought fast. "Girls, I'll be back in a minute..."

"Where are you going?" Emma asked.

"I, um, just need a word with Kev. I'll be back. Trust me."

What the hell am I doing?

She raced to get to the bar before him, a plan quickly forming in her mind.

Where the fuck is Kev? Ah, there he is!

"Kev!" she shouted.

"What's up, Meg? More drinks?"

She'd introduced herself properly earlier in the evening. She'd been chatting with him a lot while picking up their drinks.

"No, actually... yes! Two beers, a napkin, and a pen."

"Okay," Kev stretched the word out, "not the most bizarre request of the night, but certainly up there with the best."

"Napkin and pen first, quick, quick!" Kev gave her the items she requested and she scribbled the word balcony on it. Her name went underneath. Looking around to check that he wasn't right behind her, Megan passed the note back to Kev, who had just reappeared with the beers. "When you see him—and I know you know who I mean—pass this to him." She gently touched his hand. "Thanks, Kev, I owe you."

She grabbed the bottles and drifted out onto the outdoor balcony, looking back over her shoulder. She didn't know how she managed to time it perfectly, but as she turned to look back, she managed to catch Aidan's eye as they made their way down the stairs. Instead of smiling at him like a teenager with a crush, she flipped her hair and averted her eyes.

***

"Watch your step Owen, for God's sake. You're going to break your bloody neck." Aidan grabbed him by the back of the neck and guided him down each step. "Who ever said best friends were assholes?"

He let his eyes wander as he guided his friend. There she was again, heading away from the bar and looking incredibly good in doing so. *These girls are going to cost me a small fortune.*

He laughed to himself in amusement. He watched her walk out onto the balcony. As if she could feel his glare, she turned to look back over her shoulder with a *come-hither* look in her eyes.

"Interesting." Aidan helped prop Owen up at the bar. "Guys, I'm just going to check in with Kev. Five minutes, okay?"

"Aid... dude. Seriously mate, what are you doing? You don't even know her. She's like..." Owen waved his hand to and fro, signaling to Tom and Aidan that he was well and truly away with the fairies. What he was saying made zero sense, mainly because he didn't even know what he was supposed to be saying himself.

Aidan patted his head. "I'm just gonna pretend I understood what you meant."

"Bro, you are so done for the night. Bloody lightweight. Time to take you home to your nagging wife," Tom said.

"Ah, little brother, you're a good little brother." Owen hiccupped.

"Holy hell! If you're going to be sick, I'm calling you a cab. There's no way are you going to be sick in my car."

"I'm okay, I'm okay! Anyway, you don't even drive that car," Owen slurred back.

"Yeah, okay, five minutes. Kev?" Aidan called out towards the bar.

Kev appeared out of nowhere. "Aid, glad you're here. Got a note for you." He passed the napkin to him.

Aidan read it with a smile.

"How do you do it? Seriously, how?"

"Let's just see what happens next, shall we?" he replied. He headed for the door.

"Could someone please explain to me how this is happening?"

"The guy's confident, Kev," Tom leant on the bar, "and when he wants something—or in this case, someone—he usually gets it."

"I mean, it's seamless. And she went to him, Megan went to him. Went! He waited, she did the approach. That needs to be taught in schools or colleges or something."

Tom laughed and nudged Kev on his shoulder. "I've got a feeling we'll be seeing you again, mate. There'll be plenty time to show you the ropes of how to be confident like a CEO."

***

"Well, well, well, Mr. Costello."

Aidan heard the voice from one of the side tables. He turned to see a lady holding a white rose to her chest. He had to wonder if they'd stalked him. This wasn't what he needed right now. She was waiting for him. He turned again to see five women all looking at him like they were about to jump him.

"Ladies, I'm glad you like the flowers, I really I am. However, as lovely as you all are, my hands are tied this evening. Have a good night."

"Tied hands, eh? You know, I could make that work."

He turned to walk away. Looking skyward, he shook his head. "Fuck's sake." There she was, standing by the edge of balcony, looking out over the city skyline.

She must have been cold standing there with a backless dress on, but she didn't seem to show it. Aidan breathed in deeply and took a moment to admire her before he approached. She was slim, but not stick-thin. Her curves were in all the right places.

The late September weather was beginning to turn and dark clouds were closing in. At eyelevel, the city was painted in darkness, but down on the streets below it glowed beneath the street lights. Taking his leather jacket off, he placed it around her shoulders, making her jump. He could hear the five women behind him complaining at the scene.

Aidan leant on the wall and looked out to where her eyes had been. They were now locked on him. "Beautiful, isn't it? Looks like a completely different city at night," he said, taking in the view.

Megan smiled. This man was definitely full of confidence.

"You know, accepting a drink from a guy in London can be considered risky, but to meet that same man alone at night, well, that takes courage."

"I thought it would be nice to actually meet our drinks provider. It was extremely generous of you, er..."

He smiled. She clearly had no idea who he was, and he liked it. "Aidan."

"Aidan? Nice name. I'm Megan, as the note said." She passed him one of the bottles. "Beer on you?" She confidently elbowed his side, grinning to herself.

He tapped their bottles together and had a drink. "You're very welcome, and from what I could see, you were taking full advantage of the open tab." He paused. "It worked though... I had to think of something quick that would keep your attention."

"Omigosh, you are so full of it." Megan laughed. "You were watching us?"

"Watching you," he corrected. "Looked like you were planning on cleaning out my accounts."

"Hey, you offered! Can't blame us for taking advantage of such a generous offer."

"That's a good point."

There was a pause as they looked at one another.

"Thank you for your jacket, by the way, I hadn't realised how cold it had gotten out here." Wrapping it around her frame a bit tighter, she could smell his scent in the fabric. She tried to control the butterflies it gave her. "I didn't want to meet in a loud room. This was the next best place."

Aidan's eyes widened and he smiled in amusement. "Now who's watching who?"

He looked into her green eyes and breathed deeply as a thought went through his mind. She had to be the most stunning woman he'd ever seen. He had no intentions of this being their one and only meeting. He didn't know if Megan felt the same, but during their brief chat, he'd felt a connection. It was as if they'd known each other for years.

"Listen, you might think this is crazy, but I've got one hell of a drunk friend who's shouting about getting some food. We were about to get some pizza at one of the late markets. Why don't you come with us?"

"Oh, I don't know, we don't even know each other. And plus my friends are still here." Megan pointed in the direction of the dance floor. As she rolled her eyes around, she noticed some women who were watching. She frowned in confusion. Why were they watching their private meeting?

Aidan took her spare hand in his to bring her attention back, causing her to stop breathing again.

"Tell them you've got a date and that you'll meet them later."

She turned back to face him. Her eyes were wide with uncontained excitement. "This isn't a... we're complete strangers."

He looked at their intertwined hands. "I wouldn't say *complete* strangers."

"Okay, then... we don't know a thing about each other. We've only just met."

"So, come along and we can get to know each other better."

Not so confident now, sweetheart.

Which he thought was incredible adorable. The fact that she didn't know who he was felt amazing. He could actually be himself and not have to deal with yet another woman who only wanted him for the perks of dating a successful businessman.

You have no idea that I negotiate deals for a living, do you?

He could see that she was trying to think of another response that would have probably started with umm, uh, or we, so before she could come up with some kind of comeback, he placed his hand behind her neck and pulled her into a gentle kiss.

Megan was shocked by his strong and confident move. No other man she'd met on a night out had ever had the confidence to do what Aidan just did. Her whole body was rigid, but after she'd gotten over the surprise of what was happening, she relaxed and kissed him back.

He looked at her, holding her close. "Definitely not strangers anymore." Aidan found himself biting his own lip, admiring her. "How about now?"

"That, hmm... that wasn't... you can't just do that and expect—"

"My God, you're still arguing?"

"No... yes, but anyway—"

"Just shut up." Aidan pulled her in again, but this time deepened the kiss, not giving a damn about their audience.

Megan slowly brought her arms up around his neck. He firmly held her waist, catching his own jacket as it slid from her shoulders. His kiss was more than anything she imagined, gentle but claiming. Her hands began to wander, cutting paths between the soft waves on his head.

She pulled back, her arms still around him. "You have a problem with not getting your way, don't you?"

"Always been kind of an issue." He ran a hand across her back, making her pulse quicken. "Pizza? More drinks? Whatever you want, it's yours."

"What if I say no?"

"I'll keep kissing you until you say yes."

"And you don't like the word no!" she said. She thought to herself while he stared at her, looking like he was about to move in again at any moment. She sighed. More time with Aidan would indeed be a treat. She had been searching for him the whole night just to get another sneaky glimpse. This was way more than she'd expected. "Okay, but–"

"There's a but?" He pulled her close again to kiss her but failed when Megan moved her head away, exposing her neck. He opted for that instead, making her voice shake. "Yes, there's a but. First off, I need to let my friends know where I'm going. They'll worry otherwise. And second," she pointed her finger to his chest, making him lift his head. "Don't think for a one second that you're going to get lucky tonight."

Aidan couldn't help it. He burst into laughter. "Megan, even though we've just met, you seem to know how to crack me up." He ran a hand through her hair. "Trust me, I have no such intentions. Taking advantage of you was never on my mind. Sex can wait. I'd just like to get to know you and see where this goes." He smiled. "If that's okay with you, of course?"

Finally, a guy who's not just after one thing. I hope that line wasn't a play at getting his own way.

She smiled and this time pulled him into a kiss. When they parted moments later, she pulled her phone out. "Let me message the girls so they don't wonder where I am."

Aidan placed his jacket over her shoulders once more and picked up their drinks. "I'll be at the bar." He kissed her hand, letting her message her friends in private. The eyes of the five women followed him back into the venue—they were glued to him the whole way. These other females were clearly pissed at not getting a shot with Aidan. Megan could feel the envious glares as they turned their attention to her.

Yes, he was kissing me. Stare as long as you want.

She gave them a false smile before glancing back down at her phone.

He's mine tonight.

Chapter 9

Ignoring the women who made a second attempt to get his attention, Aidan worked his way through the crowds. He thought about politely asking people if he could get by, but people were getting merrier by the second. A good shove from behind soon made them move. He walked up to his friends at the bar, and was greeted by Tom first when he saw him carrying two bottles.

"Went smoothly then, did it?"

Aidan didn't say anything at first, he just smiled and took a sip of his drink. He put Megan's on the bar.

"Take that smugness as a yes then?" Owen slurred.

"Absolutely, Owen, absolutely," he happily said, ruffling his drunken friend's hair.

Owen looked like he was about to pass out on the bar stool. "Ah, get off. Bad influence you are, Costello."

Aidan smiled, watching the opening to the balcony like a hawk. He may have been a bad influence, but now? Now he was focussed on Megan. When was she coming back inside to join him? Feeling like a teenager, he shook himself before his friends started to take the piss. He spun around and tapped the bar to get Kev's attention. "Kev. Monday afternoon at around three? Come by the office for a chat. We have things to discuss."

Kev nodded. "Certainly, and thank you. It's been a pleasure to meet you all. Made my shift tonight a lot more enjoyable."

Aidan gave him his personal mobile number. "Call me when you are on your way so I can make sure I'm not held up in a meeting."

***

Back out on the balcony, the wind was picking up. Megan held a hand to her head to prevent her hair from spiralling out of control. She'd spent a lot of hours getting ready, and she sure as hell wasn't about to let some wind ruin her appearance. With her free hand, she pulled out her phone, texting Emma and Lucy to let them know that her night was enduring an unexpected change of direction.

GIRLS, HOPE YOU DON'T MIND, BUT I'M HEADING OUT FOR SOME PIZZA WITH THE GUY FROM THE BAR THAT I TRIED TO POINT OUT TO YOU EARLIER. WE'VE BEEN CHATTING AND IT SEEMS REALLY POSITIVE. WANT TO GET TO KNOW HIM BETTER. I'LL MESSAGE YOU TO LET YOU KNOW WHERE I AM. BE HOME LATE. LOVE YOU BOTH. THANK YOU FOR PERSUADING ME TO COME UP FOR THE WEEKEND. M XXX

Her phone notified her that the messages had been delivered. As soon as one of them had read her message, she knew the other would know straight away. She placed her phone back in her bag and went in to find Aidan. Pulling his jacket around her, she breathed in deeply.

God he smells as amazing as he looks! Okay, let's see where life wants to take me now.

On her approach, she could feel that stupid smile on her face again. The busy dance floor made it hard to get through, and she had to get rough with people to make it across. That didn't hide the fact that she was excited to see the man she just kissed. If she had to dropkick a few people to kiss him again, then so be it.

Aidan saw her walking through the crowd and held his hand out to her, which she quickly took. He pulled her around so she was next to the bar, hiding her from any potential onlookers.

"Meg, this is Tom, and that mess is one of my closest pals and Tom's brother, Owen. And Kev I think you already know." Aidan looked at her in a cheeky 'he's-been-on-my-side-the-whole-time' kind of way.

Megan smiled at Kev and mouthed the words thank you to him. Owen waved a hand in an attempt to greet her. Tom smacked Aidan's arm, resulting in Aidan giving him a stern look.

"Well, Megan, we've been hearing a lot about you this evening." Tom held a hand out. "Nice to meet officially y-you."

They shook hands, but Megan started to wonder what exactly had been discussed. "What's been said? Aidan, what's been said?"

"It's okay, he's winding me up. These Turner brothers try to make a habit of it."

She gave him a questionable look.

"Just how stunningly beautiful you are," Aidan whispered in her ear, kissing her cheek, making her smile and bite her lip.

"Is he okay?" She spotted Owen leaning on the bar. "Looks like he needs some water or something."

"He's okay, doesn't drink too often. Aid always makes it his personal mission to get him hammered whenever we get to go out. Isn't that right, bro?" Tom shouted in his brother's ear. Owen smacked him away and leant on the other arm.

"Yeah, he's going home in a taxi. Just had the car cleaned," Aidan said.

Owen shook his hand at him. "You've always just had one of the cars cleaned! I'm fine, I'm fine. The air will do me good."

"It's probably best to introduce Owen again when he's sobered up. I'll remind him of this on Monday if he doesn't remember anything." Aidan finished his beer. "Right, you okay helping your brother downstairs, Tom?"

"If I absolutely have too." He placed Owen's arm around his neck. "Sure it'll be more amusing to watch him struggle."

Everyone bid Kev goodbye and thanked him for a great night. Aidan added that he'd see him Monday, reminding him to call.

***

When they reached the lifts that they'd taken to get to the club's floor on their arrival, Tom pressed the button to call it. Aidan held back, quickly sent a text to his driver, never once letting go of Megan's hand.

"Is it worth asking Drew if it's clear out front?" Tom asked.

Aidan frowned, then looked gently at Megan. "That would probably be best." The question was about the possibility of paparazzi waiting outside to capture shots for the following week's papers. He didn't want the world knowing that he had a possible new girlfriend quite yet. "I'll check with Drew at the door."

Megan frowned, confused. "Sorry. Clear out front?"

Aidan's eyes widened. She really didn't have a clue who he was. "Parking."

"We asked the owner, when we arrived, to keep the space clear out front," Tom said, backing Aidan up. "Parking is a real bitch in the city."

Aidan acknowledged his support with a slight nod of the head.

The doors opened and they rode down to the ground level. Aidan held Megan close to him the whole time; she kept her arms clamped firmly around his waist. She felt safe near him, even though they'd only just met. When they reached the exit level, Drew was at the front desk with a staff member.

"Ah, Mr. Costello! I trust you've had an enjoyable evening with us? I'm thrilled that our staff took good care of your needs." Drew glanced over at Megan.

She was watching intently, taking in everything around her.

These guys seem to have the club's staff running after them left, right, and centre. Is there something I'm missing?

"It was great, thanks. Everything clear out front?"

"Yes, all taken care of."

"Excellent." He quickly checked a message that came through to his phone. "And the car's here, so we are ready to go. Thank you for your hospitality, Drew. It's been perfect." Aidan started to make his way out, but turned at the last second, snapping his fingers. "One more thing before we go, though. Kevin Hunter. That guy could do with a bonus or something. He's been great tonight and he's an extremely hard worker. You're lucky to have him. You'd best take care of him. I keep a keen eye on good prospects."

Aidan winked at Megan.

They didn't wait to hear Drew's response. They all headed out the door. Walking out into the cold London air, Megan shivered. Aidan put his arm around her shoulders to keep her warm. She smiled at him. He was being quite the gentleman. When she looked back in the direction they were walking, she almost froze. There was a large black car parked at the side of the road. It had huge alloys and tinted windows. It must've belonged to a footballer. It was the nicest car she'd ever seen.

Megan froze when a well-dressed man got out, smiled their way, and opened the doors. "This is your car?

"One of them, yeah," Aidan replied, helping her climb inside. "Owen? Coping okay there?" Owen leant against the side of the car, taking a moment. The fresh air clearly *wasn't* doing him much good. "Shall we drop you guys off and call it a night?"

Owen shook his head. "Why do I let you do this? I should know better by now. I'm going to be in so much trouble with Clare."

Tom smirked. "Not half as much trouble as Aid when she finds out who's to blame again."

Megan was admiring the interior when the guys climbed in. Owen fell onto the seat opposite her and looked like he was about to fall asleep. Tom kicked his feet out of the way so he could sit next to his drunken brother. After giving instructions to the driver, Aidan was the last to enter. He slid in smoothly beside her. It was clear that he was used to getting in and out of these kinds of vehicles, but what she couldn't figure out was why.

Okay, so he's got money. That much is obvious. And he said this was one *of his cars? How many does he own? He must have a decent job to be able to afford them all? And then there was all that with the club owner.*

All of her thoughts went out the window when Aidan moved in and kissed her once the car finally pulled away into traffic.

"Dude? Time and place."

"Don't care. My car, my rules." Aidan threw back at Tom while they continued kissing.

Megan agreed with him. "Sorry, I'm siding with Aidan."

"Great! Another one who likes to get their own way."

Aidan grinned. He placed a hand over her folded legs, pulling her closer to him.

Megan looked away to try and hide the fact that she was finding his mockery funny. Tom joined their laughter, startling Owen. He sat up quickly.

Aidan looked over to him. "Excuse this expression, Meg. Owen, you about to throw up in my car?"

"Um... no, no I'm fine. In fact, the fresh air seemed to have done me some good." Owen said, a bit less drunk now. "Your car? It's a company car."

"Out to argue tonight? You know you won't win."

"Oh, here we go! I was wondering how long it would take for you two to start." Tom laughed. He stage-whispered at Megan. "Owen likes to think he can keep up with Aid's talent of negotiating."

"Well that explains a lot." She looked at Aidan in amusement.

"Doesn't usually end well," Tom added, so Owen could hear him.

Megan smiled at the banter between them.

Aidan kept his eye on Owen, ready for any comments that would come his way. "And I haven't witnessed a time when Owen has won an argument yet, Megan. Are you sure you want to be out with these two?"

She laughed, then smiled at Aidan. "Pretty sure." She couldn't help but think about Emma and Lucy and their friendship. She'd check her messages when she could to see if they'd replied.

"Megan." It was the first thing Owen had said to her since they'd met. "First off, it's a pleasure to meet you. And second, I do apologise for my state this evening. I have Aidan to blame for that. My wife will probably grill him for it later."

"You agreed to come out if I agreed to have a relaxed weekend." Owen gave Aidan a just-don't-try-it look, which only made him laugh even more.

"It's nice to meet you, Owen." Megan was going for answers now. She had to figure out who these guys were. "If you don't mind me asking... you two look like you've got a history. Known each other for a long time? There's like, a brotherly connection? No offence, Tom."

"None taken." He laughed. "Clare, Owen's wife, says they're like a married couple sometimes. You should hear the stories she could tell you."

"If they're anything like I'm imagining, I'd love to hear them some day." She then directed her attention to Aidan and Owen. "And you work together also?"

"I work," Owen said. "Aidan nags."

"I do not nag! You try running a business. Let me know how it pans out after a week."

"Yeah, I'm seeing that married couple thing, Tom."

Aidan looked at her. "Owen and I met, what, fifteen years back? And I haven't managed to get rid of him since."

"Says the guy who wanted me to tag along with him? You big ponce." Laughter filled the car.

Megan smiled, enjoying listening to the banter filling the car as it smoothly rounded the streets of central London. She watched the bright lights of the city fly by her until the driver announced that they had arrived at Dalston Yard Food Market.

Megan Turned to Aidan. "Could you give me a minute?" she requested. "Just wanna check if the girls have replied."

"Sure, I'll wait outside the car." Aidan let her have a moment of privacy so she could check her messages.

Three texts had come through. The first she opened was from Emma.

JUST BE SAFE, OK? IN FACT, DROP ME A MESSAGE WHEN YOU CAN. HAVE FUN. WANT TO HEAR ALL ABOUT IT LATER. WHAT'S HE LIKE? LUCY LOOKS LIKE SHE'S GOT A CATCH TOO, SO THAT JUST LEAVES LITTLE OLD ME. LATERS, EM Xxx

The second was from Emma again.

SO LUCY HAS GOTTEN HER FELLA TO INTRODUCE HIS FRIEND TO ME. LOOKS NICE. WE'RE GOING TO FIND SOMEWHERE A LITTLE QUIETER. MUST BE MY AGE, BUT THIS CLUB IS GETTING LOUDER BY THE SECOND. EM Xxx

Megan laughed, which prompted Aidan to tap on the door. "Everything okay in there?"

"Yeah, I'll be right out," she called back. Last but not least, was Lucy's message.

DRESS WORKED THEN? I WANT TO KNOW EVERYTHING WHEN YOU GET HOME. BE SAFE. LOVE YOU. LUCY Xxx

Megan smiled. She couldn't imagine her life without either of them. She quickly responded to them both.

HEY LADIES, GLAD YOU ARE BOTH HAVING A FABULOUS TIME. WE'RE AT THE DALSTON FOOD MARKET. HE'S AMAZING AND I'M TOTALLY SAFE, NO NEED TO WORRY. SEE YOU BOTH LATER. LOTS OF LOVE BACK. M Xxx

Opening the door, Aidan gave her his hand to help her out of the car. He'd pulled his jacket hood up now, probably to keep warm in the cool night air. She'd almost forgotten that she was still wearing his leather jacket.

"All okay?" he asked.

She held his hand, hugging his arm. "Better than okay."

Taking her hand again, Aidan escorted Megan into the market to search for pizza.

Chapter 10

The market had everything—drinks and food choices in enough styles and sizes to satisfy everyone in London. The aroma of different stands molding together was enough to make anyone's mouth water. Mexican, Italian, Chinese, Portuguese, Thai—you name it. The place had it all.

The full capacity made it hard to walk through, so Megan let Aidan guide them through the crowds. The colourful rustic seating areas, bunting with giant balloon lighting and old wooden stands, gave the area a warm and inviting atmosphere. Anyone who was anyone could come and relax and enjoy the snacks. Owen and Tom had already gone on ahead to find the pizza stand.

Megan was in awe. Breathing in the flavours while they walked hand in hand towards a pizza bar, she sighed. "This is amazing! If I'd known about these places, I would've have moved to London sooner. There's nothing like this back home."

"You're not from London, then?" Aidan asked. He took a taster sample from a chef as they passed through. From the next bench, he took two samples of locally made cider and handed her one.

"Not yet," Megan began, taking a sip of the cider, "but I'll be moving up here in about a month. My friend, you see, got this promotion in the company she works for, and offered me a job in the department that she's now head of."

"Congratulations. Hence the celebrations this evening, then? Try this." Aidan had stopped by a stand that had all sorts of flavoured hummus. Dipping some flatbread into one, he passed it to her.

"Oh my God." Looking towards the chef, she asked, "Are these all freshly made? Aidan, you can leave me here and I'll catch up."

"I'll take good care of your lady, Sir," the stand's chef offered.

Aidan laughed, but shook his head. Megan wasn't going anywhere without him. They both took another sample and thanked the chef.

Aidan looked in the direction Owen and Tom went, but couldn't see them anywhere. They were alone, despite the busyness of the market. Walking on, he slipped her hand in his, pulling her close as he guided her. "What's the new job then? Something exciting I'm guessing?"

"I hope so. It's an office sales role. I've been in retail for many years, shop floor to personal shopper, and Emma, my friend who got the promotion, said I could do it with my eyes shut. I feel so lucky. I've been trying to get to that next level for so long now, you know." Megan was gesturing the next level with her hand, raising it that bit higher. "I'm hoping that this is what I've been searching for."

"So," Aidan started while eating some more bread, "what's the company? Anything I'd know?"

"Um, it's called JMC."

He coughed, almost choking.

Megan smacked his back to try and help in some way. "Oh my God, are you okay?"

"Yep, yeah. Just took me by surprise, that's all." He coughed again. "JMC, huh? Big guys."

"You've heard of it?"

He nodded.

"What's it like? Emma loves working there. Which is a good sign that I'll like it too."

"I'm sure you will! I'd say it's a pretty good place to work. I know it extremely well."

"Really? How's that?" Megan spotted Owen and Tom sitting on a bench, eating their pizzas, and began heading over to join them.

He took a second, thinking about how to respond.

Because I'm your new boss?

Shaking his head, he took a different path. The last thing he wanted was to scare her off and ruin what had turned into a magical night. "Owen and I work there too, and Tom. He was the head architect for the build when it moved to Canary Wharf."

"Small world. What, does everyone in London work for them?" she joked. "So this," she pointed at Owen and Tom, and then back to them, "would probably be against employment regulations?"

"Yeah, small world. But no, I don't think the boss would be too worried." He resisted the urge to smile as they continued forward through the crowd. Megan was unravelling the mystery all by herself. Pretty soon, the cat would be out of the bag. Reaching the table, Aidan gestured to Owen. "Feeling better now?"

"Loads. You know pizza always does the job."

"Talking of jobs, Megan was telling me about a new one she's starting here in London soon. Why don't you tell the guys your news?"

Megan was smiling with excitement as she told them about her job offer and her plans to move to the city. Aidan watched Owen's reaction the entire time.

"Wow, and when do you start?" Owen asked.

"In a month or so."

"Well that certainly is exciting," Owen said, looking from Aidan to Megan and back to Aidan again.

"Yeah, I've already told her that the boss won't mind what we're up to," Aidan said. He pulled Megan closer, wrapping his arms around her.

As he chewed a mouthful of pizza, Tom cottoned on to everything. The guys were going to drop the news to Megan that she was actually already with her future boss—that was for sure. He decided to keep quiet for now. Until the right opportunity to join in came up of course.

While Aidan went to get some coffee for him and Megan, Owen carried on asking questions. "Emma works at JMC, right? What's her surname? We probably know her."

"Emma Rowe?"

"Yeah, think I've actually been in a few meetings with her. Long, brown hair? Almost black?"

"Here, I'll show you a picture of her." Megan showed him a recent photo on her phone. It was taken while they'd had lunch in Covent Garden that same day.

Tom looked too. "Damn, she's hot! Single?"

"She's managed to find herself a date tonight, Tom. But I can introduce you if there's ever a chance. If you'd like me to, of course?"

Tom nodded. "Awesome, yeah. Thanks."

Aidan retuned with the coffee and handed one of the mugs to Megan. He sat next to her, his legs either side of the bench so he could hold her close.

"Thank you." She smiled while taking a sip and sighed as it instantly warmed her. "Hey, Aid, you've met Emma Rowe, haven't you? Sat in a meeting with her just the other day, didn't we, with the CEO?"

The meeting was to discuss the promotion that she did eventually get. Megan showed him the photo on her phone. "Yeah, now you mention it. Didn't realise she was *the* Emma."

"What? She didn't say that she had the meeting with the CEO. Must have been one hell of a meeting. Mind you, she did tell me a fib about it to get me up here." She laughed at the thought. "So, you both work alongside the boss often?"

They both nodded. "What is he like?"

Tom answered, he couldn't resist anymore. "More down to earth than you'd expect, but likes to get his own way."

Aidan raised one eyebrow before giving a slight nod in agreement. Tom wasn't wrong.

Megan tapped his knee. "Sounds like someone else I know."

"Royal pain in my ass from time to time," Owen added, a blatant dig at Aidan for getting him drunk again.

Aidan frowned. *We're going there, are we?* "And would probably fire someone for backchat. But luckily, that doesn't happen often."

"Like to see him try." Owen's responses were getting quicker, which meant he was sobering up.

"Sounds like a demanding guy. But I suppose most bosses of big companies are.

Think I'll stick to my level to get settled in before meeting him."

Tom was ready to burst. "Trust me, Megan, you are way past your level already."

"What? What do you mean?" she asked, taking a sip of her coffee.

"You've already met the CEO."

"How could I have already met the CEO? I haven't even moved here yet." She noticed that Aidan and Owen were keeping quiet during their exchange. She looked at them both questionably. "Wait a minute." She started pointing towards them.

"Would anyone be so kind as to tell us what JMC actually stands for?" Tom looked at Aidan. "Aid?"

Megan looked at him, a sense of panic starting to settle in.

Aidan closed his eyes, sighed, and then looked at her unblinkingly. "Megan, JMC stands for James and Marie Costello. The company is named after my parents, in their memory."

Shocked, she sat up straight and stared at him for a brief few moments.

Owen and Tom watched in fascination.

"Oh my God! Well... this is incredibly unprofessional." She watched as Aidan burst into laughter. She looked at him. Her face was glowing red with embarrassment. "This is not the place for laughter."

"Come on, Meg. It's not like we knew each other's history when we met. Neither of us had a single idea who the other person was."

"But–"

"There's that but again. Come with me a second, we need to talk." Aidan took her hand and stood up. He turned to Owen and Tom. "Can we meet you back at the car in, say, fifteen minutes?"

"Take the car. We can get a cab back to mine. I'll send you the bill," Owen suggested.

"Fine. See you Monday."

***

Megan couldn't speak. She didn't actually know what to say to him, so she just let him lead her back to the car. Once they had battled the drunken crowds, Aidan opened the car door for them and they climbed in. Now that they were sitting side by side again, she felt like she had been called to the headmaster's office. She couldn't look at him.

What the hell. I'm already embarrassed. Might as well do what I do best and make a joke out of it.

"Well this is great, isn't it? I can't wait to get back to the flat later. 'Hey Meg, how was the market?', 'Fabulous, Em, one little thing though. That job you offered me? Well, I spent most of the night snogging the boss!' That's really going to go down well."

Aidan couldn't help but laugh again at her perfect sarcasm, winning him a stern look.

"Seriously, are you going to keep laughing about this?"

"Yeah, I am. Megan," he held one of her hands, "you are an amazing woman and when I saw you earlier, I knew right then that I had to meet you. There was no way I was going to let the night end without at least getting your name. We had no idea who worked for who, there was only that feeling I felt when I looked at you. That's all I was going off. And that's all you were going off too. Tell me I'm wrong."

Megan couldn't deny that she felt a strong connection too. "But surely if word got out that you were seeing one of your own staff members. . ."

"That could be an issue, yeah. But right now, you're not one of my staff members, so we're okay."

She sighed sadly, looking at her feet. "And when I am? We call whatever this is off? If this actually is anything." She was getting ready to hear the worst. She didn't want what they had started to end, even though he was her boss-to-be.

"How about we keep it quiet?"

Megan whipped her head up to look at him. "What?"

"No one but you, me, and the guys need to know. And Tony the driver." Aidan gently held the side of her neck and looked into her eyes. "I know it's crazy, and probably a bit risky, but I don't care. And since I'm the boss, I call the shots. The only person who'll try and say it's not the greatest idea will be Owen, and you heard Tom—he's not won a single argument since he's known me."

Megan smiled, tapping his knee. "Like the married couple you are?"

"Exactly." He lightly brushed her cheek with the back of his hand, enjoying the warmth of her skin. "So, what do you say? Fancy living life on the edge and seeing where this goes?"

Megan thought to herself briefly. When would she ever get another chance to date a man like Aidan? Was this the universe's way of telling her to take a chance for a change?

"We're actually going to do this?"

Aidan smiled at the thought of having Megan as the woman in his life. "If it's what you want, although I will never push you into anything you don't want."

Looking into his blue eyes, she couldn't help herself. With a mixture of adrenaline, nerves, and excitement of something new, she threw herself at him. He leant back to take the blow, holding her above as she kissed him in a way that answered his question perfectly.

"Okay, but there are going to have to be some rules," she said.

He looked up at her, puzzled.

"Here's your first. Learn to accept the word no as an answer every now and then." They both laughed. "And there's no way you're getting your own way all the time."

"I'll try, but I'm not promising anything." Aidan repositioned them so that Megan was lying fully above him, sprawled out on the back seat of the luxurious car. He held her tight. He took his phone out of the inside pocket of his leather jacket. Megan still had it wrapped tightly around her wonderful frame. "It's still early. Anywhere you want to go?"

Megan lifted her head. "Seeing as I don't know many places, I'll let you decide."

"Give me a minute." Aidan moved to the front of the car and tapped the divider. "We're going to need you for a bit longer, Tony. How much was I paying you tonight?"

"Five hundred for the night, I think."

"Double it. Could be a late one."

"Really? Thank you, Aidan." Tony shook his hand and moved into traffic after Aidan told him where to drive next.

"Where are we going?"

"Somewhere about half an hour away. I want to show you something."

Chapter 11

W hen they got out of the car, Aidan took her hand. They walked a short distance to Parliament Hill, to admire the nighttime view. She should have been admiring its beauty, but instead felt herself snigger when a thought popped into her head. It looked like someone had set all the traffic lights on amber. The red warning lights at the top of building twinkled making the sky above glow.

"It's quite weird how down there, the city's crazy, yet up here, it feels so peaceful."

"And pretty soon, you'll be calling it home."

To Megan, that thought still felt surreal. "So we're north of the city right now?"

"Yeah. The Shard is just ahead." He pointed out in front of them. "And if you look left, there's Canary Wharf. Home of JMC. After a particularly stressful day, I sometimes come up here to relax. To get away from it all."

"I can see why." Megan turned and hugged him. "Thank you."

"What for?"

"For sharing your getaway place with me."

"Trust me, Megan, it's the city that should feel lucky. Think of the view it gets when it looks up here." He rubbed his thumb across her cheek. "This is where I sit on an evening. This is where I think about life." He gestured to a bench behind them. "Come. Sit."

They sat down on the bench, entwining themselves in one another's clutches. It suddenly dawned on Aidan that Megan was the first girl he'd ever brought up to the viewpoint he used as an escape from work. She felt special to him. There was something about her that he'd never felt with anyone else before. He had a feeling she was encountering the same.

They stayed up on the hill for an hour, enjoying the view (both of the city and each other), before Megan began to look tired. She leant her head on Aidan's chest. Her eyelids were becoming heavy. He looked down at her, sensing her tiredness.

"When did you arrive in London?"

"I caught the early train up this morning." Then it dawned on her. "Omigosh, I've been awake for almost nineteen hours."

"Thought you were looking tired. As much as I don't want to leave you, we should be getting you back." He gently placed a kiss on her forehead.

Aidan didn't want the night to end. He wasn't ready to go back to his apartment alone. He didn't want to spend the rest of the weekend wondering where Megan was and what she was doing. He wanted to sit here with her all night long, talking about life and how crazy it can be. Because it *was* pretty crazy. Tonight was proof of that.

"Come on, then. Let's get you home." Aidan stood, dragging Megan up with him. As they walked away from the bench and the beautiful view of the city's skyline, he wondered if this was the last moment they'd ever truly spend together.

***

After a twenty minute drive, the car pulled up into a side street near the building in Hammersmith. They climbed out and walked to the front door together, hand in hand. Megan looked up and tried to figure out which flat was Emma and Lucy's.

"It looks like they're home, but I can't remember which one's theirs." She laughed, trying to count along the windows.

Aidan made sure his back was to the flats so that if anyone were looking, they wouldn't recognise him. "Any luck with your counting there, Einstein?"

"Shut up!" She lightly punched his chest. "So how are we going to do this? I can't exactly say that I didn't catch your name."

"Where's your mobile?" Megan searched her bag and handed it to him, unlocked. He typed in his number and showed her the screen. He'd saved it as Adam, along with his direct lines at JMC. "Problem solved. You've been out with Adam, not Aidan."

"That's so simple."

He grinned at her.

"Don't get cocky. I'm not having any of that." She laughed and looked up again, feeling like she was being watched.

He pulled her head down to his and they lost themselves in the moment. Deepening the kiss, Aidan ran his hands through her hair, pulling her closer to him so there wasn't a single gap between them. Reluctantly parting, Aidan laid his head against hers.

"When do you go back?"

"Tomorrow, on the two o'clock train from Waterloo. But I'll be back in a couple of weeks. Em and Lucy want me to come and look at bigger flats with them."

Aidan sighed. "Yeah, not sure I can wait that long."

"You're gonna have to. Besides, you'll probably be too busy running the company."

"Telling me what to do already? That's not going to end well."

Megan looked at him disapprovingly.

"Learn to hear no, I know. I get it." He smiled, tucking a strand of her hair behind her ear. "Message when you're on the train, okay?"

"Of course." Megan began to take off the leather jacket to give it back to him.

He stopped her, placing his hands on her shoulders. "Keep it until next time." He kissed her once more before reluctantly letting go.

"Is that a tactic, Mr. Costello? Leave me your jacket so you have an excuse to see me again?"

He spoke without looking back. "You bet."

Opening the front door, she smiled. She paused for a moment as she watched him walk back to the car. Here she thought she was only visiting London to celebrate Emma's promotion, not a promotion of her own, and she definitely didn't expect to leave with a new man in her life. A night with endless possibilities. Her mind quickly found its way back to Aidan. She wrapped his jacket around her, relishing the scent of him that lingered on it.

Excitement overcame her. She threw her arms in the air and let out a squeal. She didn't care if she'd woken the entire neighbourhood. She was loving life.

Before Megan could get through the door, Emma and Lucy pounced on her with questions about her evening and date. Who was he? Where was he from? What was he like? Whose jacket is that? Are you seeing him again? She had to think fast when she answered so they didn't suspect anything.

She told the girls that Adam was from London, that he worked for some insurance company, and that they were going to keep in contact and would meet up again when she next came to the city. She was feeling proud of her quick responses, but the truth of who she was actually dating was far more exciting.

Megan kicked off her shoes and slumped down on the sofa—her temporary bed for the night. "So, what about you guys? How did your dates go?

"Never mind our dates, Meg. This is a top of the line Armani." Lucy pointed to the designer label on Aidan's leather jacket. "Looks like you've bagged a good'un."

"Yes I have, Lucy, yes I have."

"Right ladies, I am off to bed. It's been one hell of a day." Emma stood up and stretched, clearly satisfied with the amount of questions they'd thrown enough at one another. "And as amazing as it's been, I am knackered."

"Me too." Lucy nodded as she stood to her feet. "Night Meg. Night Em."

"Good night, girls." Megan waited for them to leave the room before she messaged Aidan.

UNTIL NEXT TIME. NIGHT, M Xx

Moments later, Aidan responded.

YOU TEASE! DON'T YOU MAKE ME TURN THIS CAR AROUND, I'M ALMOST HOME. SWEET DREAMS BABY. AID XX

Megan smiled at her phone. Her life was beginning to change at such a fast pace, and all in the space of a couple of days. If someone had told her at the beginning of the week that she would be offered a job in the city and would be starting a new relationship with a CEO, she would have told them to move along and stop talking crap.

Her phone buzzed, signalling another message.

SO, YOUR TRAIN LEAVES AT TWO FROM WATERLOO? WHAT TIME ARE YOU GETTING THERE?

What is he up too?

DEPENDS. AM I LIKELY TO FIND A CERTAIN SOMEONE WAITING FOR ME?

"Megan," Emma called from the bathroom. Megan hid her phone just as she rounded the living room door. "Do you want us to travel down to the station with you tomorrow?"

Perfect.

"I should be fine, Em, no point in you guys coming all the way down. You'll only have to come back again. Sleep in. I'll message you when I'm on my way home."

"Are you sure?"

"Sleep, Em. I'll be fine."

Emma waved at her, then headed along the corridor.

GOOD NEWS. I'VE TOLD EMMA TO HAVE A SLOW START TOMORROW, SO I'M FREE AT ANY TIME. WHEN AND WHERE? M Xx

Chapter 12

The next morning, dressed in her skinny jeans, oversized jumper, scarf, and Converse, with Aidan's jacket over her arm, Megan waved goodbye to both Emma and Lucy (who were still in bed) and caught the London Underground to Waterloo. Part of her wanted to stay, but she knew she had to go back to break the news to Ben and her work. She needed to tell them that she would soon be leaving them both for the bright lights of London.

Her phone, picking up the Wi-Fi as she passed a station, announced a message from Ben.

GOOD NIGHT? HOPE YOU GAVE MY LOVE TO THE GIRLS. CALL ME WHEN YOU CAN. FROM LUCY'S FACEBOOK STATUS, IT LOOKS LIKE YOU DEFINITELY HAD AN ENJOYABLE EVENING. WHO'S ADAM, BY THE WAY? BEN XX

Oh Great! Nice one, Lucy. I was hoping to not have to deal with that until I got home.

Changing trains at Westminster, Megan caught the Jubilee Line down to Waterloo. As soon as her phone got full signal, she called Ben, who answered on the second ring.

"Who is he?"

"I'm great thanks. It's nice to hear from you too."

"Megan. . ."

"Okay, fine. Someone you would approve of, okay? And since you asked, yes, I had an amazing night."

"Are you seeing him again?"

"Ben, sweetheart, you're not my parental guardian." She looked around her. "Hang on, I'm lost." She lowered the phone. "Excuse me? Where's the main entrance to the station please?"

Ben heard someone give her directions, followed by Megan thanking them.

"And yes, I am seeing Adam again. Right now, actually." Aidan had replied the night before to say he would meet her outside the station. Megan walked down the main stairs to wait for him.

"Hmm, okay. But I'm going to need details, baby girl, lots of details."

"And you will, when I get home. Listen, I have some news to tell you when I'm back. Nothing bad, actually it's really g–" Megan lost all form of speech when she spotted Aidan crossing the road.

Goddamn, he's gorgeous. Even better in daylight.

His hair was tamed back under a cap and he was wearing his amazing smile. His clothes clung to him like they were custom-made. The jeans, baseball shirt, and hoodie made him look like a celebrity who was attempting to keep a low profile. He came up to her, smiled, and kissed her, wrapping his arms around her waist like they had spent the past year apart.

"Good morning, beautiful."

"Hello? Ashton?" Ben's voice came through the phone. She'd almost forgotten she was talking to him.

Megan pointed to the phone, signalling to Aidan that she'd just be a minute. He twisted them around so he was leaning against the wall edge with Megan leaning against him.

"Are you still there, Meg?"

"Yeah, I'm still here."

"So, what's the news?"

"I said I'd tell you when I'm home. I want to tell Martin as well. Is he coming over for dinner tonight?"

Aidan turned Megan around so she was facing him. She looked into his eyes as he played with her hair, her spare arm resting on his shoulder.

"I can't keep him away. I may need you to move out eventually, if you get my meaning."

She could feel his smirk through the phone. "Ben, seriously, you have such a one- track mind. Listen, I'm catching the two o'clock train back, so I should be at the station by five and home by six at the latest. Would you be a darling and order some dinner?" Megan pleaded. "You know what I like."

"Anything for you, Meg. Message when you're a couple of stops away."

"You're a lifesaver. Thank you." She hung up and threw her arms around Aidan.

They melted into a kiss, enjoying the taste of one another.

"Who's Ben?" Aidan asked, pulling back to look at her.

"One of my closest friends, we share a place together back home."

Aidan groaned, mumbling under his breath. Megan placed a hand on her hip. "What?"

"Nothing." He placed his hand over hers. "Just not sure I'm happy about your current living situation."

Megan tried not to laugh. "Ben has his boyfriend, Martin, around this evening. I don't think either of them will try and make a pass at me." She laughed, unable to hold it in any longer. "So, you've got me for a few hours, what do you want to do?"

Aidan looked playfully at her, trying to hide his jealousy.

"Come on. You're as bad as Ben."

"Can you blame me? Have you seen yourself? No wonder that other guy was trying to make a move on you last night."

Megan's eyes lit up in amusement.

"Yeah, I saw that. Nicely dismissed by the way."

She tapped the front of his cap. "What happened to waiting?"

He planted a kiss on her forehead. "Lunch? At least let me make sure you've had a decent meal before your journey home."

She leant back and smiled at him. Taking his hand, she let him escort her to wherever lunch was going to be. Aidan hailed a cab down, and she climbed in after him. She didn't know where they were going; as long as Aidan was there, she really didn't care.

The cab stopped. Megan looked around, not seeing a restaurant or a cafe in sight. Had the driver gotten lost?

After Aidan paid, he reached for Megan's hand. They walked from the main road, hand in hand, down an alley and within moments she was gazing upon the London Thames. A beautiful brown-bricked building rose high above her. Its high arches made her glance up to take in the architecture.

***

Opening the restaurant door, Aidan looked behind to check they hadn't been followed by any photographers. Happy that they hadn't been seen, he took his hat off and ruffled his hair.

Megan glanced around anxiously. "It's quite busy. Do you think it'll be a long wait?"

"Mr. Costello, a pleasure, Sir," the restaurant's host said. "Table for two?"

Aidan shook his hand, and quietly asked him to find them a private area in the restaurant.

"Right this way, Sir."

"I see. Big name comes with big advantages, does it?" Megan felt an envious glare from the customers who were waiting for a table to become free.

They were escorted to a private dining room where they would be undisturbed. Aidan stopped the restaurant's host before they walked through. "I need you to forget what you've seen here today. If you speak to anyone, or tell anyone we were here, there will be trouble. We good?" Aidan had his hand out ready to shake the host's, knowing that he would agree to his terms—especially when he felt the note that Aidan was about to slip him.

The man smiled as he took Aidan's hand. "Absolutely, Mr. Costello. Not a word will leave this restaurant."

"That goes for the staff here as well, understand?"

"Yes, Sir. Fully." The host nodded and walked off, leaving Megan to stare in amazement.

She couldn't believe the power Aidan had just displayed. The host was all but in his back pocket. Damn, why was she finding this so ... attractive?

"So, do people usually do as you tell them?"

"Yep." Aidan scooted his chair around and held her hand. "Megan, I'm not going to deny the fact that keeping our relationship a secret is going to be hard. At times, it'll probably feel bloody impossible, but if we begin now, we'll have more of a fighting chance. We need to keep it out of the media."

"Media? Hence the hat, then?"

"Yeah. Wait till I'm in work mode, it gets worse. I need you to know that if we're out anywhere and I push away from you, distance myself or whatever... I'm only protecting you. The last thing I want is for you to become a target for photographers. You're far too precious to me to see you get hurt by what they can do."

Megan was trying not to feel overwhelmed by her emotions. She couldn't remember the last time a man had said anything so nice to her. And that was in any amount of time.

This had come within the twenty-four hours of their time together.

"If you ever feel like this is too much, or if you feel pressured in any way, please tell me. My life can get crazy sometimes, so if you ever want out–"

Megan stopped him mid-sentence by placing her finger on his lips. "Keep talking like that and I'll walk right now." She stroked his cheek. "Aidan, I'm not planning on going anywhere. Last night, I hoped I'd just get to see you one more time before I went home."

Aidan smiled and placed his hand over hers.

She understood that if she was about to begin a relationship with a successful high flyer, it would come with some hard work. They'd work through it together.

Pulling him close into a kiss, she thought she felt something that she was sure shouldn't be happening so quickly. Aidan looked at her, and his blue eyes seemed like they were looking into her soul. It felt... right.

Their moment of passionate silence was interrupted by a knock on the door.

"Just a minute!" he called out. "Megan, I've waited too long for you to come into my life." He kissed her passionately, and she melted from his words once more.

The waiter knocked for a second time.

"Are we ready to order, or shall I give it another five minutes?" "Meg?"

"I'm good to go."

They ordered their lunch and settled back to relax over a coffee. They spoke of all sorts of things, from how Aidan built JMC, right through to life in Megan's hometown. There were no awkward moments, like the ones you sometimes found on first dates. There was just the enjoyment of each other's company, of getting to know one another properly for the first time.

After they finished lunch, Aidan paid and asked the waiter to call a taxi. He wanted it to be ready at the back entrance of the restaurant.

"Do you ever want your jacket back, by the way?"

"I told you last night, not until next time. This isn't next time yet." Aidan placed his jacket over her shoulders again. "Take good care of it. I know you will."

"If it's as expensive as it looks, I'll guard it with my life."

Aidan laughed as he walked them out of the restaurant, shaking the waiter's hand as they passed him.

Megan wrapped an arm around his waist, breathing a sigh of contentment, making their way back down the corridor to the road. She was happy, happier than she'd been in years.

Aidan turned to her, cupping her face with his hands. "When did you say you'd be back in London?"

"Two weeks on Wednesday."

Aidan groaned. "Two weeks? My God."

"It's really not that long." Megan opened the back door of the taxi while he handed the driver more cash than was needed for the fare, probably to keep him quiet as well.

"You're a woman, you can handle two weeks." He flashed that smile at her again. "How about you come up the day before and we can spend some time together before you meet the girls?"

"Not a bad idea. I may be a woman, but even women have limits on how long we can wait, my dear." She placed her bag on the back seat and turned to look at him. "Are you getting in?"

"I wish I could see you off properly, Meg. I promise it won't be like this forever."

She ran her hand through his hair. "Don't worry, I understand. I'll call you every day."

"You better. Mornings and afternoons are best; the middle of the day can get insanely busy."

He gave her a goodbye kiss that made her crave more than what he was offering. She waved goodbye to the man of her dreams. Then she sank back in her seat and watched him walk off in the other direction.

Chapter 13

The Monday morning meeting at JMC had run smoothly when compared to Friday's. Even still, Aidan felt exhausted. But exhaustion wouldn't stop him today—things were going great. His employees were fully up to speed as to how he wanted the negotiations to be handled. He'd informed everyone to keep him updated via email.

After dismissing his staff to their respective departments, he sat back in his conference room chair to gather his thoughts.

Owen came back into the room and sat in the chair next to him. "Well, that went better than Friday. Should have half the deals sorted by the end of the week if there are no hiccups."

Aidan stood, gathered his belongings, and checked his phone. No message or call from Megan yet. He figured she was probably busy getting ready for work. "I need coffee. Joining? I need a quick word too."

"Sure," Owen said.

"Lois, coffee?" He asked, turning to his personal assistant as he called the lift.

"Yes please. Thank you," Lois said gratefully. "Can you pick up a chocolate muffin too?"

Aidan didn't respond, he was too busy messaging Megan.

"Earth to Aidan?" Owen tapped his head. "Has someone hit your off button?"

Aidan glared at him, stepping into the lift. "Fuck off. Yes I can, Lois, of course."

The lift doors closed. As they rode the lift down, Aidan took the private moment to update Owen on his relationship with Megan.

"Are you insane? She's going to be working for you in a month's time."

"I am fully aware of that, Owen," he said in a voice way calmer than his friend's.

"And what happens if someone finds out? It could mean trouble—a whole lot of trouble for you ... and for Megan."

"And that's exactly why no one will find out. For now, at least. So if you could pass the message to your brother to keep quiet too, I'd appreciate that." Aidan turned to face him. "Don't rip it out of me, Owen, but there's something about her that seems right, you know? Like when you met Clare. And we want to explore it. It might work and it might not, but it's something we want to find out together." Aidan looked right at him and waited for an answer.

"Okay. Just try not to fuck anything up. I'm not helping you clean this one up if it goes sour."

Aidan smacked his back in thanks. The lift doors opened and they stepped out onto the ground floor.

Seeing their boss heading for the coffee shop, staff members moved out of the way so he could walk through undisturbed. Aidan spotted Emma in the reception and couldn't help but smile. He felt a surge of energy when he looked at her. If only she knew.

"Mr. Costello. Mr. Turner." She greeted them with a smile, large coffee in hand.

"Emma," Aidan said, enjoying the scrunched expression on her face. She was clearly confused by him knowing her name.

Waiting patiently in line, Aidan checked his phone again. Owen looked down, and realised why he wasn't the usual talkative CEO he'd grown to know.

"You really like her, don't you?"

Aidan smiled, remembering how Megan looked when he saw her for the first time. *God, she was so fucking hot.* "Yeah, I do. I don't know for sure, but I think I can see a future with her."

*****

That same afternoon, Kev came to Aidan's office for their afternoon meeting. He was offered a job in the customer service department, and a salary that put his old job wage to shame. He was extremely grateful and thanked Aidan for the opportunity to work for such a large company.

"While you're here, Kev," Aidan stood and closed his office door, "I need to update you on me and Meg."

"How's it going?"

"Pretty good. We met yesterday before she left London." He shrugged, leaning against his desk. "Listen, after we left the club, I found out she's starting here in a month. And, since it's all official now, I need you to do me another favour."

Kev lifted an eyebrow.

"I need you to help us keep the relationship quiet."

"Oh right, because you'll be her boss?"

"Got it in one. Owen and Tom already know."

"Consider it a secret I'll take to my grave."

"A bit dramatic, but I'm grateful." Aidan stood up straight, changing the subject. "So, we'll be seeing you here in a couple of weeks then."

Kev stood and shook Aidan's hand, before hugging him instead.

"Come back at the end of the day, we'll grab some after-work drinks."

Chapter 14

E arly Tuesday morning, Emma came up to Aidan's office to inform him of the sales projection and targets of her department. He knew all about Emma and her close friendship with Megan, along with Lucy.

Aidan's phone was on his desk facing upward when it began to ring. Emma glanced down to where the noise was coming from, only to see Megan's name flash up on the screen. Shocked, she stood up straight, and started to try and say something. She failed. Miserably. She looked to Aidan for some kind of answer.

He put his hand up and answered the call instead, all the time watching Emma. She looked like she'd frozen solid. "Hey, how's your day so far?"

Megan groaned. "Better now, after hearing your voice. Is it legal to beat the living shit out of people?"

"Bad morning?"

"You could say that. Some people should come with a warning bell. I've had three arguments and I haven't even had a chance to touch my coffee yet."

"Not long now, sweetheart. A couple more weeks and you'll be working for the best company in the world." Aidan smirked. *Well, that's what you think.*

"God" Megan sighed. "I hate that I'll have to come back and work in this hell hole for another two weeks before I can move to London for good"

Aidan was finding it harder and harder to hide his smugness hearing her complaining. He held back a laugh as

Emma's eyes lit up in even more shock. "Are we still on for tonight?"

"Yeah, I'm finishing early, so can catch the next coach..." Megan paused to look at the time table. "At four. Then I'll get the tube to Canary Wharf."

"Coach? No way, I'm sending you a car."

"You don't need to ... oh no, wait. You're not going to let me say no, are you?"

"Argue all you want, a car will be waiting for you."

"Fine, you win. I'm not going for four arguments before midday!" They both laughed, but Megan thought there was something different in the tone of his voice. "Is something wrong?"

"Now that you mention it, yeah, there is something."

"What's the matter? Do we need to cancel?"

"God no! These past couple of weeks have been enough torture, thank you very much." Aidan paused, considering the best way to put it. "How exactly do you get Emma to start moving again? It looks like she's frozen on the spot."

Megan nearly fell to the floor. "What? Omigosh! Is she in your office with you?"

"*Yeah.*" Aidan dragged the word out.

"Shit! It's usually safe to call now. Does she know you're talking to me?"

"She's got some idea, yes. Saw your name come up on my phone and hasn't moved since."

Megan could already picture her. It was hard not to find it funny. "Is she sitting down?"

"Nope."

"Sit her down before she collapses. Can you put me on speakerphone, please? I'll sort this."

Aidan put his phone down, pressed speakerphone, and pushed Emma's shoulders so she sat in one of the chairs opposite his desk. "Done."

Megan tried to get her friend's attention. "Emma? Em, you there?"

"Huh? Yeah, I'm here," Emma replied in a high pitched voice. "What's going on, Meg?"

"Okay first of all, I'm sorry I didn't tell you straight away, but the guy I left the club with that night was Aidan."

Emma coughed and began to stutter. "W-what? H-he... What?"

"Could you get some water for her please, Aid?"

Aidan walked over to his drinks cabinet and grabbed two glasses. He poured Emma a glass of wine and a Jack Daniels for himself. He remembered her drink of choice from that night out. He walked back over to his desk.

"Aidan is Adam?" Emma's voice went up another octave. "So the guy we saw you with outside the flat was... sorry, *is*... my boss? And soon enough, he'll be your boss too."

"Hence the need to keep it quiet," Aidan added, handing her the wine. He mentally kicked himself for letting her find out about him and Megan so easily.

"Thank you," Emma whispered, taking a large mouthful of rosé.

"Have you got some water now, Em?"

"Of sorts," Aidan answered for her.

"Listen Emma." Emma heard Megan take a deep breath. "Yes, yes Aidan and I are seeing one another."

Emma glared at Aidan. "And when may I ask did this happen?" Aidan broke the connection, trying to look busy.

"The night we went out."

Emma groaned and dropped her head on the desk. "My brain hurts." She didn't know whether to ask more questions, or let Megan simply explain what went on that night. Her best friend was dating her boss. It was the last thing she expected to learn when she woke up that morning. Aidan, her boss, and her best friend. She lifted her head and ran her hands through her hair, trying to compose herself.

"Could I have a moment with Meg please?"

"Sure, I'll be outside." Aidan gave her his phone so they could speak and took his drink out to his private balcony, along with the tablet Emma came in with. Aidan opened the door of his office and stepped outside. He admired the skyline.

The tall buildings of Canary Wharf and the surrounding areas always took his breath away. He counted himself lucky that he was able to build his empire in the heart of the city. Sitting down, he balanced his feet on the edge of the balcony, focussing on Emma's spreadsheets. Reading her forecast for the following year, he found it hard to concentrate. All he wanted to do was peer around and see how their conversation was going. It wasn't like they were taking about something simple. It was about him and Megan.

Was Emma happy about it? Was she going to approve, or would she warn Megan to stay clear of him? For the first time in years, he felt himself panicking. Megan was special to him. Best friend or not, Emma wasn't about to stop him from seeing her. He jumped in his seat when Emma tapped on the glass of the balcony door, almost dropping the tablet.

He rejoined Emma in his office. "All good now?"

"Yes, sorry about my reaction, it's not every day you find out your boss is dating your best friend."

***

Megan knew exactly who was responsible when Laura told her she was able to leave today, two weeks earlier than expected.

"The gentleman on the phone was very polite, but he was also very demanding," Laura said, folding tops after some kids had messed them up.

When I see Aidan tonight, we're gonna have another chat about the fact that he's not going to get his own way all the time. She laughed aloud to herself.

"What's so funny?" Laura asked.

"Nothing, nothing... just a funny joke Ben told me last night. Wasn't even that funny really," Megan said. She tried to cover up another giggle.

"Anyway, we'll be sad to see you go, Meg. You've been such a great member of our little team. But I know you've wanted to explore a different career for a while now."

Megan smiled. Her boss was opening up to her.

"It will certainly be exciting though, working for JMC. I hope you keep us updated as to how you get on. I've heard the CEO is quite the looker you know."

Megan shrugged, stifling her grin. "Well, if I meet him, maybe I'll pass your number on." *Never gonna happen!*

Opening the work laptop, Laura searched for JMC Ltd online. "I mean, can we just stop for a moment please to appreciate the beauty that is Aidan Costello? He's hot. I wouldn't say no."

I haven't. Megan looked at his pictures, and if she had thought Aidan was gorgeous in his casual clothes, this was something else. In his business suits, he hit a whole new level of the word. She hadn't searched the internet for him while they were apart. She didn't know if she'd be able to stop herself from driving straight to London to be with him.

Shit. I can't wait to see him later. For one reason or another. She laughed at her own thoughts again, which made Laura give her another questionable look. "He's very cute, Laura, I'll give him that." *And that's all he's getting until tonight.*

"I wonder if he's single." Laura began clicking on the news section of Google.

Megan rolled her eyes. "Look, I've got a few hours left to make myself useful here. Shouldn't we stop looking at guys we'll never have a chance with and get back to work?"

That you'll never have a chance with, I mean. That CEO you're drooling over is all mine.

"What's this? Meg," Laura waved her back, "come here."

Returning to the counter, she looked at the laptop and saw an article that showed Aidan, Owen, Kev, and a redhead (hanging onto Owen's arm) at a bar in the city. Megan guessed that she must have been Owen's wife, Clare. Both of them were laughing with Kev, Aidan was on the phone just off to the left. Standing next to him was a stunning blonde, clearly trying to make a move on him. It seemed she'd been completely unsuccessful though.

Aidan's hand was up in front of her face, signalling that he wasn't interested. The woman looked horrified that she was being turned down by such a well-known man.

Megan smiled as Laura read out the caption.

"Is Aidan Costello off the market? Would you turn this woman down?" Laura thought to herself for a moment. "Hmm, well if I was a man I wouldn't turn her down."

Megan was intrigued. "When was this photo taken?" She tried to sound casual.

"Last Friday at around six-thirty, apparently. Must have been after-work drinks."

Megan tried to hide the smile that beamed onto her face. She knew exactly who he was on the phone with. She remembered the conversation they were having very well.

"Well, whoever is on the other end of that phone must be very lucky."

"They sure must be." *Yes, I am.* "But anyway, let's stop drooling over millionaire CEOs and get back to work, shall we? Like I said, you've only got me for a few more hours." *And that means there are just a few more hours until I get to see that beautiful smile again.*

Chapter 15

L eaving the company garage at around eleven a.m., in his black Mercedes Benz, Aidan began maneuvering through the busy London traffic from Canary Wharf to the West Country. He wasn't twenty minutes into his journey when he received a message from Emma.

> **MEGAN FINISHES WORK AT 3. BE OUT THE BACK OF HER SHOP BY THEN. SHE'LL BE OUT ABOUT FIVE MINUTES LATER. SHE USUALLY HAS HER EARPHONES IN TO WALK HOME, SO YOU'LL NEED TO PARK SOMEWHERE SHE'LL SPOT YOU. GOOD NEWS THOUGH, SHE'S PACKED ALREADY. MIGHT JUST NEED A FEW MORE THINGS, DEPENDING ON HOW LONG YOU'RE PLANNING ON KEEPING HER AT YOURS. EM.**

Aidan had asked Emma to keep him updated as to where Megan would be when he got to Somerset. If he was going to surprise her, he was going to do it properly; and Emma was more than willing to help. She must've called Megan to get the required information as soon as he left her office.

His media control unit asked if he wished to reply.

"Yes, reply," he ordered in a stern voice. He didn't know why he even had this function in his car. He spent more time shouting at it in frustration than he did anything else. The damn thing had a mind of its own sometimes.

> **THANKS. DRIVING THROUGH THE CENTRE OF LONDON NOW, WILL HIT THE M25 IN ABOUT AN HOUR IF TRAFFIC ISN'T TOO BAD. SHOULD BE BACK IN LONDON BY 7PM FOR EVERYONE TO GET OVER FOR 8.**

As he neared Embankment, the traffic began to slow, which he predicted it probably would. Winding down his window, he looked out over to the Thames. The river was beautiful. He loved looking out into it and getting lost in the view. He was just about to begin his daydream when a group of young women spotted him. They waved and looked like they were about to run over to his car while he was temporarily stuck in traffic.

Please don't come over, please don't come over. Shaking his head, he looked skyward. *In your own time, London. Today would be nice.* As if on cue, the traffic started moving, and he sped off as fast as possible, much to the women's disappointment.

***

It had only been an hour since Emma called her, requesting information about what time she was finishing work. Megan had her suspicions, of course, but she'd hung up the phone before the interrogation could begin. That's why she was glad Emma was on the phone again right now. Megan wanted answers. They were up to something here, she could sense it.

"Has this information been requested from a certain boss of yours, Emma?" She asked quietly, to prevent Laura from hearing.

"Aidan's really busy in a conference meeting and asked if I'd mind getting timings and what not," she lied. "He said he's going to try and organise some kind of dinner at his apartment for us all."

"Us all? Who's us all?"

"You, me, and Lucy. Owen and his wife, Clare. Owen's brother, Tom, and Kev."

Perfect! That'll be a great moment to introduce you to Tom as promised. "That will be lovely. Saw a picture of Owen's wife earlier, Laura was googling Aidan! She's stunning."

"Isn't she? She's lovely. Met her a couple of times briefly. You'll definitely get on with her."

"I'm looking forward to it. Aidan mentioned how supportive she is." Megan coughed. "Talking of Aidan. Did he tell you that Laura had a call from the recruitment manager earlier about me being able to finish today?"

"Ha! Yeah. Played that well, didn't he? It's why he's the top boss, Meg. He can pretty much get anyone to do anything he wants."

"Well, we'll see about that," Megan joked. "I better get back to work, Em. Laura is giving me a suspicious look. I'll message you when I've finished."

Hanging up, Megan gave her apologies to Laura and carried on working.

***

The journey to Somerset didn't take as long as Aidan had originally thought. He'd received many calls from his office about the up-and-coming contract deal between the UK and the USA. That had killed some time, and had gotten him excited. A software company signing up with a hardware computer company? This was going to be a walk in the park to finalise.

Emma had texted him the postcodes he needed to find Megan's work and flat, and he was getting closer by the second. In fact, he was so close that he was going to be early. He pressed a button on the steering wheel to reply to Emma.

"Got some time t–"

"I'm sorry," the automated system interrupted. "I did not get that. Please speak clearly."

"Fuck off! I am speaking clearly," he said.

"I'm sorry. I did not get that."

Aidan pulled the car over, slamming on the brakes, and picked up his phone. "I'm sorry, I didn't think a car this expensive could be as shit as it is," he mumbled to himself. "Fucking crap bollocking piece of fuckery."

GOT SOME TIME TO KILL, EMMA. GOING TO BE EARLY. ARE THERE ANY DECENT CAFES OR ANYTHING NEARBY?

He sighed and pressed send.

***

Emma sent him some brief directions to a coffee shop situated in a shopping village. Finding the coffee shop, he parked up and went in to order his usual black Americano. The barista took his card to process the sale and gave him his order. And best of all, she didn't have a single clue as to who he was. It felt great.

Don't get used to that, Costello. Probably just a one off.

Aidan leant against one of the exterior walls near the coffee shop and took in what he saw around him. Groups of students sat around carelessly, gossiping about what their crazy friend had done and telling the others not to repeat what had been said.

Aidan had to smile. He remembered life when it used to be that way, living carefree with zero obligations or responsibilities. The worst part was that those kids didn't even know how good they had it. He would be a fool for being angry about that though. When he was their age, he hadn't known either.

He downed the rest of his coffee in one gulp, tossed the cup into the bin, and walked off, heading for his car. He smiled all the way there. Today was a good day.

He climbed into the car and drove off, being careful when leaving this street and joining the next. He made the transition smoothly, blending in with the traffic, and then kept driving. He still had some time to kill.

The town looked rundown—almost like it had been forgotten about—and it was a shame. At one time, it was probably a town you could feel proud to live in. These days though, it was on its last legs.

The buildings he passed were shabby and outdated, with cracks in the brickwork and cardboard where windows should be. It wasn't pleasant to look at, and Aidan felt almost guilty. Megan deserved better than this. He couldn't wait to take her back to London and show her what life would be like with him by her side.

He glanced around the town as he drove, taking in the surroundings once more. He tried to imagine Megan walking around, doing her day to day shopping and found it hard to see her among the local townsfolk. She was too glamorous for a town so run down.

Stopping his car outside the back of her shop, just before three as instructed, he waited for Megan to appear so he could give her the shock of her life.

***

Laura gave Megan the biggest hug she'd ever received and wished her all the very best. "I'm sorry we haven't got you a card or something, we had planned on getting you some flowers when you left. I wasn't expecting that call to come through today."

Megan hugged her now ex co-workers. "It's okay, really. A hug is perfectly fine. Besides, I'll be back at the weekend. Maybe we can all go for some drinks?"

"I'll look forward to that." Laura paused a moment, thinking about what to say next. She didn't want to cry. Not in front of everyone else. "Now get out of here, before I change my mind and tie you to the staffroom door!"

Megan laughed and hugged Laura again. "I'll see you guys."

Putting her earphones in, and texting Emma as promised, she waved goodbye to everyone and opened the back door of the store. She kicked the door closed behind her and stepped off the famous back step for the very last time. *Shit, this was it.* The first step on the road to the rest of her life.

She halted as she looked up. "What the fuck?"

She pulled her earphones back out. Parked outside was a metallic black Mercedes Benz with tinted windows and a personalised number plate: AC JMC. *Well I wonder who sent this...*

Her attention was on the car—which she had to admit was beautiful—meaning that she hadn't noticed the figure leant up against the wall, next to the backdoor. She heard a cough and assumed it was the car's driver. She turned around to address the driver.

"I'm guessing this car has been sent–" Her breath caught in her throat when she saw Aidan standing there, looking as gorgeous as he had on the computer screen hours earlier. "By you?"

Aidan pushed off the wall and began towards her. "I do believe I said there'd be a car waiting for you, didn't I?"

Her breathing quickened. Dropping her bag, she launched herself at him, wrapping her legs around his waist. He happily took her weight, spinning her around. He pushed her against the wall. Their kiss left nothing to the imagination when it came to what they both wanted next.

"I can't believe you're here. When did you... shit... I don't even care. Just don't you dare go anywhere."

"Yes, Ma'am." He saluted, putting her down.

She looked Aidan up and down. "You know Laura—who I think you may have spoken to earlier? Well–"

"Don't know what you're talking about," he said, chiming in.

"—she was searching for photos of you online and was quite taken aback by your business attire. She also wondered why you'd turned that hot blonde down."

Aidan grinned, saying nothing.

"But seeing you in front of me, in what seems to be a Dolce and Gabbana..." Megan couldn't find the words to finish the sentence. She was too busy imagining what was under his black fitted suit.

"You know your labels, eh? Very impressive."

"When you have a friend who dresses celebs in designer gear," she ran a hand over his shoulder, feeling the fabric, "you tend to pick up a few things."

"And for the record, that woman was being a pain in my ass. She wouldn't get the hint and leave." He began to gently run his hands underneath the back of her top, making her shiver.

"Oh my God, you're gonna have to stop your hands from exploring. I'll end up getting us arrested."

Aidan looked like he was contemplating carrying on and screwing what the police thought. He traced a finger up the back of her spine, loving how her eyes began to burn for him. Megan couldn't control herself. She grabbed the lapels of his jacket, pulling him close. She wanted him, in more ways than one. Closing the distance, their lips met in a heated kiss.

There was a crack as the door opened. "Yeah, yeah, five minutes" They heard Laura's voice from inside the shop. "I'm just nipping out for a smoke." Aidan lifted his head. "Quick, in the car."

They hopped in and he gunned it away, rounding the corner just as Laura stepped outside. "Lunatics," she said, at the sound of the screeching tires.

***

Megan rushed around her flat, trying to pack another bag to take with her to begin her new life in London. Should she bring everything with her? She had struggled to find a dress for the night out, how was she going to decide what to take for however long she was going to be in London this time? Sitting on the edge of the bed, she composed herself.

No need to stress Meg, it's just packing a bag. Or two? Maybe three.

She leant on her hand, looking across the hall to see Aidan leaning forward, speaking on the phone. Before he could spot her watching him, she ducked back around.

Plus the biggie: the possibility of sleeping with him later.

She smiled, biting her lip just thinking about it. Changing into fresh clothes while Aidan sat on the sofa, she ran around, throwing clothes and necessary items into a rucksack.

He joined her in her bedroom and leant against the door frame.

"The signal here is crap. How do you actually manage to stay in contact with people?"

"Wi-Fi code's behind the TV."

"Nah, it's going." He looked up once he'd managed to send the email. "Have you changed? Without me?"

Megan wasn't listening anymore. She was too busy double checking that she'd packed all she could think of. "Okay, think I have everything I need for now. Are we in a rush to get back?"

Aidan groaned and stepped closer, but to his surprise, it was Megan who turned him around, pushing him onto her bed. She took his suit jacket off and happily allowed his hands to wander again, before he strongly swapped their positions so he was above her. Megan stopped him, placing her finger on his lips when he tried to kiss her.

"Wait," she ordered.

"God, Megan. You're killing me."

"I have a question."

"Now?!"

"Do as you please if I get it wrong."

"You're wrong, whatever it is... so wrong."

"Very funny." She wiggled beneath him, doing nothing for his train of thought. "Were you or were you not planning a dinner or something at your apartment tonight? Emma happened to mention something about it earlier. If so, should we actually be getting back before everyone turns up? But believe me. I would very much like to continue this, you know, later on." Megan hinted at their intimate position.

He moaned into her neck.

"I'll take that as a yes, then." She smiled. "But, Aid, tonight, I'll be in *your* apartment. And there, *you* get to make the rules."

Aidan moved quicker than expected, pulling her up with him. Throwing his suit jacket over his shoulder and picking up his Armani leather (the jacket that Megan had hijacked), he leaned in closely. "Tell me, how are you with speed?"

Chapter 16

The journey back to London went quicker than the drive down. Megan finally got to admire the beauty of his car, but she kept her hands to herself. It looked very expensive and she was feeling clumsy. The last thing she wanted to do was break her new boyfriend's car.

Aidan kept hold of Megan's hand as he drove, only releasing it to indicate and answer calls from his office. When they stopped briefly for a break, Megan took the opportunity to call Ben and let him know she wouldn't be back because JMC wanted her to start the following week. She felt terrible feeding him this lie, but she couldn't tell him the truth quite yet. She promised to call him and keep him updated daily.

Aidan came out of the service station with cold drinks and leant against his car. Passing her some lemonade, he smiled. "Wanna drive it? You'd look good in the driver's seat."

"Eventually, maybe ... but right now, I'd probably crash it. I don't want to know how much that would set me back. It looks expensive."

"It's only a car, don't think of the price."

"Says the multimillionaire!"

***

The closer they got to London, the heavier the traffic became. Aidan took all the back roads he knew to bypass the traffic to Southbank, where his apartment was. There was only a few times the traffic came to standstill, which annoyed the hell out of Aidan, but gave Megan a chance to admire the city she was about to call home.

"So, does everyone in London drive a Mercedes?" Megan noticed a large amount of them on the roads.

"Not like this one. It's custom-built. One of a kind, you might say."

"Another reason I'll wait to have a go in it."

They pulled up to his apartment building at around six-thirty, parking in the underground carpark. He opened Megan's door and helped her out. He'd arranged for everyone to arrive at around eight, so they had an hour or so to themselves.

"You live next to the Thames?"

"Wait till you see the view from the top, you can just about see the restaurant we had lunch in."

He threw some of her bags over his shoulder and locked the car. Taking her hand, he guided her to the stairwell that led to the main foyer of the apartment building.

The doorman of the building greeted them. "Good evening, Mr. Costello, Madam."

"Evening George," Aidan said, before entering the lift. "Good day?"

"Not bad." George looked between Aidan and Megan. "Not bad at all."

As she opened the door to his apartment and stepped inside, Megan was welcomed into a reception room first. Then on into the open-plan living room and kitchen that was a mixture of bare brick walls, wooden ceilings, and sliding doors that opened onto a stunning garden balcony with lounge chairs and a decking.

"Aidan, this is . . .wow!"

The mixture of rustic and modern furniture worked well and it took her breath away.

Putting one of her bags down, and placing his jacket on the back of a chair, Aidan simply watched her explore before he couldn't hold on any longer. "You can have the full tour later."

He grabbed her waist to turn her around and kissed her until her breathing became restless. He slipped her jacket off and she removed his shirt. He was toned with broad shoulders—he was everything she'd expected and more. He moved to kiss her neck, only stopping to remove more clothing. Megan ran her hands over his back. There was no way they were going to make it to the bedroom.

Now that they were fully undressed, Aidan lifted her and laid her on the large corner sofa in the middle of the room. He leant over her, breathing heavily. "I don't know what it is that drives me crazy about you, Megan." He groaned when her lips found his chest. "That certainly helps." He playfully held her wrist above her, moving in for a kiss. Stopping at the last second, loving how Megan complained, he smiled down at her. "Say you'll be mine?"

Megan grinned, stroking the side of his face with her free hand. "Aidan Costello. It would be an honour."

His eyes filled with happiness. "You're amazing. You know that? And I have to say," his eyes ventured—he wanted to admire every single inch of her, "absolutely stunning."

Megan bit her lip. "Is it bad that this is all I've thought about for the past two weeks? Aidan whipped his head up and gave her a cheeky look, before lifting her so she was straddling him. He held her waist. "Not bad at all. Ever since your bathroom tease, I've had to stop myself from driving down to you every single day."

"My God." She moaned softly and leant in close, whispering in his ear. "You should have."

**

Just before eight, Megan was finally dressed after a longer-than-usual shower. They'd pushed it right up to the line and if she hadn't stopped him, their guests would have arrived while they were still exploring one another.

Aidan came up behind her and kissed her neck. "Are you sure you want to host guests tonight?"

She turned to face him. He was back in his casual attire, and was sporting dark jeans, a grey designer t-shirt, and a pair of glasses that she found absolutely adorable. *Was this real life?*

"I can cancel, but I'll let you explain why—as long as I can listen in? Sorry guys, go home. I need to keep my man busy in bed all night."

"I doubt that even the mighty Aidan Costello could pull that one off," she challenged, pushing her face into his.

They both smiled when the doorbell sounded.

***

Clare was as lovely as Emma described and Megan could've listened to her stories about Owen and Aidan all night. She had mid-length red hair and green eyes with a pale complexion. They were getting along like they were old school friends, catching up and telling each other about their life stories since they had seen each other last. It was like a friendship that had been put on hold. Megan could tell that they would be spending a lot of time together while their men ran JMC.

She poured Clare another glass of wine, enjoying the comfort of the sofas, while Aidan and Owen stood in the kitchen catching up on how the rest of the work day went. The others had better hurry up. There wouldn't be any wine left for them with the way she and Clare were going.

The rest of the guys (other than Lucy, who was held up at work) arrived shortly after, and it didn't take long for everyone to settle into their respective spots. Kev planted himself with Aidan and Owen in the kitchen, helping himself to the beers in the fridge.

As promised, Megan introduced Tom to Emma and had found them a private spot at the bottom of the stairs. It was clear Emma was interested in Tom by the way she kept twisting her hair around her finger and giggling at everything he said.

He was like a smaller version of Owen, and anyone could tell you they were brothers with nothing more than a glance. Every now and then, Megan looked over to Aidan and they smiled at one another.

Clare spotted it every time. "He's not going anywhere, Meg. He's completely besotted by you. Hasn't stopped talking about you for the past two weeks. I knew we'd get on from what he told me."

"Sorry, I just can't believe I'm with a man like Aidan."

"I'm just glad I have another lady to have lunch dates with while Owen's busy at the office." Clare grabbed her arm in excitement. "We should get lunch tomorrow actually, sound good?"

"Sounds fabulous, I'd love that."

Lucy turned up a bit later, after a meeting with one of the designers who were supplying the wardrobe for a photoshoot that ran on longer than expected. She spent the first ten minutes staring at Kev before they spoke over a glass of wine, after being introduced to everyone else. She had admired him from afar at the club, but didn't have an opportunity to talk properly since he was being kept busy by his then boss. Even though he was a couple of years younger, she didn't seem put off.

All the girls were getting on brilliantly, which was a relief for Megan. In the past, women found Lucy and Emma a bit intimidating. But then, Clare was married to a business man, so she was probably used to strong women. Whilst they were all chatting amongst themselves, Emma slid over to Megan and Clare.

"Ladies, a word? Outside?"

"Wonder what she wants to speak about?"

Clare looked at Megan like she was dumb. "Maybe the fact you and Aidan haven't been able to stop looking at each other? Seriously, I've never seen Aidan look so protective over a woman, or anyone for that matter."

They laughed, causing Aidan and Owen to look concerned. *What were they up to?*

"Lucy," Megan tapped her arm, "we've been summoned outside."

***

Once the women came back in, the night continued. Aidan decided to lay the takeout on the large coffee table that sat in the centre of the room, encircled by the sofas. Megan watched her closest friends as they sat talking to Tom and Kev, sitting side by side. She smiled, feeling blessed to have them in her life and to see them getting on so well with men that their parents would approve of.

Aidan leapt over the back of the sofa to sit between Megan and Owen with a couple of fresh beers in hand, and began loading his plate.

"How are you enjoying the new job, Kev? Are these two being good to you?" Clare asked as she plated up some food.

"Why do you always assume we're up to no good?" Owen demanded, dropping his fork on the plate. Aidan frowned at her as well.

"Because, my darling, you two are usually up to something. Megan," she leant back, literally talking behind their backs, "word of advice, keep an eye on these two. Especially when that one's around." She pointed at her brother-in-law.

"Hey!" Tom objected, "don't bring me into this."

"It usually gets a lot worse," Clare added.

"It's true. I've heard the rumors at the office about misbehavior from the top floor."

"That promotion can be taken away if you're not careful, Emma." Aidan raised a finger and shook his head. He tried hard to hide his smile.

"Ah, but you see, Aidan, you now have a problem."

"And what's that?" Aidan leant forward.

"Megan." Emma hugged her. Aidan caught the look the both of them were giving him and instantly started laughing. "Remember, best friend outranks boss?"

"So, now that your best friend is the CEO's girlfriend, that makes you safe? Is that so? Interesting concept."

Megan smacked his arm. "Yeah, it does. You've got Emma for life now."

"Does that mean I have you for life then?" He sat up, not giving her a chance to respond.

Megan just stared at him, smiling.

A silence fell over the room as everyone dug into dinner. The only sounds were when someone fancied seconds and couldn't quite reach the dish they were pining after. It was clear that not one of them were going to leave any food uneaten.

Kev placed his dish down. "Oh, in answer to your question, Clare. It's going great, thank you"

"Huh?" she said, through a mouthful of food.

"You asked how the job was going."

"Hmm." She swallowed. "Yes, I forgot. Sorry."

He smiled wryly at everyone. "I'm very thankful for the opportunity. Think I'm doing a good job." Kev looked at Aidan and Owen who nodded back at him in approval.

"It's funny, isn't it?" Lucy randomly said. "Somehow we've all got a connection with JMC."

"How'd you mean?" Aidan asked, drinking his beer.

"Well, obviously you three work there, as will Meg soon. Clare is married to Owen. You own it." She pointed to Aidan. "And you're sleeping with Meg."

Megan looked at the ceiling, not believing Lucy just said it out loud.

"Tom built the building, is Owen's brother, and is building something with Em, if you know what I mean? And Kev and I are, well . . ."

"Continue with it, Lucy. I'm not letting you get away with it after what you just announced about me and Aid."

"Soon to be shagging also?" Aidan continued Lucy's speech for her. Kev almost choked on his food, Tom smacked his back to try and help.

"Exactly. Thank you, baby." Aidan and Megan shared a fist bump, laughing at the embarrassment they caused for Lucy and Kev.

"As long as it's not happening at the office..."

"Oh yeah, because that wouldn't be the first time that's happened." Aidan smirked, sensing he was about to get a bollocking, "Would it, Owen?"

Everyone looked at Clare in shock, who was now reliving the embarrassment she had felt on the day Aidan's PA walked in on them having an extended lunchbreak. "Thanks, Aid. Very grown up of you."

"You're welcome. Took Lois a good week to be able to have the courage to approach you after that." Aidan laughed, as Owen and Clare joined in.

After about five seconds, the entire group was letting out unrestricted streams of belly-aching laughter.

***

After dinner, everyone was relaxing in the living room. Aidan and Megan were on the sofa in the corner with their feet up. It was the same spot they'd found themselves in earlier that day. He was whispering to her, reminding her about that moment. He was telling her that he couldn't wait for everyone to leave.

Lucy felt exhausted because of her late meeting, so decided to head home earlier than everyone else. Kev insisted that he would give her a lift. Megan made her promise to reveal everything at the girls' lunch date on Friday—they'd also arranged that, as well as tomorrow's occasion with Clare, meaning she now had two lunches planned. That was two, in two days. She couldn't wait to catch up on the gossip. It had been a while since she'd spent regular quality time with her girls and she loved the buzz of it.

The rest of the gang remained. Owen lay flat on the carpet, hoping it would help his dinner go down, while Clare tucked her feet up on the sofa.

Emma leant forward and stretched her arms out in front of her. "I fancy a coffee."

"Tom! Note this down. If you want to see Em again, make sure you get her coffee right," Megan joked. "Fussiest woman I know when it comes to caffeine!"

Emma was about to voice a comeback, but instead nodded in agreement. "I'll give you a hand," Tom said, getting up to follow Emma to the kitchen.

"Oh and Em?" Megan called to her in a relaxed voice. "Just because you'll have a buzz on doesn't mean everyone has."

"There really is two of them now, isn't there?" Owen said, getting up to sit next to his wife. "Does this mean I have to go through the both of you to get things done at the office?"

Aidan laughed. "Just because we're together doesn't mean I've signed my company over. Sorry baby, you're not getting that quite yet."

"Wouldn't even know how to begin running it. It'd probably be bankrupt after a few days."

"Highly unlikely." He kissed the top of her head and looked down at the screen on her phone. "Are you taking a picture of our feet?"

"Yeah, it's cute. Don't worry. No one will recognise you from your socks."

"Unless they're designer socks, Meg." Owen teased.

He was quickly smacked by Clare. "Leave him alone. Can't you see they're having a nice moment?"

"This is a one-off, Costello. Next time, when the wife's not here–"

"Anyway," Clare interrupted her husband, sensing another debate brewing between them. "We should probably get going. I'd imagine you two would like some alone time?" Clare winked at Megan, who grinned back at her.

Aidan noticed the look. "Owen, I'm not liking this. They've got that secret exchange thing going on already. Means we aren't going to be able to get away with half the stuff we usually do."

"See, Meg?" Clare pointed between them. "That's exactly what you need to keep an eye out for."

Megan and Clare said their goodbyes and promised to maintain their lunch plans for the following day. They exchanged phone numbers, setting a time that would be best for both of them.

"Bro, you getting a lift back with us? Em, we can drop you off too if you like?" Owen smiled at each of them.

Emma was delighted for the lift; she and Clare could chat more on the way home.

Megan put her coffee into a travel mug, handing it to her before saying her goodbyes to Tom and Owen.

"I never thought I'd see my Megan so happy again. It's like looking back in time." Emma scrunched Megan's face between her hands, then turned to Aidan. "Be good to her, Aidan. I'll be watching."

Aidan held his arms out by his side with his palms facing the ceiling. "You can bet your life on that."

Closing the door behind them, Megan jumped up onto Aidan.

This time they managed to make it to the bedroom.

Chapter 17

I t had been over three years since Megan felt safe with a man. Aside from Ben, there wasn't a single guy she had spent time around that made her content and worry-free. Her ex-boyfriend, Jay, had mistreated her when she needed his support the most. No one expected him to react the way he did when Megan broke the news about her parents' nasty divorce.

They'd moved to separate countries, leaving her in England. It broke her heart, and she needed the support from the people she was close to.

Jay had been supportive at first, but as the year aged, he began drinking more, getting angry, and taking his rage out on her. It went on for a long time and Emma and Lucy had been there to witness the bruises and tears. They supported Megan every time she told them she was okay, and not to worry about her. Megan was alone, and felt as though no one could do anything about it. That was, until the day she called Ben from the hospital.

Ben drove over to Jay's, demanded an explanation, and threatened him, saying that if he ever came near her again, he'd be mopping up his own blood. He called Lucy and Emma, updating them on her health after he arrived at the hospital, and he made a promise to them both that he would never let anyone hurt her again. It was a promise he kept.

But that was then, and this was now.

She was now in the arms of a guy who made her feel that nothing bad would ever happen to her again. She knew Ben would approve of him—even though she couldn't tell him about Aidan quite yet. Megan shifted so she was leaning on one elbow to get a better view.

"Are you watching me sleep?" he asked, his voice rough and his eyes still closed.

Megan smiled down at him and sighed. "Just admiring the view."

Aidan reached out pulled Megan down to hold her, taking a deep breath. "Well stop it. It's weird." He reached for his phone to check the time and groaned. "Baby, I've gotta get up."

"Nope." Megan decided that wasn't going to be an option, and clung onto him tighter.

"As much as I'd love to stay home with you, I've got big meetings I have to be present for today." He rolled her over and kissed the top of her head. "Promise to be back as soon as I can."

"If you say so." She released her grip reluctantly, letting him get up. She sat up and pulled the sheets up to her neck.

He turned back and smiled at her. "Shower?"

Megan was out of bed and in his arms before he had a chance to say anything else.

***

The hair salon was like something she'd never seen before. The hi-tech machines and gadgets made her head spin. Was this a hair salon or the inside of a UFO? Megan didn't know. It was a glorious morning—that much she knew. Megan had spent it getting up to nothing, enjoying her stress-free days while she still could.

Clare had texted while she was in the middle of that nothing, proposing that they make a day out of their lunch plans. Megan had no objections.

"So yeah, I'm getting the impression that I'm not going to need to look at bigger apartments with Em and Lucy quite yet. What do you think?" Megan asked Clare.

"Certainly sounds like Aidan has no intention of letting you out of his sight. I believe you moved into your new home last night."

"Is it not too soon? We've only known each other a few weeks."

"Too soon isn't in his vocabulary, Meg. You think he made a name for himself by taking things slow? Hell no, he gets shit done quickly." Clare scooted closer. "Besides, he wouldn't have driven down yesterday to pick you up in person if he wasn't taking your relationship seriously. Trust me, this is the real deal, and for the record, Aid's never acted this way with any other girlfriend before."

"Really?" Megan's eyes lit up. She was thrilled that the new man in her life appeared as excited about their relationship as she was.

"People think he has women hanging off his arm constantly, because, speaking the truth, he's an attractive guy. But they couldn't be more wrong. He broke up with his last serious girlfriend almost five years ago." Clare looked like she was looking back in time, a look of sadness on her face. "Thinking about it, Owen and I had only been together a year when it happened. He was going out with this girl, Sophie, and we all thought they were set. But one day, I came to JMC to meet Owen for lunch, and I overheard her on the phone to someone in Aidan's office. She was speaking about how they could use Aidan's fortune to build a future together. That's when I guessed she must have been speaking to another guy." She paused, taking a steady breath. "Another guy on the side."

"What?!" Megan quickly apologised to the nail technician, after almost spilling the nail varnish over the white towels in shock.

"Yeah, I know." Clare shook her head. "Anyway, I kept listening in, right? And turns out she was only staying with Aid to take advantage of his status, fame, and money. I was so angry. I told Owen about what I heard straight away."

"What happened?"

"Owen was furious, like, ready-to-storm-in-and-demand-she-tell-him-everything furious. But I told him not to, because she'd probably deny it. I used to be a lawyer. I know what guilty people will do. So he followed her after she left Canary Wharf, before he told Aidan. He saw her meeting with a guy down near Blackfriars underground and they were definitely more than friends. Owen got photographic proof before retuning back to JMC. We sat Aidan down and told him everything. Those two have always looked out for each other. They have this connection which is way stronger than brothers. I didn't understand it until I saw how protective Owen became that day."

"So, did Aid break it off that day then, after you both told him?"

"We waited for the ultimate shit storm to explode, and believe me, it did! He waited until she came back the following day. I've walked into that office when they're both in foul moods before and it's not pleasant, so I can imagine how unwelcoming an atmosphere it was for Sophie when she arrived. Owen told me it was an overdramatic scene: her denying everything and claiming that he owes her for the past two years together. She was after a serious amount of money. Aidan told her she would never get her hands on it."

"For her and her other man?"

"Ha, yeah! Aidan had his security escort her out of the building." Clare sat back, remembering. "That's when he put his barriers up, Meg."

"Barriers?"

"To protect himself. He began trusting very few and threw himself into his company, working day and night, turning JMC into one of the top computer software companies in the country."

"Poor guy. I can only imagine how upset he must have been."

"You have no idea. Owen dragged him to Vegas for a messy weekend to try and cheer him up."

"Did he hear anything else from her? From Sophie?"

"She tried to get him back, hanging around the building hoping to run into him, but he was having none of it. Megan, you are the first woman in five years he's let the barriers down for. Five years, Meg! Which means. . ." Clare projected a troublesome grin.

"Means?" Megan shook her head slowly, knowing what was coming next.

"It means he trusts you more than you could ever imagine. Sure, he's had a few flings since, but nothing serious." Clare put a hand on her leg. "So when I say that this is for real, believe me, it's real. It's only a matter of time until he's declaring his love for you."

Megan looked down, feeling sad for him. She'd been through heartbreak herself and could empathise all the way. She knew how it felt when someone you thought you could trust, and who you thought cared for you, turned out to be taking the piss instead. It hurt. It hurt like fucking hell.

"Let's take it one day at a time, Clare."

Chapter 18

Aidan didn't get Megan's message until the end of the day. The video conference with the American computer hardware company, Norfolk Computers, went on longer than expected. Aidan was pissed at that. But now he was just happy to hear from Megan. Her update messages always managed to brighten his day.

"Owen!" Aidan shouted from his office door, almost deafening Lois. She covered her ears. She knew what was coming next. "Clare's gone back home, said she'd meet you there."

"Yeah okay," Owen yelled back.

"Can you two please use your intercoms? Or text one another?" Lois begged. Aidan walked behind her desk, giving her a hug to sweeten her up. "Oh, that's not fair."

They stepped into Aidan's office, doing as she requested, so she could at least get

some work done in peace.

"Megan messaged, asked me to pass it on."

"Thanks." Owen walked further into the room. "So, Clive seemed pretty confident about that meeting." He put on his coat. "Are they finally getting their asses in line now? They're taking their bloody time, I know that."

"At least we are in some sort of agreement. Although, I still think we can push them for more."

"Sales and marketing split is pretty big, Aid. Plus their connections in the States—we can go for other companies over there once we sign this contract. Surely we should start small?"

"I'm thinking more along the lines of getting JMC offices out there."

"Always aiming high, aren't we?"

Aidan grinned at him. "You know it."

"So what's your plan for tonight? Taking Meg out for dinner still?"

"Yeah, although she's asked if we can meet back at the apartment instead of here."

Owen nodded. "Probably wise, dude. Don't blow it yet. I can see how special she is to you."

They both rode the lift down to the ground floor and sighed when they saw the amount of people leaving the numerous offices of Canary Wharf all at the same time. It was like everyone was piling into a venue to watch their favourite band, pushing one another to get to the front of the stage.

"I hate this time of the day. It's like a fucking cattle march with everyone heading for the underground at the same time."

"Lucky for us, then. We have the luxury of hiding in our cars." Aidan smacked Owen's back as he walked off to the car park. "See you tomorrow. I'll message you if I hear anything else from Clive."

"Later, Aid."

***

Aidan pulled up to the private parking at his apartment half an hour later. Climbing the stairs to the foyer, he was once again greeted by the person he called 'the commander of the building'.

"Evening, George. Good day?"

"Wonderful, Aidan. Cheers."

"Meet Megan properly?"

"Yeah, she's lovely." He nodded. "And by the way, the secret's safe with me."

"Good lad, thanks."

Aidan rode the lift to the top floor and gave a sigh of relief. He was finally home. Stopping before he unlocked the door, he realised he could smell cooking from inside. An aroma of freshly marinated chicken, with a hint of cheese. Something told him she and Clare had been gossiping. As he opened the door he called out, "Meg, baby? You home?"

He walked into the kitchen and noticed she had been cooking. He had dreamt many times of coming home after a stressful day to a home-cooked meal made by a wonderful woman. He'd been invited to Owen's many times, where Clare had a meal ready for them both, but to come back to his own apartment to find that Megan had cooked for him... that made him smile like an idiot.

"Aidan!" Megan ran up and hugged him, giving him a welcome-home kiss. "I hope you don't mind my little fib, but I couldn't resist giving you a nice surprise. I hope you like pasta bake?"

Aidan lifted her up and held her tight. "You are amazing, thank you. And yes, it's one of my favourites."

Megan smiled over his shoulder. *Nice one, Clare!*

"Right, now that you're back, keep an eye on that," she pointed to the oven, "while your girlfriend changes into non-fabulous mode." She kissed him again. "Back in a minute"

He watched her climb the stairs, then opened the fridge and grabbed a bottle of wine, pouring Megan a glass. His last girlfriend, Sophie, hadn't once cooked dinner in the two years they were together. She just expected him to take her out, order dinner, or cook himself. He did enjoy cooking for her, but the pleasure of cooking for someone who seemed unappreciative soon wore off.

"Omigosh, Aidan!"

"What have or haven't I done?"

Megan came back downstairs dressed in knitted leggings, fluffy socks, and an off- the-shoulder jumper. Her hair was pulled back into a tight ponytail. "You could've told me I had sauce on my face."

Somehow she'd managed to flick cheese sauce on her forehead. Aidan had noticed, but thought it was too cute to point out. So he'd simply chosen not to. He shrugged. "I thought it looked great."

She got a damp cloth from the sink and wiped her head. "Have I got it all?" she asked, looking at the cloth.

Aidan took the cloth and wiped the remaining sauce away, trying not to laugh at the look Megan was giving him for not telling her. "There, all clean again."

"Stop laughing."

Aidan couldn't hold it in any longer. He burst. "I'm sorry, that was just too adorable. How did you manage to get it in your hair?"

Megan pushed her hand through her hair, noting the stickiness in her fringe, and frowned. "Bloody hell, I'll get it later. You go and change while I finish dinner." She pointed to the stairs.

"Yes, Miss." Aidan did as he was told. Without a need to rush, he rummaged in the wardrobe of the main bedroom to find his favourite jogging bottoms. A burgundy pair that should have been thrown out years ago. "So, who's the boss again?" He called from upstairs.

"Me. You told me so this morning." Megan leant against the kitchen island and drank the wine Aidan had poured for her. She needed to text Emma and Lucy. She still wasn't sure what her living situation was, but she thought it was best to check in with the girls. The whole reason she came was to look for an apartment with them after all.

EVENING LADIES. SO WE WERE MEANT TO BE LOOKING AT APARTMENTS, ALTHOUGH, NOW YOU BOTH KNOW ABOUT AIDAN, I'M NOT SURE WHERE IT'S ALL STANDING. SHALL WE MEET UP TOMORROW AND SEARCH AROUND ANYWAY? I DON'T WANT TO ASSUME THAT I'M MOVING IN HERE. PROBABLY BEST TO KEEP THE OPTIONS OPEN, IF YOU KNOW WHAT I MEAN? IT HAS ONLY BEEN A FEW WEEKS AFTER ALL! CALL ME WHEN YOU CAN, WE'RE IN ALL NIGHT. LOVE YOU, M Xx

Aidan came back downstairs sporting that rock star look again. He was dressed in relaxed clothing and wore a facial expression that matched. He hugged her from behind and Megan stood up. He turned her around and lifted her onto the kitchen island.

"Dinner going to be long?"

Megan sighed. "Not long enough for what you're thinking." The buzzer sounded on the oven, signalling that it was ready. Megan tapped his shoulders, pushing him back so she could get to the oven. "Before I forget, I messaged Emma and Lucy while you were upstairs. You know, about meeting up tomorrow."

"Tomorrow?"

"Yeah... You know, the whole reason I was coming up this week?" Aidan looked confused. "To look at bigger places with them? Come on, Aidan, you're intelligent enough to follow."

"Oh right, yeah." Aidan frowned. He'd forgotten that they were going to search for a bigger apartment to share, and the thought of coming home every day to a Megan-less apartment wasn't something he was particularly fond of. He'd not known her long, he got that, but there was something about Megan. She had broken all the rules he had set in place after his last serious girlfriend, and he didn't care. No moving in, no rushing into a relationship, and certainly no falling for anyone. She was seeing him for him. Not the boss of a large corporate company. Not the self-made millionaire. Just Aidan.

He was brought back to reality when Megan served the food and handed him a plate of what he had to admit was one of the best-smelling bakes he'd ever come across. "Meg... shit, this is amazing. You can definitely cook this again."

"Glad you like it. I got the recipe from the chef at the local pub back home. Nagged him until he handed it over."

"Same pub you were at when I called the other night?" he asked, taking another mouthful of pasta.

"The only decent pub back home." She shook her head playfully. "So, how was your day? Anything exciting happened?"

And now she's asking about my day? Good God, she's not going anywhere. "It was okay. We're pushing a deal with an American company at the moment. We finally managed to get some kind of agreement out of them today, but I still think we can push for more. Did you have a nice day with Clare?"

"Mm hmm." Megan nodded. "We had so much fun."

After dinner, they settled on the sofa and cosied together in a ball of happiness. The plan was to watch a movie, but the bump in the road lay right where it always did when enjoying a movie was on the agenda. What were they going to watch?

"Drama?" Aidan asked, stopping on a movie selection.

"Hmm, no."

"Rom-com?"

"Yuck! No!"

He chuckled at the look on Megan's face at the mention of such a genre. "Ok, action?"

"Now you're talking."

They finally decided to settle on Iron Man, a mutual favourite. An hour into the movie, Aidan started to question the plotline, much to Megan's amusement.

"Yeah, but if he's got that much cash, surely he'd have better security who'd expect an attack... or at least be ready for it? Dumbass!"

"Leave Downey Jr. alone, he's only going on what the script told him. Or are we talking from experience?"

"No, I'm just saying. I wouldn't leave JMC without a security team patrolling the building. There's stuff in there other software companies would love to get their hands on."

"I'm sorry, are you comparing yourself to Iron Man?" Megan laughed.

"Maybe I am Iron Man."

"Bollocks!" She slapped his leg. "Mind you, you did have a bit of the Tony Stark ego when we met."

"Hey, I'm not that bad. At least I wasn't all, 'Hey baby, I've got a shit load of cash, let's hook up—that's too much."

Megan snuggled further into him, laughing at his rant. "Are we going to be like this towards every make-believe millionaire character we watch in a movie? Or are we just singling out Iron Man?"

Aidan tried to say something back, but realised that he had just been brought back down to earth by his girlfriend's comment about millionaire businessmen. "Depends. Can I open a department at JMC that can make the Iron Man suit?"

"If it'll keep you happy."

Aidan put a hand on his chin. Where would he set up such a department? How much funding would it take? Was it actually possible? He shuffled in his seat, mulling over the fantasy.

"Wow. You're actually thinking about doing it, aren't you?"

"I mean, why not? Gotta keep all the doors open."

"Well, maybe because it's insane? The British military would shoot it down in a heartbeat."

"Would be fun though, right?"

As the movie went on, Aidan noticed that Megan was falling asleep. Her first day in the city must have taken it out of her. He placed a pillow on his lap and put his feet up on the coffee table. He gently stirred her enough to guide her head onto the pillow. He placed his arm around her waist, stroking her hair with the other hand. He wanted to let her sleep.

***

Moments later his phone rang, he answered it in record time so it didn't disturb her. "Yeah," he whispered, looking at the screen to see who was calling. "Emma?"

"Hey, Aidan, sorry to call so late. I've been trying to get hold of Meg. She okay?"

"She's fine, fast asleep. What's up?"

"She messaged Lu and I about meeting up tomorrow. We weren't sure what the situation was."

"How do you mean?"

"Wow, this is awkward."

Aidan waited. He knew what Emma was going to say. *Is she moving in with you, or are we still looking for a bigger place together?*

"Do, umm... how long are you planning on letting Meg stay at your place?"

"Probably best you got hold of me then, Em. I was thinking about bringing this subject up."

"Looks like I called at the right time then, huh? The way I see it, she's probably going to be spending the majority of her spare time at yours anyway, if you catch my drift?"

"Do you think she would?" He ran his hand through her hair, looking down at her as she moved beneath his touch.

Emma giggled. "Ask her, you never know. It may take a small amount of persuasion because she'll want to make sure everyone is okay with the change of direction, but yeah." She paused for a moment, considering what to say next. "Just let us know what she says tomorrow, okay?"

"Will do. Thanks, Em, I really appreciate it." Aidan hung up and smiled down at her. "Megan?"

She stirred. "Hmm?"

"Come on." He lifted her up off the sofa and carried her upstairs. She looked up into his blue eyes as he laid her on the bed.

"Am I being put to bed?"

He stroked her forehead. "Meg, I want to ask you something. Where do you see yourself in, let's say, a month's time?" Megan tried to begin to answer. "Actually, don't answer that. You wanna know where I want to see you? Right here, waking up next to me every morning in this bed."

She sat up. "Are you asking what I think you're asking?"

"Like Em just said, we'll probably be spending the majority of our time together, so why not? Unless you think it's too soon, of course."

"Emma?"

"She just called." He paused, taking it all in. "So how about it? Want to live in a top floor city apartment? And also in Farnham?"

"Farnham?"

"Have I not told you about it? Okay, so technically, this isn't my main home. We should drive down and spend the weekend there. Beautiful barn conversion in the country with–"

"Aidan, Aidan, whoa... slow it down." Megan was speechless. Part of her felt cautious—just over two weeks ago, she didn't even know him, and now he was asking her to live with him. Yet, there was a spark inside her that made her feel alive every time they interacted. *Live a little, Megan. This could be a once-in-a-lifetime chance to have everything you have ever wanted and more. Look at him! So much more!*

"Well, I suppose it would make sense. I can't stand being away from you for more than a day." She grabbed the sides of his head and pulled him closer. "Those two weeks apart were a nightmare. But . . ."

"Dear Lord, not another but. You know what happens when you use that word."

"But, is this one of those times where you won't hear the word no?"

Aidan smiled.

"Then I suppose I don't have a choice, do I?"

Aidan's smile grew larger as he looked down at her, before pulling her into a crushing embrace to express his happiness.

Chapter 19

F riday was here. Aidan had organised for the ladies to use one of JMC's limos so they could go out for lunch in style. It didn't look suspicious that they were using the car, since people knew Clare was married to the second in command of the company and was good friends with the CEO. It just looked like she was treating her friends.

Heads turned when the car—with its personalised number plate—pulled up to the side of the Italian restaurant in Greenwich. Megan felt a bit exposed, being seen getting out of the limo that was owned by the boyfriend she couldn't tell anyone about, but Emma reassured her, holding onto her arm as they entered the restaurant.

Taking their seats, they admired the delicious menus, each one of them finding it difficult to decide what to choose. Lucy called the waiter over, asking him to describe each meal in a hope it would help her make a choice. Eventually she settled on the skewered chicken, served with Mediterranean vegetables. It sounded interesting, and because the others hadn't made a choice, they all ordered the same thing. Once drinks had been ordered and the meals had arrived, Clare homed in on the subject they were all interested in.

"Didn't I tell you a home-cooked meal would work?" Clare asked as they ate their main course. "You've got him eating out of the palm of your hand. Wait until you see Farnham. It's gorgeous."

"We're heading down there after he finishes work tonight to spend the weekend together."

"Spend the weekend? Is that what the kids are calling it now?"

"Well, since we are the same age, Lucy, I'd say we probably have no clue what the kids are calling it. Last time I heard it was just sex."

Clare almost choked on her wine at Megan's blunt response to Lucy's mocking. "You guys are crazy." She laughed.

"Way to be subtle, Meg." Emma laughed too.

Megan shrugged her shoulders and smiled. "Anyway, we all know where me and Aidan are in our relationship, I think it's high time you two," she pointed towards her two best friends, "spill the dirt on Tom and Kev. Don't you think so, Clare?"

"Oh, absolutely."

Megan and Clare stared at them, waiting for one of them to start talking.

"It's only been, what, two days?" Emma tried to defend their position, hold their ground.

"How was your lunch date with Tom? From what Owen told me it involved flowers," Clare said.

Emma smiled. "It was lovely. Owen told Tom how busy it's been at work, so he brought lunch to me. Turned up with flowers and chicken salad."

"That's so cute." Megan sighed.

"We're going to take things slow and see where they go."

They all nodded, and continued eating their food. They shared a quiet booth in the corner of the room, too far out of earshot to care. The place was huge. The only way the other people here would overhear them would be if they got really crazy about something. Megan hoped they would. This place needed some excitement.

"Lucy? You look like you have something you need to share." Megan gave her a knowing grin.

"Kev and I slept together last night at his place."

Megan and Clare both screamed in excitement, disturbing the other diners. It was the exact noise Megan had been dying to make. Finally, some personality in the room at last. The place was beginning to give off old-people's-home vibes.

"So that's why you were home late last night?" Emma asked, slightly shocked.

"That's two of us who aren't taking it slow." Megan hugged Lucy. "Are you happy?"

"Yeah, he's a real gentleman, Meg."

"Yeah, yeah, that's great." Megan leant on her elbows. "How'd it happen? *Progress*, if you will."

Lucy took a slow slip of white wine, watching each of them carefully. She knew full well that denying them the gossip would only heighten their excitement. She gently set the glass down. "He met me after work, took me out for early evening cocktails."

Emma threw her hands in the air in an over the top gesture. "He got her hammered. Lucy and cocktails? You were all over him after one drink, weren't you?"

"Actually, Miss Rowe, I was not."

Megan nudged Lucy's side. "Two then."

"You're both arseholes." Lucy turned to Clare, ignoring her so-called long-term friends, who were in hysterics. "As I was saying. We went out for drinks, and we were getting on like a house on fire." She smiled, the memory of the night before still vivid in her mind. "After we'd had a few he offered to accompany me home."

Emma and Megan let out a hooting noise, indicating they knew what was coming.

"But, not before I insisted we pick up some dinner, and Kev insisted he would pay and cook for me."

Clare covered her heart. "Adorable. He does have that cuteness factor about him."

"So that's how you ended up back at his?" Emma said, pointing at Lucy.

Lucy nodded. "We were so near his, it made sense."

"You ended up back at his, you had dinner, and I'm guessing more drinks, but who made the move?" Megan demanded.

"Both of us."

"Both of you?" Clare asked.

"We moved in at the same time." Lucy sighed. "It was like a scene from one of those romantic films where the director calls action, and the actors suddenly perform." She clapped her hands together. "Action! Boom!"

Emma sniggered. "In more ways than one. Am I right?" She held her hand up for Lucy to high-five.

"Waking up next to him in the morning... It didn't feel weird at all."

"I know what you mean," Megan said. "When I woke with Aidan, it was like it was where I was meant to be." She reached for Lucy's hand. "Most importantly though, and sex jokes aside, are you happy?"

Lucy face lit up as she grinned. "Happier than ever!"

After polishing of the main courses and delightfully indulging in the most delicious desserts Megan had ever tasted, they ordered coffees to finish their extended lunch date. It was nice, taking the time to relax before going about the rest of their day.

"So, are you heading back to Southbank after this, Meg?" Clare asked.

"I'm meant to be meeting Aidan at JMC, but I'm not sure how I'm going to be able to get into the building, and to the top floor, without it looking obvious. No one will actually know who the hell I am."

"That's easy. I know how we can do it." Emma sounded full of confidence as she pulled her phone from her purse. "Excuse me, while I call your boyfriend."

Lucy, Megan, and Clare stared at her in fascination.

"Aidan, hi... yeah, we're all here, having a nice lunch. Listen... no, we're not far... Okay, hang on... listen a moment. I'm bringing Meg in... yes, into the building." Em covered the phone and rolled her eyes. "Does he ever listen?"

Megan laughed at Emma as she tried to get a full sentence into the conversation with him. "That's Aidan for you." She leant closer to Emma. "Aidan? Listen," Megan called down the phone, even though she had no idea what Emma was up to.

Emma put the phone back up to her ear. "He says he's sorry." She laughed. "Okay, so Megan and I will be at JMC in about an hour. I'll bring her up to your office, but... yeah, that's why I have a plan... so people can see early on that neither of you know each other and are clearly not in a relationship. Yeah, hang on. One of us will message you when we're in the building. So, if you're not in a meeting or whatever, be in the reception and walk right past us like you don't even know we exist. Yes, I know... genius. That's the idea, yeah. Yep. Okay. Bye."

"So," Lucy began, "you're sneaking Meg in?"

"In a way, yes, but as a new JMC recruit, having her first introduction to the company. Aid wasn't convinced until he twigged onto my plan."

"That is genius, Emma," Clare said.

"I've done loads of introductions for new starters too, so it will seem totally normal to anyone who happens to see us around the building."

Lucy shook her head in disbelief. "To Emma's genius." She raised her glass and the rest of them joined her.

Emma raised hers too, clanking it against the other three. "Hell, I'll drink to that."

***

The lift buzzed in front of them. They were on the top floor, and had been for the past hour. The building was everything she'd expected and more. It was a modern masterpiece with architectural assets beyond any she'd ever seen. Every glass panel was crisply sealed and etched, each surface was polished to perfection, and every room they'd been through boasted tall ceilings and enough natural light to grow a field of crops. It was paradise, and Megan couldn't believe that she was going to work here.

But now that it was time to leave, she was feeling anxious. "This plan has worked great and all, but how exactly do we *leave* the building together?"

The lift doors opened. Aidan typed in a code on the control panel of the lift and smiled. "Leaving was never going to be a problem." The code he typed in meant they were able to ride directly to the basement—where his car was—without any interruptions. He asked for her phone, which she gave him. Opening her notes, he typed in the code. "Not even Owen has this. Keep it safe."

"Does he even know it exists?"

"Nope." The lift doors opened in the basement, right next to his black Mercedes.

"So, is this your secret 'I-don't-want-to-be-bothered-by-anyone' escape route then?"

"Pretty much. I leave by the main doors usually, but sometimes I don't want be caught by staff needing me for one more thing." Aidan opened the driver's side door while Megan got in the passenger's side. "Or the media waiting to grill me about the company."

Megan leant across and kissed his cheek. "Such a hard life."

He glanced sideways at her and smiled. Starting the car, Aidan drove out of the basement and into London traffic. The workers of Canary Wharf watched on as the head of JMC escaped the building for the weekend.

***

The drive had been a nice length—not so short that it felt pointless and not long enough to cause a crick in your neck or a pain in your arse. Neither of those; it was just right. And now, smiling contently, they drove through Aidan's hometown.

When they reached the outskirts of the built up area, it was like looking back in time to a simpler way of life. The buildings had character and it felt like a real homely area. The stores that lined the old high street were charmingly delightful, filled with shoppers supporting the independent traders.

People waved at the car as they drove through the high street. They knew who the car belonged to and were welcoming him home. Aidan drove carefully through these streets compared to how he drove in the city, turning left then right, until they reached a quiet area in town.

Aidan turned to Megan. "Do me a favour. Close your eyes."

She gave him a suspicious look, but did as he asked. Her senses were heightened, and she tried to use her ears to see. She heard the sound of an electric gate opening when Aidan pressed a button from within the car, and then the sound of gravel under the wheels as they drove forward. Another button was pressed and a door opened. It sounded like a garage door. She jumped when the car door swung open and then jumped again, a little harder, when she felt his hand on her shoulder, guiding her out.

"Relax," he said. "Why so tense?"

The garage door was still open. She could feel a breeze on her neck. She heard him open and close the boot of the car. Then everything was still.

"Okay, this way." He guided her out of the garage and closed it behind him. "Stay right here."

"I'm not a puppy, Aidan."

He laughed and put his arms around her waist, standing behind her. "Open."

She did, and then she lost her breath and took a step backwards. Aidan kept hold of her, helping her to stand upright when he felt her sway. He let her take it all in, admiring the barn conversion in all its glory.

Megan turned around to see where they had driven in and saw a long driveway that swerved off a private road. She spun again and focussed on the building itself. It was frighteningly beautiful. Original bare brickwork that was mixed with floor to ceiling glass made up most of the external walls, and there were high archways framing the main double doors and extensions on either side of the building.

Aidan snuggled into her neck when she tried to say something. "Welcome home, baby."

"Home?"

He smiled at her befuddled expression. "Come on." He pulled her towards the front door, pausing only to turn back and cast a wink in her direction. "And this time, I promise we can look around first."

He turned off the alarm and led Megan into the large open-plan reception room, where the ceiling went all the way up to top of the building. Ahead of her, there was a curved staircase leading to the first floor and a hallway that led off behind it.

Part of her felt as though she should wait for him to escort her around. It was his house. She also felt like she could have got lost without him showing her each room. The place was huge.

"Megan? You're doing a great impression of a statue right now."

"Sorry? Statue. Yes."

He laughed at her first impression of the house. "Damnit, you're so cute."

Megan's legs began to work and she wandered through a double door that filtered into one of the largest kitchens she'd ever seen. She absorbed the sight, shaking in excitement, and headed back into the reception. The next door she walked through led to the living room, and that's where she paused to look at him. "Does every place you own have the same theme? Bare woodwork, chrome, glass?"

"Yeah, I suppose it does."

Megan nodded. "It's beautiful, Aidan. Really stunning."

"You've not seen anything yet." He grabbed her hand and took her back into the reception and through the hallway behind the staircase.

It only took her a couple of seconds to realise that the main staircase hid another set of stairs that went down behind it. Megan's chin dropped when Aidan opened a door for her, revealing the personal gym and basement swimming pool.

"It's heated. And the one outside as well. Well, not right now, but they can be."

Megan stared at him in amazement. "You have too much money, Costello."

He twirled Megan around to face him. "And here I was thinking you weren't interested in the money."

***

Once Megan had put the majority of her clothes away, she made her way down the staircase towards the kitchen. Her eyes immediately shot up to the wooden beams, supporting the roof, then down, gazing at the brickwork of the original building. Finally, they landed on Aidan, who watched her taking in the room. He stood in the centre of the kitchen, and was busy preparing dinner at the island in the middle of the room.

Aidan threw the dough down and slid over to the refrigerator, handing Megan one of her favourite beers. "Had them brought in the week after we met. You know, just in case."

"Thank you." Megan took a sip and sat down at the island. "What do you mean you had them brought in?"

"Running a company and stocking two homes at the same time? Becomes a bit of a handful. Mrs. Miller, Angela—an old family friend—she keeps me organised and takes care of this place when I'm away. She loves you, by the way."

Megan smirked. "Been telling people about me already? I thought we were keeping the relationship a secret?"

"She doesn't count. She pretty much raised me as a kid. I can't keep anything from her."

"Raised you?"

Aidan looked at her, realising what he'd said. "It's a delicate subject. I'll tell you some other time. Let's not spoil our first night here together." He sighed when he saw the puzzled look in her eyes.

"I understand if you don't want to talk about it. But if you do I'm all ears."

Aidan nodded, set down his cooking equipment, and walked around to her side of the counter. He sat on the stool beside her, swiveled it around so they were facing one another, and rested his palms on his knees.

"Mrs. Miller's my Godmother. My parents died in a car accident when I was six, after dropping me off at my grandparents' in Dublin for a week. Fatal crash. Killed them instantly." He worked through the details effortlessly, as if he were discussing the plot of a movie. "I ended up living in Ireland until I was, umm, eleven I think. Then, after my grandparents passed away, I moved in with Mrs. Miller. That's the whole reason behind JMC being named after my parents."

Megan rested a hand on his, massaging his skin with her thumb. "Oh God, Aidan. I'm so sorry."

"Don't be. It was a long time ago." He tightly held her hand. Her support radiated through him. "It can still be upsetting around Christmas time—that's when it happened. And it's pretty shitty knowing that they'll never see what I've achieved." Aidan pushed a strand of her hair behind her ear. "But I had a group of strong women looking out for me growing up. They put me on the right paths and supported my decisions. One of those women in particular, was Mrs. Miller." He stood and returned to the cooker, knowing he had a pot of bubbling sauce to attend to. "And they all want to meet you, so get ready for some serious hugging."

Megan stood and held his waist, feeling heartbroken for him. "I'll look forward to it. Maybe they'll tell me some stories about you growing up."

Aidan put one free arm around her shoulders and kissed her head. "Most likely."

"Oh, and before I forget." She flicked some flour up, getting it on his face and in his hair, before making a dash to the other side of the kitchen. "Now we're even."

Aidan stirred the tomato sauce he was preparing. "Miss Ashton, that was a bad move." He lifted the spoon from the pan, watched as a droplet of redness splashed back into the contents, and then turned his gaze back to her. "Dare to try that again?"

Chapter 20

T he café was always a great place to be on a late Friday afternoon in the JMC building. There weren't many people around, and Megan tended to favour that when she was at the office. The whole Aidan situation had been stressing her out more than she ever thought it would. And on top of that, the work itself was putting a beating on her. *Seriously, why couldn't things just be easy?*

She smiled internally as she looked around the ground level of the building. People were beginning to wind down for the weekend, casually chatting to one another. The reception staff were laughing at what she could tell was an inside joke. She couldn't quite believe it had only been a week since their girls' lunch, yet here she was, working for one of the most established, well known computer tech companies in the country. The weekend after the lunch date, she and Aidan had spent the first weekend of their lives together relaxing in Farnham. Taking full advantage of having an entire barn conversion to themselves to do more than just talk.

"I still can't believe how quickly you picked everything up. It's only been what, about a week? And you're smashing all your targets. I mean, seriously Meg, you're doing better than any of the others when they first started." Emma complimented her over their coffee.

"Thanks, Em, really. But—"

"Don't start with that 'but' nonsense. I know what you are going to say."

"How?"

"Because you have that nervous sound in your voice." Emma tilted her head to the side. "Please don't tell me you're still feeling awkward about being here? You're doing great."

"I know; I shouldn't, I know!" Megan waved her hands. "But Em, you studied so hard to be here. The guys on our floor did too, and I've just waltzed in with some retail experience. Surely it's got to feel unfair to some of the uni graduates who are working their arses off to get to my position." Megan pulled Emma closer, and whispered, "And I'm sleeping with the CEO. Wouldn't that look a bit of a coincidence if it got found out?"

"Please, you've had life experience, worked the shop floor for years, that's more than enough to be able to do what you do here. And, may I add, you're in a *serious relationship* with him. Get that right, young lady."

"Young lady? Really?" Megan snort-laughed. "I was chatting with Kev yesterday, and he said that people were talking about how well your department was doing since I started. Not that it's all me, of course." Both of them laughed, causing some gentlemen to look their way. "Almost gave myself an ego boost there."

"Sorry, private joke," Emma told their onlookers. "Surely Aidan can see how well you are doing?"

"We don't talk about work once we're home, not now that I'm here, anyway. It's kinda weird otherwise, you know? Coming home to have sex with your boss while at the same time talking about targets and sales? So wrong."

"Yeah, that's got to be a bit bizarre, I'll give you that. I suppose before you were just dating this guy you met on a night out, now you're dating the CEO."

"That doesn't help, Em!"

Emma checked the time of her phone. "Four thirty. Time to get back to work. Ready?"

Megan drank the rest of her coffee. "Am now"

Emma thanked the baristas and they both walked across the bright white reception

toward the lifts. "I do appreciate you two living together, though." Megan called the lift. "How do you mean?"

"Now we don't have to move. Can you imagine the stress it could've caused trying to find a place in the city at this time of year? We'd probably be signed off with stress."

"And would probably have killed each other by now."

The lift doors opened, ready to take them back to their floor. "Exactly. As much as I love you and Lucy, moving is too much." A thought crossed Emma's mind—one that hadn't hit her until now—and clicked in her brain just as fast, exploding into something with substance. Megan was crazy to feel the way she did. "I still can't believe you're doubting yourself up here. You should be the most confident person in the entire building."

"Why would that be?"

Emma faced her. "Listen, I should probably warn you about this anyway. A lot of the women here," Emma waved a hand in the air, " have tried to hit on Aidan."

"What! People have tried to?"

"Tried, failed, and handed in their resignation afterward through embarrassment." Emma laughed. "But don't worry about it. Sure, you may see women flirt with him, but you know Aidan will dismiss it straight away." She shrugged. "That's why you should be confident. The guy who everyone wants only has eyes for you."

"I thought you were calming me down, not telling me about all the women who've made a move on him. That just makes me more nervous than ever."

"Trust me, Meg... with the way he looks at you, you have nothing to worry about. You two are in it for the long haul, I can tell."

Megan rolled her eyes so far back they were looking in on her brain. "Have you been talking with Clare?"

"Just as long as I get to wear a beautiful dress to your engagement party. I need to keep Tom on his toes."

Emma had met up with Tom a few times now, and they had started dating. It was lovely for Megan to see her with such a great guy. They had a similar sense of humour and talked about taking a holiday together in the New Year. She was happy for her friend. *Emma deserved to find her smile.*

Megan couldn't hide her grin. "Will you lot stop going on about engagements and marriage please? I had this off Clare the very first week I was up here." She sighed. "We've not even said ... *you know*, yet." Megan looked down, trying to hide her expression.

Emma was having none of it. She could read Megan like a book. "You do, don't you? You love him." Emma grinned.

Megan met her eyes, and smiled a shy smile. "Just don't tell anyone. Not before I've told him. I'm trying to find the right moment, and he's been freaking out about this latest deal in America."

"Your secret is safe with me." They walked into the office, trying to appear as calm and casual as they could.

"Are you coming out for drinks with us tonight, Meg?" Karen, one of Megan's new work colleagues, called from across the room, making her jump. "We're heading out to

Southwark's Understudy Bar after work. Come with us. Just for tonight? *Please.*"

Megan held her tongue for a moment while she gathered her thoughts. Karen had been asking her to join them all week, and she really hadn't felt up to it. *Why her? What made her so special?* But Megan couldn't think of an excuse this time. Karen had put her on the spot. She had no choice. "Yeah sure, why not? Should I meet you there?"

"Guys, Meg's coming out!" Karen called to her friends, who all cheered at the fact that they had finally managed to persuade the newest member of their team to join them. "We'll start at the Understudy and see where the night takes us."

Megan and Emma took their respective seats, next to each other of course, and wheeled themselves under their desks.

"Sounds great," Megan said. She smiled at Karen, who then turned her attention on Emma—it was her turn now.

"You're coming too, right Emma?" Karen was doing a butt-shaking dance in the middle of the office, not caring about who might be watching in the slightest. "It's party time, guys!"

"Yeah, sure. But Tom's meant to be meeting me this evening, so he'll probably come along later if that's okay?"

"Of course it's okay." Karen kept dancing as she spoke. "But seriously, how did you manage to bag Owen's brother?"

As Karen danced back towards her desk, Emma leant on the back of Megan's chair and whispered, "Wouldn't she like to know?"

Megan and Emma sniggered to one another, acting like teenagers.

Emma looked up and found the entire office starting at them, confused as to what was so funny. She coughed, and gestured for everyone to get back to work.

"I'd best just let Aid know. He and Owen were thinking about having a lads' night. I think they're dragging Tom out too," Megan whispered.

"Really? They kept that quiet. We've got to watch these three, you know."

Megan nodded. "These four, you mean. Let's not forget Kev. They're all just as bad as each other."

Emma put her finger in the air, signalling the acknowledgement of Megan's point. "You think it's a guy thing? It's got to be a guy thing."

Megan shrugged. "You know how the song goes."

"What?" Emma looked beyond confused.

"Boys will be boys."

Chapter 21

The bar, located in the middle of Southwark, was filled with people from the surrounding media buildings. Everyone was enjoying after-work drinks, celebrating the end of the working week. The music inside was turned up to such a volume that Jimmy, one of Emma and Megan's fellow workers, had to shout at the barman to place an order.

"You two go and find us a spot," Emma instructed. "We'll bring the drinks out."

Megan and Karen shrugged and waltzed off into the broader section of the bar to find them a drinking spot for the evening.

All the tables were taken, but they found an empty squared bench that they quickly descended upon before anyone else spotted it.

"So this is ours for the night. Look, here come the others. Hey!" Karen waved to their work colleagues, Carol and Brendan, who ran over to drop their bags off before they hurried in to order drinks. Emma and Jimmy came over from the bar, greeting the others as they passed. When they got to the bench, they placed the drinks down on little side tables and sank down themselves.

"Who do I owe?" Megan asked.

Jimmy shook his head. "These are on me."

"Thank you, Jimmy. I'll get the next round in."

The evening flowed with remarkable ease. Everyone mingled, conversed, and enjoyed each other's company. It felt less like one of those awkward nights out with work colleagues you hardly know, and more like a casual gathering between a close group of friends. There was none of that 'my husband does this' or 'my girlfriend does that.' It was just a group of people existing within the confined mutuality of alcohol and atmosphere.

Seeing as she'd apparently had one too many drinks, Karen decided to turn the conversation to Emma's love life. Testing the waters a little, Megan mused.

"Okay, Miss Rowe, spill it. How exactly did you manage to get with Owen's brother?"

"That, my dear, would be telling." Emma shrugged. "But since you keep nagging me, we met when I had to take some files up to the top floor," she lied. "Tom just happened to be in reception while Owen and Aidan were finishing up in a meeting. We got talking and, um..."

"He brought lunch in for you the next day, wasn't it?" Megan finished her sentence. She could clearly see that Emma was struggling to keep the white lie going.

"Yes, came in with flowers and... what was it again?"

"Chicken salad. You messaged me after he left and told me he brought you a chicken salad."

"Chicken salad. Yes. He's such cutie." Emma laughed nervously. Their work colleagues stared at them in confusion. When they looked away, she turned around and whispered into her friend's ear, "Thank you."

Megan winked at her before having another drink.

"Well, I don't know about any of the other ladies here, but if I was upstairs—not that Emma ever gives us a chance to visit—I would definitely have taken a shot at Aidan."

Megan almost spat her drink out in shock. Emma smacked her back and laughed.

"He's your boss, Karen. You can't hit on your boss."

"Why not, Jimmy? He's hot. And you ladies can't tell me you haven't thought about it either."

"What's Aidan Costello got that we fellas don't?" Brendan demanded.

"Erm, where do we start?" Karen replied sarcastically. "He's gorgeous, successful, in amazing shape, and—"

"Yeah! Yeah! You can hold it right there before you take it too far." Brendan stopped her, waving his hand in her direction. "We get it, you're in love with your boss."

Megan looked around the other women, who were shyly looking into their glasses.

"I have to admit," Carol added, making Megan's eyes widen, "you do have to wonder what it would be like to wake up every morning in those strong arms. I bet he knows how to treat a woman."

Karen nodded. "I bet he knows how to satisfy a woman, Carol. A guy like that must know a thing or two."

"Karen, seriously!" Brendan laughed.

"What? I'm just saying out loud what you ladies are all thinking. Emma excused, obviously."

"Jesus, Karen." Emma was trying not to laugh at the look Megan wore on her face. She knew Megan was mightily pissed off because of the frown and her raised eyebrow, which was being directed at Karen.

Carol groaned. "Have you seen him when he's not in a suit?"

"Carol. You can't say that! Sounds like you've been stalking the CEO." Jimmy burst out laughing.

"Oh my God, Jimmy, you don't get it. It's like he's a movie star. Insanely hot."

Megan glared at her. *I'm gonna punch her, I'm gonna bloody punch her!*

"Blimey, Carol. Have we just touched on a subject that needs to be discussed in a private room or something?" Brendan joked, leaning against the pillar behind him.

Jimmy broke Karen and Carol's train of thought. "You know he's got someone on the side though, right?" He got a stern look from the single ladies, and a panicked look from Megan and Emma. "Oh, I'm sorry. Have I just ruined your vision, girls? Remember that photo of him in the papers a few weeks back? He was on the phone when he was out with Owen, Clare, and that other dude? Who was that guy, by the way?"

"Kevin," Emma answered.

"Kevin, right." Jimmy nodded. "But yes, he was blatantly dismissing that blonde chick. I'm sorry, but who pushes that away if you're not already seeing someone else? Meg?"

Oh shitting hell! Megan looked even more panicked now. It was as if the mention of her name acted as confirmation. Confirmation that yes, they were currently sat around in a huddle, discussing their chances at getting into her boyfriend's pants.

"Did you see it?"

"Um, yeah, I think so. But he could have just been asking for some privacy to finish the call, right?" *The call where we were talking about my next trip to London and spending our first night together. Bastards!*

Karen pointed to Megan and nodded in agreement. "See, not everyone is in a relationship just because they are on the phone, Jimmy."

"Shut up, Karen. You're just in denial."

Emma's phone began to ring and Tom's name appeared at the top of the screen. She showed it around the table in an excusing gesture and moved away to answer it, pulling Megan with her.

"You okay, Meg? Bit weird hearing them talk about Aid like that, right?"

Megan nodded, then gestured that she'd give Emma a moment. She returned and sat back down on the bench, reentering the conversation her work colleagues were still having about how much they wanted to fuck the man she was in love with.

Emma returned to the group, hanging up the phone. "If it's still okay ladies and gents, Tom's on his way over."

"Lover boy's coming out to play," Jimmy teased, nudging her. The rest of them giggled.

"Thank you, children, very grown up of you." Emma quickly looked at Megan, who already knew what she was going to say. "Owen and Aidan are with him too."

"Omigosh." Carol sounded like she was hyperventilating.

"They were going to have a lads' night, but Tom messed up the plans, so they're meeting me here. Please behave yourselves and try not to get fired." She looked between Carol and Karen. "They've just left Aidan's, so should be here in about twenty minutes."

"I feel I need to check my makeup." Karen shot off to the bathroom, followed by Carol.

"I feel I need a stronger drink," Megan said, sliding closer to Emma.

"And a restraining order, perhaps? Can't say I didn't warn you." Emma giggled as they stood, and linked Megan's arm. They each took a deep breath, spun in a one-eighty turn, and headed to the bar.

***

As she sat back down on the bench and hugged her beer (not her usual favourite), Megan tried hard to hide her laughter. "For goodness sake." She nudged Emma in the direction of the bathroom door. "If there's one thing I've learnt so far, it's that Aid isn't attracted to mountains of makeup."

Emma put her hand over her eyes once she saw what Megan had seen. "Mountains is right. That's like Everest and Kilimanjaro's love child."

Karen and Carol had indeed applied more makeup, in an obvious attempt to try and get Aidan's attention. They were heading back to return to their seats.

Megan sighed. "This is going to be beyond uncomfortable, isn't it?"

"How do you mean?"

"Those two, Em, and the rest—drooling over Aid when I can't do a damn thing about it."

Megan's phone vibrated in her back pocket, making her jump to her feet.

Emma laughed, grabbing her hand as she regained her balance and helped her sit back down again.

Unlocking her phone, Megan laughed while she read the message Aidan had just sent her.

BABY, YOUR ASS IS LOOKING INCREDIBLE IN THOSE JEANS. DON'T WORRY ABOUT REPLYING, WE'LL BE WITH YOU BEFORE YOU FINISH READING THIS...

"Hey gorgeous." Tom pulled Emma back from behind them for a welcoming kiss, making her scream.

Megan almost swore.

"Don't mind us dropping by? Hi Meg." He gave Megan a hug while she continued to read Aidan's message.

TOM'S HAD AN IDEA. DON'T FREAK OUT BY WHAT YOU'LL HEAR ME SAY ON THE PHONE IN A BIT, OKAY? JUST TRUST ME. Xx

"Evening, Tom. Being good to my Emma?" She pocketed her phone.

"As always, Meg, as always." Tom addressed the rest of the group. "Hey guys. Good night so far?"

They all greeted him, but were looking around, probably wondering where Aidan and Owen were.

"Aid's already made a beeline for the bar, do you need another drink? He's paying."

"We're good, babe," said Emma. "Meg just got these in." She pointed at their drinks.

"So, Aid's already been buying drinks then?" Tom whispered between them so no one else heard.

Megan laughed sarcastically at him. She didn't have to hide the fact that she'd met Tom already. He was dating her best friend, of course they would have already met.

"Tom!" Aidan's voice boomed across the main seating area, making heads turn, including those of his own staff. It was clear that he had no intentions of staying quiet.

Megan looked over and instantly wished she hadn't. Aidan was wearing his favourite baseball top, and that same zip-up hoodie he'd worn on the night they'd met. Her eyes melted, and pretty soon, they'd be two measly puddles on the table.

"What?" Tom yelled back, looking at what Aidan wanted. He was waving his hand for him to come to the bar to collect his drinks. "Yeah, okay!" Tom turned back to Meg and Emma. "Back in a minute"

"Shit, Aidan looks hot again tonight." Carol stared at him in awe before snapping to attention. She'd apparently only just become aware that she'd just said it out loud. She turned a shade of pink.

Everyone else looked at her, trying not to laugh. Everyone except Tom, who couldn't help but snigger. He raced to the bar and returned shortly afterwards with drinks, along with Aidan and Owen.

"How's it going, Em?" Owen greeted her, trying not to acknowledge Megan like they had known each other for almost a month.

"Owen, can I slap your brother for scaring the living shit out of me and Megan please?"

"Yeah, as long as we can film it?" Aidan answered for him. "Em, your boyfriend needs punching more often these days. Keeps him on track."

"Fucker!"

"Beautiful come back, Tom, absolutely superb." Aidan applauded him.

Just the sound of his voice melted Megan right on the spot. She looked at him, but quickly realised what she was doing and returned to her drink.

"Megan," Emma began, trying not to laugh while she introduced the guys to her friend, "this is Owen, Tom's brother." Megan shook his hand as he went in for a friendly hug. They too were both trying not to laugh at the situation. "And this is Aidan. Guys, this is Megan."

Aidan looked up from his phone and went in for a friendly fake-first-greeting hug. He smiled as they embraced and, almost silently, whispered, "Evening beautiful." He pulled back. "So, Megan. Emma's latest? We've been hearing good things about you."

He didn't give her a second to respond, and instead turned his attention to everyone else, including Karen and Carol, who hadn't stopped staring at him. "How's the night so far, guys? Going good?"

A resounding murmur came from the group, who weren't quite sure how to respond to their boss in casual mode.

"Take that as a yes?"

There was a brief pause. Emma stared at all three of them, begging for one of them to think of something to say. Giving up, she turned her attention to Karen. "Karen, what's the plan this evening? You seemed to be in control of this earlier."

"Well ... Umm ... I don't really know. Start here and head further into the city later?" She was trying her absolute best to sound calm but was failing badly.

Jimmy nudged her back into reality. "Maybe Soho?"

"Ah, Soho." Emma smiled. "Meg, you remember when we went out to dinner there, that night when you came up for the weekend? We should go there again soon. I want to try the fish this time."

Megan shook her head. "Remember? How can I forget the restaurant where everyone thought you were about to propose to me? We got a round of applause, Em, it was incredibly awkward."

"You loved it!"

They both laughed as they sat back down. Megan thought back to that very night and felt herself smile as Emma reminded her what went down at the restaurant. Yet Megan was thinking about what went down later in the evening. Aidan's smile, the way he admired her and the way he made her feel when their eyes locked. Her heartrate quickened and she had to tell herself not to jump on him as the adrenaline surged through her entire body.

While they sat talking, Aidan's phone began to ring. He pulled it from his pocket. "Hey sweetheart, you in town yet?"

Megan looked around, already understanding what their plan was. Aidan was about to fake a call from his 'girlfriend,' making it clear that she definitely was not Megan.

Owen sat down next to her and typed on his phone, angling it so Megan could clearly read what he was writing.

DON'T WORRY, HE'S TALKING TO CLARE.

Happy that Megan had read his secret message, he pretended to send a text and put it back in his pocket.

People began talking again now that they were getting over the initial shock of seeing both of the top bosses in a relaxed environment. They managed to turn the conversation around to work, but Megan listened instead to what Aidan was saying to Clare.

"So you're not coming out tonight? Shame, gonna be one hell of an evening... They're always messy you know that... Nah, he's said he's not drinking, well, not much." Aidan laughed. Clare must have been warning him about getting Owen drunk again. "Maybe... I've been thinking about it, yeah, I'm not gonna lie... Let's just see where things go, shall we?" Aidan managed to catch Megan's gaze while everyone was talking. "Driving down again this weekend?"

Megan gave the slightest smile, which meant *yes please* to his last sentence, which was clearly directed at her. A weekend where she had him all to herself? Who wouldn't say yes to that? Certainly not her work friends, that was for sure.

"Ok, tomorrow morning... Bye." Aidan hung up and was happy that his fake call was heard by his members of staff. "Sorry guys, what are we chatting about?"

"Elle not able to make it out tonight?" Owen went along with their plan a bit further, making up a fake name in the process.

"Got a last minute family dinner or something. No biggie." Jimmy leant into Karen. "I bloody told you."

"Lucky woman, huh? I'm actually pretty gutted. Maybe it won't last."

"His last relationship latest a while," Jimmy countered.

"What are you guys being so secretive about?" Aidan said, even though he knew exactly what they were talking about.

"Nothing exciting," Jimmy said.

"Fair enough." Aidan finished his drink. "Anyone want another?"

This time Megan happily accepted his offer. "Please, if you don't mind?"

"Sure, what will it be?"

"Something different to whatever that last one was. I'll give you a hand if you like, it'll give me a chance to see what else they have to offer." *And some alone time.* She stood and followed Aidan through the crowd.

The area around the bar was crammed with alcohol-thirsty animals, all pushing and shoving to get their nectar. Aidan pushed through the crowd firmly, dragging Megan behind him so they didn't get separated. He stopped when they found a spot near the front.

She stopped beside him and smiled. "Don't get all big-headed sweetheart, but that fake call was a genius idea."

"How'd you know it was fake?"

"Owen showed me in a text that said you were talking to Clare."

"Subtle. I didn't see that." He cocked his head to the side. "So, was that a yes to driving down to Farnham tomorrow?"

"Of course." She nodded slowly. "And maybe a promise of something else later?"

"I do love where your mind goes, Meg."

While they were waiting to be served at the busy bar, Aidan took the opportunity the crowd gave him to hold her waist. Megan lay her hand over his, massaging his knuckles with her fingertips.

"What was Clare asking you?"

"That would be telling, wouldn't it?"

Megan turned to face him, waiting for him to continue.

"She was saying that it's amazing that we're so serious about making our relationship work, that I better not get Owen hammered again, that I've never been like this with anyone else in my life before, and that she's glad I'm happy." Aidan leant in. "She also wanted to know what's in store for the future."

Megan almost jumped on him now that she knew what Clare had asked. His responses had all been promising—an indication of their perfect future. In fact, she was just about to do it. She was going to throw caution to the wind; she was going to jump into his arms, wrap her legs around his waist, and press her lips to his so hard he'd teleport out of his socks. But then she stopped herself. She saw Jimmy out the corner of her eye, and he was heading right for them.

"Megan? Mr. Costello?" he said.

"That was close," Aidan whispered. "Jimmy, right?" He asked, raising his voice.

Jimmy nodded. "First off, let's not shout my surname out too loud, shall we? And secondly, I'm not your boss tonight. Aidan is perfectly fine." He smiled.

"Sorry, my bad." He smiled back awkwardly. "Owen just sent me in. Asked if you could you grab him some crisps. He said you owe him or something?"

"Lazy bastard! Sure, I'll get him some."

Jimmy ran back out to pass on the message to Owen that his crisps were on their way.

Megan watched him disappear and ran a hand under Aidan's shirt, enjoying the desire that she saw building in his eyes. "You do kind of owe him, Aid."

Aidan shook his head. "It was Tom's idea."

"And it was your best friend's wife."

He pursed his lips, closed his eyes, and bobbed his head from shoulder to shoulder, considering her point. "Talking of Clare, she wanted to know if we're free Sunday evening for dinner. She's apparently got this new cooker she wants to try out."

"So she's testing her cooking skills on us? Charming."

Aidan laughed at Megan's sarcasm.

"Sounds great."

After asking the barman to put the drinks on a tab, Aidan turned and looked Megan up and down. "I'd do anything to kiss you right now."

Megan pressed her face into his neck and whispered, "Do it then. End all this secrecy and let's see what the future holds." She pulled back at the last second, grabbed her drink off the bar, and walked back in the direction of the table, placing great emphasis on the motion of her hips.

She smiled when she heard him groan behind her.

***

The rest of the evening went by without any awkwardness. Everyone got on brilliantly. Although when the weather took a turn, Megan began shivering. Much to Aidan's disapproval, Brendan saw a chance to make a move, wrapping his arms around her to help keep her warm. The look on Aidan's face was priceless. Pure anger.

Owen had nudged him hard in the ribs, to make him break focus and stop staring. He hated not being able to tell Brendan to back the fuck off.

As the hours passed the others decided to go further into town, leaving Aidan, Megan, Emma, Tom, and Owen to reflect upon good times. After one more drink they called it a night.

The cab pulled up to Aidan's apartment building, after a short drive. Aidan got out and helped Megan out too. He guided her to the path and leant back into the vehicle. "Cab's paid for guys. Until Sunday."

Emma and Tom waved them goodbye.

Now that he was finally able to touch his girlfriend Aidan picked her up and threw her over his shoulder, making her squeal in surprise. He carried her through the front doors of the building and made for the lift.

"So tell me, what was that lot saying about me?" he asked, placing Megan down in the lift. He stepped in beside her and pressed the button for the top floor.

She pressed her index finger to his lips. "First things first." She grabbed his shirt, pulling him into a deeply passionate kiss, making up for the fact they had spent an entire evening together but apart.

He lifted Megan's hands and placed them around his neck. He found her waist, wrapping his arms around her and pulling their bodies together. He leant her back and his hand ventured lower, lifting one of her thighs up. He ended the kiss and rested his forehead against hers. He closed his eyes and listened to Megan's breathing, thinking about the other question Clare had asked him.

Going to marry her, then?

The doors opened on their floor. Aidan took Megan's hand as they walked the short distance to their apartment. "God, I don't like having to wait to be alone to kiss you. Hated every minute of that."

"You already know what my answer is to that, Aidan."

"I can't, sweetheart, not while you're still at JMC." He cast a glance towards her. "Not yet, anyway."

"You know what the hardest part of this evening was?"

Aidan opened the front door, looking at her in anticipation.

"Having to listen to other women drool over you and not being able to say or do anything." Megan ran her hands up his chest and around his neck once more.

"That must've been uncomfortable."

"More uncomfortable than you could imagine. But then again, they don't get to come home with you."

"That's right." Aidan began kissing her neck. He wanted to continue with that what they'd started in the lift.

"They were wondering what it would be like to wake up with you. And made comments about your loyalty. They reckon you'd know how to treat a woman too."

Aidan lifted her chin and looked into her eyes, waiting. Waiting to consume her.

She ran three fingers diagonally across his lips. "They put money on your ability to *satisfy* a woman."

He smiled. "Well, from the sounds you make when we're in bed, I'd say I'm satisfying you nicely."

"Oh my God, Aidan!" She hit his shoulder.

He slung her over his shoulder and marched towards the bedroom. "Yeah, there it is."

Chapter 22

T he following week, after spending another weekend in Farnham and having dinner at the Turners' on Sunday, life at JMC had become a nightmare. Norfolk Computers were getting close to the deadline he'd given them, and there was still no official response.

Megan could tell that Aidan was getting pissed. He'd returned home ten minutes ago, two hours later than expected, looking stressed and wound up.

Megan had been standing outside the living room door for the past few minutes. She was watching him, trying to decipher the right moment. There wasn't one, really. He sat there with his head in his palms for the best part of five minutes, and judging by the sighs he was letting out every other second, that wasn't about to change any time soon.

She walked into the room, being careful not to startle him. "I know you said we wouldn't talk about work at home, sweetheart, but do you want to talk about it?" Megan asked as she began to rub his shoulders, feeling the tension in them.

"It wouldn't be fair to land all that on you."

She sat next to him and put a hand on his cheek, guiding his head onto her shoulder.

He let it rest there and sighed once more—though more of a relieved one this time. If he didn't want to talk about it, the least she could do was comfort him.

"We gave them plenty of time to come up with an answer—more time than I should have given. And when talking with them today, they still came back with nothing! It's pissing me off now."

So we do want to talk about it. Megan listened while she stroked the back of his neck.

"It's obvious they're in trouble, so why take a fucking living age to give a company, who's willing to help, an answer that'll solve their problems?" He groaned. "I've wanted to get JMC in the states for a couple of years now and this, right now, is our ticket in. But they're bloody stalling it." Aidan rubbed his tired eyes.

"When's the deadline?"

"Friday, but I'm getting impatient. I shouldn't have given them that extra month. Fucking idiot!"

"Well it's Monday, so they have three days, right? How do you work it?"

"Yeah. We're speaking to them again tomor–"

"Then," she placed a finger over his lips, "leave it until tomorrow. I have no idea what it's like to do the job you do, Aidan, or what it takes to deal with the obvious stress levels, but as a girlfriend, all I'm going to say is what I kept on having to tell my old work colleagues when they were having a meltdown." She smiled. "Chill the fuck out and leave it until the next working day!"

Aidan looked up, slightly shocked.

"Yeah, you've just been told off. So suck it up."

"I don't think anyone's ever said anything like that to me before." He sighed. "You're right though. I'm sorry, baby, today hasn't been the best. I hate bringing work home."

"Come on." Megan pulled him up off the sofa.

"Where are we going?" He asked, when she dragged him towards the stairs.

"To get you out of work mode." Megan turned to face him. "And before you get any ideas, I'm out of bounds this week."

Aidan gave her a disappointed moan.

"I'm gonna run you a hot bath, order a takeout, and then we'll chill with a movie that doesn't involve Iron Man."

***

Aidan left earlier than usual the next day. He needed to get to the office to prepare for the afternoon video conference with Norfolk. He wanted to make sure he was well prepared for anything they could throw at him. Much to his surprise, he'd actually been able to relax after his little rant last night. The bath that Megan prepared for him must've done the trick. It had calmed him right down, pulling the knots of tension from his stressed out muscles, and he'd gotten a decent night's sleep. That was something he didn't encounter often.

His mind usually went into overdrive when his head hit the pillow, filled with general overthinking, strategy planning to win contract deals, and the overall running of the company. Either Megan had slipped him something in his dinner, or her presence in general had a calming influence. Either way, he was grateful that she hadn't shied away from his obvious temper.

Not many people had the courage to try and calm him down when he was in that kind of mood. Even Owen struggled to get past his anger at times. It's part of what he liked about her. She didn't give a crap that he was a powerful CEO who controlled an entire company. He was simply a man. Her man.

"God, I love that woman." Aidan sat upright in his chair, realising what he had just said. He stared into space.

Do I? Of course I do. I can't think of spending my life with anyone else. I love her. I love her.

Owen burst into his office. "Morning sunshine."

I should tell her, but not now. I need to be focussed. Actually, keep the fact that you're in love with Meg to yourself. Don't let it slip until later tonight. Aidan smiled to himself.

Owen tried to bring him back into reality. "Hello? In dreamland there, Aid? Did you hear anything I said?"

Aidan swatted Owen's hand away. "No, what? Shut up, I'm fine." He shook his head as he took another sip—or gulp—of coffee. "What's the schedule today?"

Owen shrugged. "Win over Norfolk and get into the States?"

"Okay," Aidan stood, clapping his hands together, "let's do this."

***

Megan hadn't heard from Aidan all day. She gathered he was probably busy with Norfolk Computers, demanding that they give him their answer. The whole building knew about this latest deal—the one currently pushing their CEO's temper—since it could affect everyone positively if it went through. The staff were already discussing the growth of the company if it was successful, although they were unaware that Aidan's aim was to get JMC into America. He was keeping that piece of information on the low for now.

Megan looked at her reflection in her computer's monitor and studied the hunger in her eyes. She thought about messaging him, just to check that he wasn't stressing out, but decided against it. He needed to be focussed, and receiving a message from his girlfriend would definitely cause a distraction.

Brendan slid over to Megan's desk, producing a cup of tea. "Meg, listen, I just want to apologise for that move at the bar the other night. I had no idea you had a boyfriend. Just thought I'd give it a shot. You're a stunning woman and any guy would be lucky to have you." He held the cup out to her. "Tea to say sorry?"

"It's okay, Brendan. I probably should have told you all, it just never came up." She took the cup. "Thank you."

Brendan smiled and went back to his desk.

She took a sip and frowned at the cup. *Ugh, what flavour is this?* "Emma, I'm just nipping to the bathroom."

"Are you going via coffee?"

"I'm not about to use the downstairs loos just to get you a coffee. You have a problem."

She tutted. "Fine, I'll head down in a bit."

"If you're lucky, and a good girl, Emma," Megan locked her computer screen and picked up her bag, "I may take a detour for you."

"You know I love you Meg."

"Yeah, I know."

Smiling and blowing Emma a dramatic kiss, she walked across the office and opened the glass door. Entering the corridor that headed towards the lifts, she jumped out of her skin when she found Aidan leaning against the wall near the door, dressed in her favourite black D&G suit.

"Holy shitting hell!" She smacked his arm. "Were you waiting for me?"

It was obvious that he was dealing with an inner battle not to sweep her up there and then. "Come with me second, I need a quick word. Just pretend we're talking about work stuff." He sent Emma a message as they walked through the corridors.

EMMA, STOLEN MEG FOR A MOMENT, I'LL RETURN HER SOON.

"Work stuff? You mean about you looking stressed again?" She teased him.

"Very funny." Aidan summoned the lift and they entered it together. As soon as the doors closed, he was on her in a flash.

"So, this is your idea of a quick word? Wasn't this part of the guidelines?"

"Screw the guidelines, no one can see us in here unless we stop." He placed a kiss on her lips and let it linger. He withdrew it sharply, leaving his eyes on hers. It was a solemn look, one he rarely shared.

Megan inhaled a little too fast. She tried to hide her discomfort, but her lungs wouldn't allow it. "Aidan? Everything okay?"

The lift reached the top floor, but Aidan kept the doors closed. He looked into her eyes, searching for her soul. He didn't dare break the connection. "Megan, I have to fly out to New York."

Bugger!

"Today."

Double Bugger!

"Actually, my car is being readied now. I should only be a few days, a week max. But I had to see you before I left, to explain, for starters, why I won't be home later."

Megan studied him. He seemed genuinely gutted that he had to leave her. She hugged him. He sighed and it sounded like her nearness was taking away the pressure of the last minute flight to New York.

"Didn't go to plan today then?"

"No. Not sure what they're playing at now. Don't seem to have made any progress in terms of a decision. So we've decided they deserve a surprise visit." He kissed her. "You don't mind?"

"Actually, yeah, I do. You should be here."

He looked at her in shock.

"No, you muppet, of course I don't mind. Did you not think I'd expected this sort of thing to happen when we started dating?" Megan placed her hand on his cheek. "You really are taking this can't-always-get-your-own-way thing seriously, aren't you?"

"Anything to keep you happy."

Megan smiled warmly at him.

"God I'm lucky to be with a woman so understanding. You're too good."

She'd fallen so hard. *Was he feeling the same? Did neither of them know how to say it yet, or when the right time was?*

"Just make sure you let me know when you land in New York, and when you're heading back, okay? I'll be here waiting for you. I may even have dinner waiting as well."

Aidan laughed. "I'm sure you will."

"And watch those American women."

"No one but you, Megan." He smiled at her before they kissed. He released the button, allowing the doors to part, and stepped out of the lift, leaving her to travel back down to her floor.

A tear lingered in her eye as the doors closed once more.

***

Megan entered Emma's office and slumped into one of her chairs.

"Whoa," Tom said in a patronising way. He'd arrived earlier than usual to pick Emma up. "What's up, chicken? Bad day?

Or has Aidan done something that requires me to have a word?"

"No. No need to have a word, Tom, but thanks. Aidan's got to fly out to New York and will be gone for a few days. Told him I didn't mind, which I don't, of course." Megan started playing with one of Emma's photo frames on her desk. "I just feel a bit bummed out now, that's all. We've not been apart since those two weeks after we met."

Emma's work phone rang, displaying Owen's number. "Owen, what can I do you for?"

"First off, is my brother there distracting you?" Emma looked at Tom.

"I'm being spoken about, aren't I?"

"And second, can I borrow you and Meg please? I have a feeling she's there with you now, feeling glum about Aid flying out. This will keep her occupied."

"Sure, be up in five minutes." She smirked at Tom. "And yes, your brother's here, but he's behaving."

"Behaving? I'll believe it when I see it."

***

The door swung inwards and they stepped inside. Clare closed it behind them, gave them each a warm smile, and offered them some cold drinks with a nod in the fridge's direction. It was a warm day, and the air in Owen's office didn't fail to live up to that.

Megan nodded firmly. Emma did too.

"You okay, Meg?" Owen asked her. He tossed a couple cans in their direction.

Megan caught hers. "Yeah."

"Cheer up, he'll be back soon." They sat on the sofas to discuss what Owen had summoned them for. "Okay, the reason I asked you all here is a little strange. Before Aidan ran out the door, he asked me to finish organising something. Something, I think you ladies will enjoy."

"Me? But I don't even work here?" Clare reminded him.

"You're married to me and keep us in check, so you kinda do."

Clare shrugged. She couldn't argue with facts.

"Anyway, Aidan asked if you'd all mind finishing the planning of an event for him. Usually Lois helps with this, but because Norfolk idiots have taken their sweet ass time, they've put us behind schedule. He also said that it would be nice if friends and family could do it, make it extra special or some bollocks like that."

Clare smacked him for being cheeky. "Don't be a dick, Owen."

"Get to the point, bro. Em will need more coffee by the end of this." Tom grinned at Emma who was looking back at him.

She pointed to the coffee machine. He took the hint and headed off to make her one.

Megan decided to tease him and made the sound of a whip cracking. Everyone smirked.

Tom let his middle finger linger behind him as he walked across the room.

"Okay, okay! The Christmas Company Conference is coming up in a few weeks. Emma will tell you Meg, that it's one of the biggest events in the city."

Emma couldn't control her excitement. "Oh my God, Aid wants us to help finish planning the conference?"

Owen nodded. "This is going to be amazing! Lucy will love it! She's got so many connections for events like this."

Emma paused, a thought putting a temporary black cloud over her parade. "But, what about the end of year stuff?"

"Not to be worried about. People in all the relevant departments are going to be notified of the slight change in direction. You'll get company credit cards to splash out on, and full use of the limos."

"Fuck off! Thank you for snogging the boss, Megan, I've always wanted to help plan one of these events." Emma hugged her arm. "When do we start?"

"Right now," Owen said.

"It's quite last minute to plan, can it be done?" Megan asked.

"It can and will get done. The venue is already secured: The Roundhouse in Camden. The manager, Nigel, wouldn't dream of booking anything on the party weekend. What with the amount of cash we throw his way and the amount of media that show up. Plus, he likes to keep on Aidan's good side—such a kiss-ass." Owen grinned.

"Is there a theme or style?" Megan asked.

"Aidan said you can do pretty much anything you like. Which was brave."

Megan stood up, pacing up and down the room. "We have the venue, we have the date, we can do what we want." She stopped, facing them all with her hands held up. "And–"

"And we have Lucy, she'll pull some strings," Emma said, standing up with her. "You know the contacts she has."

Megan snapped her fingers, pointing at Emma. "Yes. Yes I do."

"What sort of contacts?"

"Oh, you know, just the top designers, bands, and celebs, Clare. You name them, Lucy can probably get them," Megan replied.

"Come on girls, let's go and spend some cash and start planning." Emma lifted Clare off the sofa and dragged her out to the lifts. "Bye boys," she shouted, without looking back.

Owen watched them fly through the door and rocked back on his heels as it slammed closed. He turned to his right and exchanged a look with his brother. Their look said the exact same thing, in the exact same manner, at the exact same time: What had Aidan let himself in for?

Chapter 23

A idan sank back into the warmth of the business class leather. London to New York was quite the flight, but as he pulled his blanket around his chest and stretched his legs out into the seemingly endless space in front of him, he figured he'd be quite alright. He pulled out his phone and checked his messages one last time.

The pilot was about to make his mandatory announcements, or rather, portray his boredom through the monotone telling of an instruction everyone knew was coming. Aidan could empathise with the poor bastard. He knew all about that.

He quickly sent a text to Megan, saying he was about to take off, but would call her every day. Remembering how she held him when he was telling her he had to go, he typed about how she drove him crazy and how he couldn't imagine how his life would be now, had he not met her at the club that night. Part of him wanted to tell her how he felt, how much he was in love with her, but he decided against it. That's not how he wanted to tell her at all. Not over a goddamn text message. He was better than that. He'd wait. Wait until he was back on British soil, when he could wrap her up and kiss her lips. He'd wait and tell her then.

Should have told her in the lift—I had the chance. No, wouldn't have been good enough. I should take her out for dinner or something. Something special.

Another message flashed up from Owen.

YOU'RE IN TROUBLE. THREE WOMEN, HEADING OUT THE DOOR WITH YOUR CREDIT CARDS? GOOD LUCK!

He laughed to himself. He knew he'd made the right decision by choosing them to plan the big event. He trusted Megan and Clare, which meant he also trusted Emma and Lucy. If anyone could pull an event that big together in a few short weeks, it was those four. No one would refuse them, but he'd love to see what reaction they'd give to someone who tried. All four of them were strong in their own ways and from what he'd learnt about Megan's capability at the office, he had no worries at all. This year's party would be a huge success.

"Ladies and Gentlemen..."

Knowing what he was about to be told over the tannoy, Aidan switched his phone to airplane mode and put his earphones in to block out the sound of the pilot's announcement.

Closing his eyes, and smiling at the thought of the woman he loved, he forced himself to think about all the ways he would win over Norfolk Computers. Two massive companies on either side of the Atlantic, working alongside each other... they could take on the world. It made Aidan rack his brains.

Why were they taking their time?

Chapter 24

Megan waited in line for a large mug of her usual coffee. The barista greeted her. She smiled politely and placed her order. She hadn't slept as well as she hoped, and that wasn't just because Aidan wasn't next to her. She felt lost in such a large bed, in an apartment she felt wasn't her home. Checking her phone to see if Aidan had made contact, she felt deflated when she found her inboxes empty.

"Large latte for Megan?"

"Yes, thank you." She took her coffee, making her way to the lifts to start her working day. Calling the lift, she decided to message Aidan, checking to see if he'd had a good flight.

AIDAN, HOPE YOU MANAGED TO RELAX AND NOT DRINK TOO MUCH FROM THE MINIBAR? I MISSED YOU LAST NIGHT, M Xxx

It wasn't until she was in the lift that she heard someone calling for her to hold it. "Which floor?" she asked, holding the door open.

"Thanks. Twelve please."

"No problem."

"Megan Ashton, right?"

Megan nodded.

"Been here a few weeks?"

"Yes, that sounds about right." Megan tried to remain calm. It was weird being questioned by a stranger.

"I'm Kelly." She held her hand out to shake Megan's. "It's nice to officially meet the woman who's made an impact in the sales departments. You've made quite the impression around here."

"Oh, thank you." Megan looked at her feet, feeling embarrassed. "Just trying to do a good job."

"While we're chatting," Kelly moved closer to her, "did you happen to notice Aidan's weird behaviour recently? It's like he's, I don't know, not as focussed as he used to be?"

"I really don't think I've been here long enough to notice a difference in Mr. Costello's behaviour. Sorry."

"I mean, this deal that's going on with the Americans shouldn't take this long surely? Don't you think? He usually has people eating out his hands. He's clearly distracted somehow, it's weird."

Megan's phone began to ring and she bet a hundred quid that it was Aidan. She quickly hid her phone but Kelly looked towards it as the doors opened on the twelfth floor.

She looked Megan up and down. "Hmm, well, it was lovely to meet you, Megan. Perhaps we could go for a drink sometime?"

"Yeah, yeah." Megan nervously laughed. "Sounds wonderful. "I'll call your office sometime then. Bye!"

Kelly left, leaving Megan alone and more worried than ever.

Chapter 25

T he eyes of everyone followed him as he stormed through the lobby, heading out of the building, and frankly, Aidan didn't give a fuck. He was at the very end of his already-short tether. There was nothing these gaping morons could do to affect him now.

He'd only been in Norfolk's head office building for an hour, but that was all he'd needed. How long did a guy need to walk into a room, announce the importance of the deal and how pissed he was, and turn and walk back out? Not long. And that meant even less time when you were Aidan Costello.

He was ten steps away from the main doors when he heard the voice. He turned to meet their Head of Legal, Clive Hillard.

"Mr. Costello, please, this deal will help us—we are aware of that. My client merely needed another couple of weeks to—"

"Like I just said, Clive, I gave you more than enough time to come up with an answer. Because of your time wasting, I've had to fly out here to get an answer, which apparently, you're still not willing to give. I'm tired of waiting. And because of the nightmare this has caused, you are disturbing any progress within JMC," he lied.

"Mr. Costello, if you could just—"

"Luckily, *we* can cope perfectly fine without the deal going through. The only question is: *can you*? You heard the terms, but I am becoming less and less interested in this contract to give a damn anymore." He was losing his patience now.

"So that's it? The deal is off?"

Aidan had him right where he wanted him. "Not quite." He paused for effect, holding Clive's gaze a second too long. "Since you've all been so welcoming, I'll give you one more week. I'd consider this to be *extremely* generous given the circumstances. If by then we do not hear anything from you, I'm withdrawing. Understood?"

Aidan turned on his heel and walked out, leaving the lawyer unsure of how to answer him. The threat card had worked before and he had no doubt that it would work on them too. If not, he was beyond caring anyway.

He heard a scuffle from behind him as he walked through the door and outside into the New York air. He knew it was the company's directors, coming to see if their lawyer had managed to calm him down. Aidan smiled to himself. He had them just where he wanted them.

He called Owen when he got to the car.

"Owen Turner."

"Really? Still?"

"I told you, it's a habit. How did it go today? Any luck?"

"Yeah. We've got them. Give it a week and we'll have an answer."

"You've threatened them, haven't you?" Aidan heard a gasp in the background. It sounded like Megan.

"Just a little, yeah." He paused, remembering the scene. "Okay, maybe more than a little. Their lawyer chased me down in the reception."

"I do love a good scene. You think they'll finally sign?"

"Still bloody hard to say right now, but after I told them we don't actually need them, they panicked. Their turnover seems to have dropped dramatically over the past year, with stocks lowering too. They'll need to sign with us if they want to get back to playing with the big dogs."

"I'll inform legal of the updates on Monday." Owen grinned. "So, are you staying in New York for the weekend, or heading back today?"

"I'm heading back right now. I just have to stop by the hotel. Can you let Megan know that I should be landing around four a.m. your time, please?"

"No problem, I'll let her know." Owen turned to her. "Hey, Meg! Aidan's on his way back. We're having a night at yours."

Aidan laughed. "You're a real pal. Would it be possible to get a car ready at the airport?"

"I'll sort it," Megan said.

Owen must have had him on speakerphone. "Thank you, baby!" Aidan shouted so Megan could hear him. "I'll message when I land, Owen."

"Safe flight, Aid."

The car pulled up outside the hotel. Aidan asked the driver to wait while he got his bags. That was the last order of business. He'd run in, grab his bags, and return to the car. After that, it was time to head to the airport. Aidan smiled as visions of Megan popped into his head. He couldn't wait to be home.

***

Aidan stepped out of the airport's revolving doors and into the London air. There wasn't any sign of Tony. Megan must have told him to wait a little out of sight because of the possibility of paparazzi. Thanking his escorts, he headed off to the left, a few photographers following. He didn't care about them anymore. It was too early for their shit.

There it was, parked on the pavement, the car he would recognise anywhere. The same car he'd picked Megan up in; the car they'd rode into their new life. Before he could properly register the moment, he saw Megan standing by the open door.

She had sensibly worn one of his large hooded jumpers and a pair of glasses so she wouldn't be recognised.

Aidan smiled.

Screw the photographers, no one's stopping me from greeting the woman I love.

He walked slowly towards her as she watched his every move. "You'll handle the car, huh?" Aidan put his bags on the back seat. "Nice touch." He pulled her into a crushing embrace and kissed her.

Flashes of lights went off around them and photographers shouted his name in excitement.

There was no way they would see Megan's face—Aidan had pulled her hood further down so they could have some privacy. Well, as much privacy as they could manage while surrounded by flashing lights and unnecessary questions.

"I've missed you so much," Megan said so only he could hear.

He kissed her again, setting the photographers off once more, then escorted her to the passenger's side of the car, still keeping her face covered. Questions were being thrown left, right, and centre.

"Aidan! Aidan! Who is she?"

"Mr. Costello, have you been seeing her long?"

"What does this mean for JMC?"

The last question baffled him. *What, a guy couldn't have a girlfriend while he ran a huge company?* He shook his head and smiled into the sea of white light. The flashes continued as they climbed into the car, slammed the doors shut, and drove away.

Once they were far enough away from the photographers, Aidan pulled over and stopped the car.

Megan pushed her hood down and took the glasses off. They stared at each other for a brief moment, before bursting into a fit of laughter.

"Owen's going to be pissed."

"Probably." Aidan took her hand, looking deep into her eyes. "Megan? I need to say something. I wanted to make this special, but I can't hang on much longer."

Megan was watching him intently, smiling. She knew what was coming.

"What? What are you smirking at?"

"I love you so much, Aidan."

He smiled at her. That was what he'd wanted to hear from the moment they met. He encircled her neck and pulled her close, stopping just before their lips came into contact. "You're all I think about. It wasn't until the day I had to leave that I've realised how much I'm in love with you."

Megan closed the distance between them, kissing him in a way that made him remember where they were. It was time to get the car moving again.

Chapter 26

It wasn't until they came into work on Monday morning that they realised how much the stunt at the airport had made an impact at the office and in the media. Aidan had gone in earlier than usual to do some ground control with Owen. He was sure he would have a fit when the pictures were released. He wasn't wrong.

Owen put the paper down on the desk. "What the actual hell, Aidan?" Owen shouted at him. "Seriously, playing it close there weren't we? You were lucky it was at night! Keep you damn phone on next time, so I can yell at you straight away!"

"Calm yourself, sunshine." Aidan repeated the nickname Owen had given him the previous week, when he was in a mood. "No one saw her."

"And if they had, what then? You've already got all the staff talking."

Aidan laughed. "Owen, listen. No one knows it was Megan. They'll just be overexcited because this place will be under the media's eye again for a while." He leant back in his chair. "Probably do us some good to get a bit more media coverage this time of year anyway."

"I hate it when you're right."

"That's because I'm usually always right, Owen."

"Even if you could have buggered it up severely," Owen mumbled under his breath. "Now that's settled, can we get back to updating the legal files from the trip please?"

***

Megan walked into JMC with Emma an hour after Aidan had arrived. She'd already told Emma, Clare, and Lucy the inside story of what happened at the airport, and they loved it. Emma said it had to be the most romantic thing she'd heard in a long time.

Looking like they were up to no good as they walked across reception, Megan whispered to Emma about how she and Aidan celebrated their love for one another over the course of the weekend. Both of them giggling like teenage girls, they hadn't noticed Jimmy bouncing over to them in a fit of excitement.

"Didn't I say? Didn't I say?" Jimmy nudged Megan, joining them. "Certainly causing a scene around here this morning. What was her name again, Mel? Elle?"

"I can't remember, Jim. Either way, it certainly is public knowledge that Aidan's officially off the market." Emma glanced towards Megan.

Jim rubbed his hands together in excitement. "Karen and Carol will be gutted now, can't wait to see their reaction. See you upstairs."

Emma sighed as she spotted Kelly walking towards them with a morning newspaper in hand. She knew what was coming.

"Oh God, here we go." Megan nudged Emma. She'd told her all about Kelly.

"Megan, didn't I tell you Aidan wasn't himself? Have you seen the pictures?" Kelly handed her the paper.

"Yeah, I saw them."

"I wonder who she is." She looked up and spotted Emma, who was eyeing her up. "Oh, hello."

"Kelly, this is Emma. Old friend and colleague."

"Hi."

Emma smiled. She hated her already.

"Any ideas? Looks like she's got brown hair." Kelly looked at Megan's hair. "And she looks to be about 5'7? That's around your height, right?"

"Okay, enough of this," Emma interrupted. "I'm sorry, Kelly, I don't know what you are actually trying to achieve here, but we have work to do. Please stop stirring whatever this is." She shook her head. "Come on, Meg."

Emma linked arms with Megan and headed for the lift. She wasn't planning on stopping at their floor. They were going straight to the top.

Megan groaned. "Thank you, Em. She's pushing it now. Maybe Aidan and I should just tell everyone. It'll stop all that fucking nonsense for good! I don't know how much longer I can–"

Emma hugged her as she burst into tears. "Don't succumb to the pressure, Meg. You and Aid can do this. It'll blow over soon enough."

"But what if it doesn't? What if it's always like this?"

"Jesus, Meg, it won't be. He loves you, and may I add, would do anything for you."

The lift stopped and the doors parted. They stepped out into the corridor and took a moment to breathe. Emma held her friend's arm, letting her know that she'd always be right there. Emma opened Aidan's office door.

He sensed something was wrong and rushed straight over. "What's happened?"

"It's Kelly. I just witnessed her grilling Meg for answers about your mystery girlfriend."

"Kelly." Aidan was furious when he saw how upset Megan was. He held her, taking her tension away. He didn't need to say anything—just being in his arms was reassuring enough.

Lois was at the door, watching in shock. Aidan locked eyes with her. He shook his head, signalling that she shouldn't freak out.

"Owen? Mind explaining this to Lois, please?"

"Sure."

Owen took Lois aside and told her the story of how Aidan and Megan had met and that they had been a couple before Megan had begun at JMC. Owen made her promise to help keep the secret from anyone else, apart from those who already knew.

"Well, Aidan. It's nice to see you happy again," Lois said, sitting down with Owen on the sofas.

Aidan smiled at her, still holding Megan. "Thank you, Lois. I'm sorry I couldn't tell–"

"No need to apologise. Anything I can do to help you both, just ask."

"Thank you." Aidan stroked Megan's hair. He lifted her head and looked into her eyes. "I think the best thing for us today is to get the hell out of this building, all of us." He turned, addressing the rest of the room. "Be in the basement carpark in half an hour. Lois, can you ask for one of the limos to be readied please? Ladies, you can show us the progress on the conference."

Megan couldn't have felt more relived that they were spending the day elsewhere. She held onto him tighter, like he was her safety net. His support radiated throughout her entire body. She felt the tension leave her every time Aidan gently stroked her hair.

"Well then, come on. Let's get going," Emma said.

"We'll wrap up in here, and be right behind you," Aidan said.

The girls left the office moments later, leaving Owen and Aidan alone. "Don't say a word," Aidan said. "Not a word."

"I wasn't going to say anything."

"You were thinking it!" Aidan snapped.

***

The car pulled up to the entrance of the Roundhouse in Camden. The glass walls of the modern foyer looked straight into a café that was full of theatre technicians taking a well-deserved mid- morning break. Megan looked up at the brickwork building to see new large posters advertising future events happening in the New Year. One in particular made her smile.

JMC LTD: PRIVATE CHRISTMAS EVENT.
CLOSED TO THE PUBLIC.

Megan and Emma went in ahead to inform the manager of the venue, Nigel, that their CEO had arrived to oversee the plans for the JMC Christmas Conference. The large reception once again took Megan's breath away. She didn't want to think about how much JMC must've paid to secure such a venue. The rest of the guys waited outside. Moments later, Nigel came out to greet them. He was wearing his brightest smile. After the formalities, he made a sweeping gesture with his arms and they all followed him inside.

As they walked through the venue's foyer, Aidan stopped Owen. "Owen, when we're done here, I'm taking Megan home. She's clearly shaken up about this morning. I don't want her going back to the office."

Owen nodded. "I'll ask Clare to go over to keep an eye on her if you like."

"I'd appreciate that, really. Thank you."

Owen tapped Aidan's back. "No worries. It's the real thing then, is it?"

"Yeah, can't imagine life without her. I love her."

"You two look like you are up to no good," Megan said from behind them, making them both turn quickly.

"Us? Up to no good? Seriously, Meg, what do you take us for?" Owen said. "Hmm, two powerful businessmen having a sneaky word?"

Aidan laughed, hugging her. "She knows us too well, Owen, I told you it's not safe anymore."

Nigel walked down the grand staircase that led to the main arena and smiled. "All is being taken care of as per the ladies' requests. I must say they have a flare for design. This place is going to look incredible this year."

"I have no doubt that it will, Nigel. If the ladies are happy then I am too," Aidan said.

"Let me show you the designs. This way." Nigel escorted them up the stairs to the venue's main arena, to show them the layout plans, and so Emma and Megan could finalise any changes that needed to be addressed. "There is an artist rehearsing for tomorrow night's concert, but I've let them know we won't be disturbing them."

"We really won't take up too much of your time Nigel," Owen said, holding the door open for Megan and Emma. "Flying visit."

Lucy had sent her fashion contacts in to draw up designs of the Christmas theme that they'd decided on. Emma told Nigel that all four of them would be there to oversee the organising on the day, but in the meantime, they were to keep Lucy's design team up to date about any issues that might arise.

Feeling brave and out of the public eye, Megan took Aidan's hand, squeezing tight.

He met her eyes with a loving smile, as they listened to how Nigel was going to deliver the women's vision.

Aidan and Owen were blown away by the progress that had been made in such a short space of time. There was no doubt about it—this year's Christmas party was going to be the best one yet. They walked around the open space that would soon be full of fans for the following night's concert, envisioning it filled with JMC staff instead. Each person laughing and wishing one another a Merry Christmas with a drink in hand.

Smiling to himself, Aidan knew full well his staff would once again have the night of their lives.

Thanking Nigel for allowing them last minute access, especially when they knew it was a busy time of year for him and his employees, they left the Roundhouse more than satisfied.

Outside, after their tour, the atmosphere was way more chilled. Megan seemed to have calmed, which Aidan was grateful for, but he still thought it would be best to have her head home. He pulled her aside as they neared the car. "Meg, I'm going back to the office, but I want you to stay at home. I'll drop you off, then head back once I know you are safe."

"I'm okay, Aidan. This morning just took me by surprise that's all."

"I don't want you to be under any more pressure than you need to be sweetheart. Owen said Clare's going to come over too. Em?"

"Yeah?"

"Take the day off and stay with Megan, please?"

Emma nodded to his request, Aidan whispered, "Paid, of course." Megan tried to argue, but Aidan shook his head. "I'm not hearing it. Not today."

***

Now that they'd managed to convince the girls to stay at home, Aidan and Owen were back in work mode, storming through the outdoor air. They rounded the final corner and froze solid when the JMC building came into view. There was a sea of paparazzi outside the building, each member armed with a camera and a voice recorder.

"Holy fuck," Aidan said. "Time to face the music, Owen."

They headed straight for the building's glass doors. Journalists lined the front path, making it hard for them to get near the entrance. They shoved their way through, jostling for position. When they reached the front of the crowd, Aidan turned to face them. Owen stood behind him. A camera man shone a light to catch Aidan's eyes. This, he'd learnt, was their way of drawing his attention to get a good picture for TV.

"It's morning? Does the light need to be on?" He looked at the guy like he was a fool, making the journalists laugh.

Chapter 27

M egan was flicking through TV channels, but stopped on a major news channel when she saw Aidan and Owen standing outside the front of JMC. She couldn't believe her eyes. The words wouldn't leave her mouth fast enough. "Emma? Quick!"

"What?" Emma ran into the living room.

Megan pointed at the TV screen. "They've got company."

Aidan answered every question the press asked him about his recent trip to New York, the company, and the secret woman he was photographed with at the airport. There was some laughter between him and the journalists, and Megan thought all was in the clear. That was, until someone asked him a question that clearly made his blood boil.

"Is it true, Mr. Costello, that this woman is a member of the JMC staff?"

"Shit, he looks pissed. Do you think that Kelly's talked?"

Emma eyed her friend. "Without a doubt."

"Who's your source?" Aidan demanded, keeping eye contact with the journalist.

"Damn, that's a stare. I wouldn't want to be Kelly right now," Emma said.

"I can't divulge that information," the journalist replied.

"I think you can," Aidan threatened, still keeping his eye.

"You know, I've heard that he does this to intimidate clients, but I've never actually witnessed it," Emma said again. "It's a little terrifying."

The cameras were now on the journalist; it was obvious that he was beginning to crack. Even through the television screen Emma and Megan could clearly see beads of sweat dripping down the journalist's forehead. His eyes darted side to side, hoping another of his peers would help him, but there was no such support. He'd dug his own grave and they knew it. They were going to let him stew. Rule number one when interviewing Aidan Costello: Don't fuck him off.

Aidan looked directly into one of the cameras, with a stare that could melt everyone around him. Megan and Emma could feel his anger through the television screen. It made them feel nervous.

"Let me just make one thing clear. And I'm talking to you here as well, pal." He gestured to the journalist who asked the last question. "The people working at JMC are loyal members of a hard working team. None of them have ever crossed the line like they did today. What I do in my personal life, in or out of this office, has absolutely no connection with the business that we run here. Is this clear? Or does anyone else have a question they want to ask that will piss me off?" Aidan looked around. No one dared to say another word. "No? Thought not. Interview's over." Aidan turned and walked through the glass door, disappearing from the camera's view.

"I'm getting a feeling Kelly won't be working at JMC after today, Meg," Emma said. She was stunned by Aidan's reaction. "I mean, wow ... that was one hell of a response."

"Hell of a response? Do you think we can still make it work after that?" Megan started panicking. "I mean, I hope we can, but surely that's got to leave some kind of dent on a relationship?"

"I have never witnessed Aidan to swear on TV the whole time I've worked for him. He was protecting the woman he loves. He was mightily fucked off, mind, but protecting you all the same."

Chapter 28

A idan flew through the amber traffic lights that were about to change red. Speeding ticket or not, nothing was going to stop him from getting home. Not after what Emma had told him on the phone. Megan was struggling to breathe. Emma mentioned that they witnessed the live interview and Megan knew straight away that Kelly had spoken to the papers about their relationship. It sent her spiralling into a panic attack.

Dodging the traffic, he pulled into the street that led directly to the underground parking for his apartment building. Parking up, not as neatly as he usually did, he ran up the stairs to call the lift, ignoring George's always friendly greeting. He tapped his thumb against the railings as he watched the lift climb each floor. The lift stopped, and he was out before the doors were fully open. Bursting through the front door, he looked around for her.

"Megan?"

Emma lifted her head, a clear look of concern in her eyes. "Aidan, thank God."

"What's happened?" He approached the sofa, finding Megan sprawled out on the cushions, unconscious. He dropped to his knees, gently holding her face.

Emma wasn't sure if she was about to see her boss break down in tears, or go off his rocket again. Instead she updated him on the situation. "She passed out a little while ago, Aid. This probably a good time to tell you she suffers from panic attacks." Emma stroked Megan's hair. "Didn't take your reaction to the media very well."

"I'm getting that." Aidan leant forward to kiss her head. He felt her move. "Megan?"

Emma sat up. "Meg? You awake?"

Megan slowly opened her eyes, blinking away the fuzziness from her attack.

"Sweetheart. You ok?" Aidan held her hand. "You had me worried for a minute there." Megan turned to find him looking down at her, a terrified look in his eyes.

"I'm ok." She faced Emma. "I'm ok."

Aidan helped her sit up, while Emma fetched her a glass of water.

"Kelly said something, didn't she?"

Aidan sat next to her, engulfing her in his arms. "Not for you to worry about, baby. You won't have to deal with Kelly ever again." He cupped her face in his hands. "Like I said, no one and nothing will ever stop us from being together." He kissed her like he was tasting her lips for the very first time. "Promise."

Chapter 29

It had been three days since the ordeal outside JMC and Megan's subsequent episode, but to Aidan, it felt more like three weeks. The time had dragged by. He'd had so many fires to put out at JMC, and a lot more commuting than he usually had to deal with. It was all worth it though. Megan was worth it.

She hadn't been back to the office building. They'd both agreed that it would be best if she stayed out of the office for a while. In making that decision, they also decided that she should stay in Farnham for a little while, away from it all. That's where the commuting part came in. Aidan had travelled back and forth every single day.

It pained him to keep her away from the office, but the realist in him knew it was the right thing to do. It may even be the right thing to do on a permanent basis. They needed to talk.

Pulling into his drive after another busy day, he parked in front of the house. Swinging the car door shut with his foot, he let out a yawn and stretched, before entering the house. He didn't want Megan worrying about what the early mornings and late finishes were doing to him.

Opening the door, he smiled when he saw her plating up dinner, and getting him a beer ready. The tiredness didn't matter anymore, he was happy to see her.

Pulling him close, she greeted him with the same kiss and hug he'd received over the past three days.

***

After dinner, they relaxed on the sofa in the lounge with their feet up on the coffee table, watching a classic comedy series. Megan was glued the screen; Aidan couldn't focus enough to tune in. He was trying to find the right moment to bring up what he knew was going to be a delicate conversation.

He took her hand, breaking her focus. "Baby."

"Hmm?"

"We need to talk about something."

Megan squeezed his hand. "Is this the talk I've been expecting?"

"I really don't like having to do this, and I know you loved your job–"

"Not as much as I love you." She dug her head into his neck.

"Are you about to make it easy for me to fire you?"

Megan moved so she faced him. "I can try and distract you while you do it. Would that help?" She ran a hand over his chest, feeling his heartbeat quicken. "But I'd say I already have you pretty distracted."

"Miss Ashton, this is the sort of behaviour that has led to your dismissal."

Megan's eyes widened in amusement. "On what grounds, Mr. Costello?"

"For looking sexy as hell in that gold dress and making the boss fall in love with you."

"And whose fault was that?"

"You could have said no."

"You would've let me say the word no?" She let out a mock gasp. "Don't believe it."

"Enough of this nonsense." Aidan ran a hand through her hair. "Do we have an understanding, Miss Ashton?"

"No, Mr. Costello. What other reasons do you have? I think you need to convince me further. I need to know for sure that this is the correct thing to d–"

Megan screamed as Aidan moved quicker than she expected, pinning her down, accepting the challenge. He kissed her, and between kisses, he continued to think of reasons.

"What else? Oh yes, you're a complete distraction. How's the boss meant to concentrate when you're around?"

Megan smiled at him when he lifted his head away from her neck. "He's a strong guy. I'm sure he would manage."

"The decision is final, Miss Ashton." He looked deep into her eyes. It was like he was trying to study what was going through her mind. "It'll all work out. Besides, it's not like you need to earn an income. You're with me, which means you're set for life."

"What use am I then? I don't want to sit around like a sponge. I want to serve some kind of purpose."

He nodded in agreement. "Okay, how about an unofficial promotion? You can assist me in the big decision making, if I hit a brick wall or something?"

"Hmm, seems fair."

"It's very fair." He smirked. "And before I forget—because you do in fact have me extremely distracted—I need to nip to the bank soon."

"Why?"

"To add you to the accounts. You're officially a millionaire now."

Megan looked at him in shock. "What?"

Aidan burst into laughter. "I love that surprised look you pull when something's shocked you, Meg." He lay a kiss on her lips. "It's the same look you gave me when you turned to look up at the balcony from the bar."

Her expression stayed hard. The nervousness in her voice didn't quite match. "Are you sure?"

"What do you mean, am I sure? Of course I'm sure. I love you."

"I guess so." Aidan always insisted that he paid for everything when they were out, or for anything they needed, but she hadn't thought that in such a short amount of time, he would be adding her to his accounts.

She remembered when Clare told her about Sophie— how Aidan told her she would never get anywhere near his fortune. *Was it the same when they were together? No access to his accounts?* It was obvious he was offering Megan something that he hadn't offered any girl in the past.

Was Clare right? Was this meant to be?

Chapter 30

Megan stood in the middle of the Roundhouse with Lucy and Clare on the day of the party, watching the stagehands raise a giant JMC sign above the stage. There was a near accident, where one side almost fell, making them all race forward while Megan raised her voice at Lucy's team. The same team she used for fashion show launches.

"Careful, that's the second time now! Do you want me to get the CEO on the phone so you can explain to him why his money's being wasted through stupidity?"

"Wow, Megan, your temper is short today," Clare said.

"Sorry Clare, it's just the second fucking time now." Raising her voice again to the stage hands, she yelled, "How can hooking something around scaffolding be so bloody hard? Swear to God, it makes building a festival stage look easy when you watch that."

"Large coffee? Tequila maybe?" Emma passed her a cup.

"Thank you!" Megan took a sip, feeling the liquid burn the back of the throat, but calming her nerves at the same time—anything to help steady the butterflies in the pit of her stomach. She dreaded having to face the entire company as Aidan's girlfriend, but tonight, the cat was out of the bag.

Lucy jumped down off the table. "Okay guys, take ten minutes. We'll test in a bit." She turned to Megan. "Meg, I know you've stopped, but . . ." Lucy offered her one of her cigarettes.

Megan grabbed it without hesitation. "Sorry, just a little tense about being back in London. Feels like only yesterday Aidan had a go at the media, not a month ago!"

"You'll be fine." Clare pointed towards to the door. "Go and get some fresh air."

Lucy and Megan pulled their coats on. Megan threw her scarf around her shoulders as Lucy held the arena door open for her. Climbing down the stairs simultaneously, they went outside for a cigarette before Aidan and Owen turned up.

Megan stared down at her cigarette. Lighting it, and taking a drag, she sighed. "One off, Lucy, just one."

"It's like being back at college, sneaking out before lessons."

They both laughed, remembering their teenage days. Megan just wished she could relax. Before another thought could enter her mind, Owen pulled his Lexus up to the front of the building and all four guys got out.

"Ah, that probably means trouble," Lucy said.

Aidan walked up behind her and grabbed her waist. "Are you still stressing about tonight?"

"Shit!" she shouted in shock. "Aid, don't do that, you know I'm jumpy as it is."

He took her cigarette and had a drag himself. "Bad habit, you know." He laughed.

"It's a one off." She snatched it back. "Anyway, didn't know you used to smoke."

"Can't expect me to build an entire company and not have a smoking habit. Bad habit to break, isn't it?" He snatched it back and stubbed it out on the wall. "Come on, let's head inside."

***

They were all gathered around the middle dining table, eagerly awaiting the demonstration Lucy had promised them. Lucy clicked on her head set, demanding that her team return to their stations as they entered the main arena.

The room was dark, so none of them could actually see how it had been decorated.

"Okay boys, don't fail me now. The heads of JMC are here." She paused, almost for effect. "Light it up."

The stage lights slowly came up, revealing the decorated room. Giant white Christmas trees circled the room and silk drapes hung from the edges of the arena, covered in what looked like a million fairy lights.

"Very nice, boys, looking good from down here. Now, a little fun maybe? Let's have a track with nice big bassline, shall we?" Lucy climbed back onto a table to get a good view of the room. "Mark? Fill the floor."

Aidan leaned down to Megan. "Fill the floor?"

"Just wait, you'll like this." Megan held his hand as the floor filled up with dry ice.

The PA came to life, playing a heavy dance track. The lighting flashed in tune with the beat. Lucy was barking out commands down her headset to her team, whilst looking around the venue to make sure all was to her standard.

Aidan was speechless. *How had all this been possible in such a short amount of time?* The lights turned, flashed, and the floor glowed, giving the room a winter wonderland feeling.

Lucy returned to stand with them all, speaking to her lighting engineer. "Yes, please." She turned to everyone. "Eyes forward, boys and girls."

The song slowed and picked up pace again as the giant JMC sign flashed, looking like it had been covered in diamonds. It was great, but what had them all in awe were the two male silhouettes, walking up to either side of the sign as if they were leaning against it. One had his elbow on the C, and anyone could tell that it was meant to be Aidan.

Tom shook his head slowly. "Good call, guys. Like these two need their egos pumped anymore."

Lucy, looking proud of her team's work, called them all to the venue's floor when the testing was over. She wanted to have a brief chat before the events began.

Everyone else walked around the room, admiring the obvious hard work.

"They certainly have made this look incredible. I wonder what it costs to hire Lucy and her team," Nigel said, more to himself than anything else.

The group stopped beside him at the main doors and turned to look back at the venue.

"Not sure you'd be able to afford them, Nigel," Aidan joked, shaking his hand. "Right, I think it's time we let the guys finish off here and get some lunch in the docks before the ladies hit the salons. It's on me." He nodded to himself. "Nigel, we'll see you later tonight."

Chapter 31

M egan looked herself up and down, and for once, when she looked in the mirror, she beamed with confidence. She was wearing a full-length, black strapless gown with a gold bodice; her wavy brown hair was beautifully pulled back into a style that showed off the elegance of her neck. She felt beautiful.

Aidan joined her and admired the view before him. He looked her up and down too, taking in the curves he knew so well. "I get to escort the most beautiful woman to one of the city's biggest events of the year? Damn, how did I manage to get this lucky?"

Megan turned around to face him.

"Your dress needs something." He reached behind the doorway. "I heard from a friend a while back that someone has a weak spot for shoes."

She nodded a little too eagerly. "That friend would be correct."

He produced a pair of gold-sparkled Louboutin heels.

Megan's eyes lit up. "Aidan! This is all too much. First this dress, now some shoes?" She shook her head in disbelief. "I love you so much."

He laughed, placing the shoes on each of her feet, running a hand up her leg as he did. "You can thank me tonight."

Megan closed her eyes and bit her lower lip, relishing the feel of his touch on her bare skin. Her mind went into overdrive imagining what she could do to him. His hand kept climbing, making her catch her breath. Stopping his hand, she met his gaze with a burning desire. "How about we forget the party and I'll thank you right now?"

He pulled back and looked up at her. "A fine suggestion, but one that wouldn't go down well. We can't have the boss skiving his own event."

Megan leant down and kissed his head. "I suppose that is true."

Aidan didn't get up. Instead, he stayed on his knees and looked deep into her eyes. "Megan, from the moment I saw you, the world around you seemed to disappear. It was like everything was out of focus apart from you. It's not been long, I know, but this life we're building together so far, it's just ... it's missing something else."

Megan looked like she had twigged as to what was happening, but Aidan raised his hand at her. "Let me finish," he said.

She put her hand over her mouth. "Yes. Sorry."

"Every time I look at you, I see a future that makes me think about growing old together, making a lifetime of memories and having to let you win the occasional argument every now and then. Megan, it makes me fall in love with you all over again."

A tear fell down Megan's cheek.

Aidan reached into his pocket, pulled something out, encircled Megan's hand, and smiled.

Chapter 32

The Roundhouse glowed. White and gold drapes hung from the centre of the ceiling, stretching out towards the edges, making them feel like they were in a marquee. The Christmas trees that stood in the arches were beautifully decorated with gold and silver decorations. The large JMC sign, that Megan was losing her patience over earlier in the day, hung high above the stage with the silhouettes of the boys at either side. Spotlights slowly moved around the venue.

The dry ice on the floor changed colour, going from ice blue to gold and silver. It looked like the room was set for a wedding reception, with all the employees of JMC sitting around tables, drinking the wine and beer that had been provided for them. Each table was set out for a three course dinner, with large vases filled with lights and decorations as centre pieces, giving each table enough light for people to see one another. The room was a buzz of talking and laughter; each person seemed to be having the night of their lives. The best part was that the evening had only just begun.

Clare held Megan's hand as they walked through to reach the centre table. She noticed she was nervous again. Most likely due to the fact that Aidan wasn't with her at the moment, and now she had to face the entire company for the first time since she'd left.

Aidan was backstage, getting ready to come out so they could get the ball rolling. Clare knew that she had to help Megan right now. She was clearly a bag of nerves.

People turned to see who the lucky ones were this year—the group that got to share the main table with Aidan and Owen. Megan glanced to her right before sitting in the chair, next to the one marked CEO. She caught Brendan waving at her. She nervously waved back.

Brendan waved at Megan and then nudged Carol's arm. "So, you still think Meg's been off sick these past few weeks? Look at her, Carol, she doesn't look sick at all."

Megan's work colleagues couldn't figure out why their new friend hadn't been in the office. They had come up with many different scenarios as to why she had suddenly vanished. Carol sat up high to get a good look at her.

"I'm sorry," Jimmy said, "but I'm not buying the 'she's been ill' nonsense either. Come on, put it together. She was fine. Then, after that day Aidan swore at the media, we don't see anything of her? And, may I add, she's seated at the main table, right next to the boss man."

"She's best friends with Emma, Jim," Karen said. "Emma is now apparently good mates with Aidan and Owen. That'll be because of her thing with Tom; she may have become friends too. There's no way . . ."

"No way, what, Karen? That she's with Aidan? She's holding Owen's wife's hand, for goodness sake!" Jimmy laughed. "Join the dots."

Carol was still trying to get a better look. "That dress she's got on is designer." She took a sip of her wine. "But I'm not believing anything until I see it."

***

Music engulfed the room, overwhelming Megan more than any festival she had ever been to. She span around, taking in the scene before her. Each table was filled with JMC employees, soaking up the atmosphere. Drinks flowed, laughter echoed, and phones flashed, capturing the memory of what was going to be another amazing night.

Tom tapped Megan's arm, offering to pour her a glass of wine from their private selection of alcohol, including three special bottles that no other table was lucky enough to get. It was a secret they were sure to keep between the eight of them. No one was going to find out they were hiding a few four–and-a-half-thousand pound bottles of champagne.

Emma took a long sip of rosé wine. "If you had told me last year that this year I would be sitting on the main table, I wouldn't have believed it."

"Em, Owen may have been working with Aidan for over fifteen years, but even he has to pinch himself to believe that this is all real sometimes. Don't tell Aid that though, he'll never let him forget it." Clare laughed.

"Looks like the world knows now." Megan passed her phone around to show them the message. "There's certainly no need to hide anymore. I think this will stay on silent for the rest of the night." Megan turned the volume down on her mobile and placed it back in her bag.

"Wise idea, Meg," Clare said, still holding her hand.

Tom leaned across Emma, addressing Kev. "How's it feel being the other side of the drinks, mate?"

"Bloody nice. My days behind the bar are long gone."

The music was playing at such a volume that they had to shout at each other, and that went on until the DJ announced that Aidan and Owen had finally arrived. The employees of JMC cheered and shouted in excitement at their arrival.

Suddenly, Aidan's voice came out over the PA—he was winding them up to an even more excitable level from back-stage. It was clearly working. People began to stand and chant. If there was a better company to work for, none of them had ever heard of it.

"Smile," Lucy shouted, taking a photo of Megan, who was looking around and feeling a bit nervous still.

"A warning would have been nice." Megan laughed.

"Kev, get one of us from your side?" Lucy asked the girls to stand so Kev could take a group shot of the four of them. Tom did the same on Emma's phone.

"Send me a copy of that?" Clare asked.

The lights went down and the giant JMC LED sign began to put on a light show.

Silhouettes moved around the screen.

"Theatrical, I like it. Nice one, Lucy," Tom complimented, as they took their seats once more.

They both walked out onto the stage, but it was Owen that spoke over the PA. "JMC? Are you out there?"

They all cheered.

"I don't know, Aid, they're not half as loud as last year. I just don't think it's acceptable. Do you think we should have annual reviews about behaviour at the Christmas party?"

Megan could make out that they were having some kind of private joke on stage, with Aidan leaning on Owen in fits of laughter. "Clare? They always wind the employees up like this?"

"Oh yeah! They love seeing the boys mucking about. Reminds them that even though they're the bosses, they're still normal."

Aidan spoke next, trying to control his laughter. "I agree, extremely disappointing. I think Owen makes a good point. Surely you can give Nigel something to worry about this year, guys, come on!"

With the command for his entire company to go crazy, the lights came up and his wish was granted. Everyone cheered, banged tables and clapped as loud as they possibly could.

"Yeah, better, although some of the noises from that table to my right are a bit questionable." He laughed. "How many of you are drunk already?"

Aidan was walking up and down the stage, looking out over the crowd, listening as they responded to his questions. Every now and then he caught Megan's eye, and couldn't resist sending her that smile, the one that had caught her unaware the first time they saw each other. "Excellent. Right, before we begin, we all need to thank and give a massive round of applause to the ladies at our table for turning this place into what I can only describe as a wonderland. Thank you so much."

The whole room filled with cheers and appreciation at the fabulous job they had done with the decorating.

"Loving this screen. Owen, stand on that side."

They both posed the same way the silhouettes were standing. Everyone took photos of them as they laughed, turning around to make sure they were copying the stands correctly.

"Amazing! When we came here earlier to make sure everything was going as planned, I'm not going to lie, Owen seemed nervous that it wasn't going to be ready. I think Clare must have slipped you something because you seem calm as anything now, buddy."

Owen gave him a look, and shook his head at the fact that Aidan had managed to get one over on him in front of his entire staff, making the pair of them laugh. "Bastard!"

"Okay, seriously now, Owen, behave yourself."

Owen turned on the spot, shaking his head again.

"We both need to thank every single one of you for the dedication and commitment you've shown in this company, for it has led to yet another successful year. Really well done. We wouldn't be where we are today without strong, hard-working people such as yourselves. This year turned out to be one of the best we've seen for a while, with profits rising to the highest I've seen them. However—and I know a lot of you are probably wondering about the outcome—the New York deal has taken a stand due to the fact that they took too long; and well, me being me, I pulled it. Told them to come back when they want us to help them out of the hole they've dug themselves into."

Laughter filled the room. They knew their boss well and also knew that if Aidan had told them where they could shove their deal, then they must have royally annoyed him.

Whilst the company cheered their boss on, Aidan glanced back at Owen for a boost of confidence in preparation for what he was going to deliver next. Owen dipped his eyes to the floor then met his gaze again.

It was all Aidan needed. He had his friend's full support.

"Next! And you know what, you can react to this whatever way you wish because we are done hiding it, but please don't go to the press—it didn't work out well for the last person who did. But I think you all deserve to know the truth, especially after the amount of support I've felt recently." He looked at Megan and then back to Owen, who nodded for him to continue.

"The past few months have been a test of commitment and dedication elsewhere in my life. Some of you, if not all of you, would've seen the papers a few weeks back, and the live broadcast where I lost it with the media for the first time."

"Here we go," Jimmy tapped the table, getting his friends' attention.

"I just want to take this opportunity to apologise to everyone for the way I reacted. By the way, magazine photographers, this is not an official story that you can print. You see this table of lawyers," he pointed to a table, "I'll have them come down on you like a ton of bricks if I see anything in your magazines. Okay? Cameras down please."

Everyone was quietly listening to their boss opening up.

"I only lost my temper because the woman I love became a target for a story, and I wasn't down with that. The truth is," Aidan took a moment, "Megan did work at JMC."

There was a gasp from nearly everyone in the room.

"Please focus on *did*. Obviously, she is not with us now."

Megan glanced at Karen and Carol again, who were now looking right back at her with shocked expressions. She dropped her head, releasing the breath she didn't realise she'd been holding. She counted to ten then lifted her head, forcing a confident smile to flash back to her old colleagues.

Tom leaned over to her. "That's it. All done. It's out there. You guys never have to hide again, chicken." He rubbed her arm.

She nodded, smiling back at him.

"Yes, we *were* hiding our relationship, and I think you all deserve to know why." Aidan began to tell the story of how they met, and why the decision was made to keep their relationship secret—because of the amount they cared for one another. He looked at her while he described the first time he saw her at the bar, smiling at the memory of how stunning she looked in her gold dress. "Now you know, and I want to thank you again for all the kind words and support you gave us when you didn't even know the truth. Meg has actually been feeling really nervous about this evening, so to have your support makes me feel blessed to have such wonderful people working with me."

Megan was fighting back the tears listening to his kind words.

Clare passed her a napkin, sensing that her emotions were close to exploding.

Megan took it with a smile, dabbing her eyes as they tears began to fall despite putting up a fight. As they fell, she could feel the months of pressure lifting from her shoulders. Aidan was right, there was no going back now. People knew about them and she felt like running up to the stage and throwing her arms around him as added proof that he was hers.

Everyone laughed as Aidan winked at Megan.

"A lot of you will have met Megan already and a few of you, where are you?" Aidan found Brendan's table in the crowd. "There you are, have been out for drinks with us. Sorry for that night, guys, we had to throw you off course. Brendan, I'm watching you, pal!" Aidan spotted him laughing and joined in. "Meg? Stand up a moment." She shook her head, but he simply waited as Clare pulled her up from her seat, "Megan, officially meet my entire staff. JMC, I want you all to meet the soon-to-be Mrs. Megan Costello. And yes, you heard that right." He pointed to Megan, who held up her left hand. The hefty ring sparkled in the disco lights.

The crowd erupted in applause at Aidan's announcement of their engagement.

He handed Owen the microphone and jumped down off the stage and walked towards Megan, pulling her into a kiss in front of everyone for the first time, right in the middle of the room.

"Hear that? Didn't I say you had nothing to worry about? That's the sound of approval, sweetheart."

"Aidan, I love you so much, but I can't believe you just did that in front of everyone."

Owen carried on the speech, after Aidan waved at him. "Congratulations again, you two." Owen clapped. He remained silent for a moment, smiling wryly as the room settled. "Hopefully now we'll have someone to keep the CEO in order."

***

The night was far from slowing down. The live band Lucy managed to book at the last minute played songs from all decades to meet everyone's tastes. Lucy and Emma dragged Megan onto the dance floor, and were enjoying the band's selection of tunes.

Emma twirled Megan around. "Did you have a part in this Meg?"

"A part in what?"

"Emma and Kev's promotions," Lucy said.

"What promotions?"

"Your fiancé promoted me again, and created an entire new department for me and Kev to run!" She held her hands up, like she was reading a banner. "Kevin Hunter and Emma Rowe: Joint heads of JMC's International Affairs."

"Both with attractive salaries to match," Lucy added, hugging the life out of Emma in congratulations.

"Means Kev and I can actually look for places to buy in the New Year."

Megan was speechless. "I literally had no idea." She opened her arms to them. "Oh, but it's amazing. I can't tell you how excited I am for you both. Everything that's happened these past few months? It's like a guardian angel has been looking out for all of us." She hugged them tighter. "I love you guys"

Emma wiped her eyes. "Don't, don't you dare make my artistic masterpiece run. You know how long this eyeliner took?"

Lucy smacked her arm. "Would have taken a hell of a lot longer if I hadn't helped you."

They continued dancing into the evening, catching up with Karen and Carol who expressed their congratulations to Megan when they finally managed to get near her. Everyone wanted to talk to the boss's new fiancée.

"We've been asked for a request." The lead singer looked around for Aidan. "Mr. Costello? Where are you?"

He waved towards the stage from the bar, where he stood with Owen, Clare, Tom, Kev, and a few other people.

The lead nodded. "A few of your staff members have decided that the newly engaged couple needs to dance. What do you say?"

Never one to back down from a challenge, he nodded and went off to find his fiancée in the middle of the dance floor. The band began playing a slow song.

Aidan took Megan's hand and twirled her around to face him. His staff cheered in approval, watching their boss dance with his fiancée.

Megan put her arms around his neck as he leant his head on her shoulder, taking a private moment to enjoy her company. Sighing like it was the first time they had held one another, he wrapped his arms around her. "Was this your idea? Or do we have Em and Lucy to thank?"

"I would love to say yes, but no, I have no idea whose idea it was. And it couldn't have been the girls—they've been with me the whole time. I have a feeling it was either Karen or Carol."

"Sneaky." He laughed. "You know," Aidan lifted his head, "this is the first time we've danced together. We never got the chance to when we met." He paused for a moment. "Well, unless you count the fact that I was watching you dance most of the night?"

"Absolutely not." She hit his arm, making Aidan and the people around them laugh. "There is no way you're using that as an excuse."

"You can't hit the boss, you'll give this lot ideas." He looked out to everyone and pointed. "You all saw that, right? Where are my lawyers?"

"Shut up!" She kissed him.

He pushed his arms out—a sign that he'd been defeated—before bringing them back around to hold her tighter. His staff laughed at the banter between them.

"Hmm, good to know," she said.

"What's good to know?"

"That the technique you use to shut me up works both ways."

"You've learnt my trick?"

Megan looked around to see Lucy filming them. She clung onto Aidan and hid her face in his neck, continuing to dance. People began to join them. When the song came to an end, the singer congratulated them again, before beginning the next upbeat modern tune.

"I need some air. Can we nip outside for a minute?"

"Got you all hot and bothered, have I?"

Megan turned and looked at him. "Is that the sort of line I'm gonna have to learn to live with for the rest of my life?"

"Yep." He grinned.

"Then I guess you're lucky I love you enough to put up with them."

"I'll grab us some more drinks." He kissed her head. "Meet you outside."

"Okay."

They both shot of in different directions. A few minutes later, Aidan joined Megan outside, on the rooftop patio. It was quieter out here—a testimony to the building's effective sound-proofing—and the lights of Camden below greeted them, giving the area a warm and welcoming atmosphere. They stood side by side, surveying the area. They'd both been trying to find a suitable quiet spot to have a moment's peace, but from what they saw out here, they weren't getting any alone time quite yet. The patio was filled with the younger members of staff, drinks in one hand, smart phones in the other.

"Are they surgically attached to their phones?" he whispered, passing Megan her drink.

"They grew up with technology as a social tool, what do you expect?"

They lingered for a short while, eyeing the room, looking for somewhere to sit.

"Mr. Costello, Sir? Spare seats?" a young lad with blond hair called from a large wooden table, where he sat with friends.

Aidan heard him and nodded back, pointing out the spot to Megan. "Thanks. Nice spot you've found here."

"You're welcome, Sir."

"No, none of that. We're not at work now." Aidan took a drink.

Megan sat down, nodding in Aidan's direction. "Doesn't like Sir—and stuff like that—outside the office." She smiled. "Hi, I'm Megan. You are?"

"Patrick O'Neill, nice to officially meet you." Patrick's friends all introduced themselves to their boss and his fiancée.

"So, tell me, Patrick, which department are you in? I can't keep track of everyone all the time." Aidan took out a pack of cigarettes.

Megan looked at him in amazement.

"What? Didn't know if you were going to freak out again." She laughed. Aidan offered one to her. She took it.

"Reception, worked for you for about seven months."

"So that's where I recognise you from." Megan nodded

"Well, that's embarrassing. I obviously don't pay much attention in reception."

Everyone laughed, nervously at first, since they'd never witnessed their boss in non-CEO mode before. "And where do you want to be? And by when?"

"Aidan, you're doing that intimidating boss stare. People are looking nervous."

He looked at Megan, then to everyone else—who did indeed looked like their palms were sweating. "Do I really do that? Shit, sorry. Takes a while to switch off sometimes. But seriously, Pat, what did you study at Uni to get here?"

"Business and Law," Patrick said, taking the cigarette Aidan offered him.

"What the fuck are you doing on reception then?"

"Just getting in the door, Sir." Aidan looked at him. "Sorry... Aidan. I want to work my way up eventually."

"Good lad, keep at it. You could be where I am one day. Not that I'm retiring anytime soon. I could do, but it's too much fun." Aidan pointed at him. "Law, eh? Explains the confidence."

"Confidence?" he asked.

"No offence to you guys," Aidan gestured to the table, "but some younger staff members still see me as this scary figure who could fire them at any moment. But you, Pat, yeah, there's something in you. Come and see me in the New Year, we'll work on getting you into legal."

"Really? Thank you."

Aidan's phone began to ring. He looked down at it in surprise and started laughing. "Well, this should be entertaining." He rubbed his eyes, going back into CEO mode.

"Who is it?" Megan asked.

"Norfolk. Why are they phoning on a Saturday? Excuse me." He began to stand up to take the call, but stopped. "Actually, who wants to see what we do on the top floor?"

Sounds of approval at wanting to hear what Aidan did on a daily basis went off all around them. He hushed everyone. They were fascinated by what they were about to witness. He pressed speaker phone so they could hear what their boss does best. Normally, if he received a work call out of hours, he'd let it go to voicemail. But it was the work party and, after a few drinks, Aidan's confidence was on a high. "Yeah, Costello." He answered, in a non-welcoming way, while gesturing for someone to fetch Owen.

"Ah, Mr. Costello, I'm glad I caught you. Apologies for calling on the weekend, we are just about to close up the office for the holidays."

Aidan took another cigarette out the packet. "So Clive, to what do I owe this unexpected pleasure?"

"The deal."

Aidan rolled his head, running a hand through his hair. "My clients would like to negotiate the terms of–"

Aidan cut Clive off before he had a chance to say another word, bringing his hand down onto the table, making everyone around him jump. "Did I, or did I not, give you a week when I left New York? Did I say that after that time, the current deal would be pulled? You took too long and I already warned you—JMC can cope perfectly fine without this whole thing going ahead." He waited for a second, letting it sink in. "I'm guessing the reason behind this late call is that you've discovered that your company may need our help after all?"

Owen turned up and asked Megan what was going on.

"The Americans have just called." She updated him as to what Aidan had just said.

Owen sat down in a chair next to him, tapping his shoulder so he was aware he had joined them. "On a weekend? This should be good. Keep it quiet, guys, you're about to see the boss at work. Soon you're going to realise why JMC is at the top of the game."

"Aidan," Clive said. "May I call you Aidan?"

"No." He lit the cigarette, his reaction both shocking but impressing his staff. Not many of them had seen him negotiate deals before. Aidan leant back in his chair.

"Forgive me, Mr. Costello. Our company does in fact require JMC's help."

Aidan gave a sarcastic grin.

"The second half of this year proved that our sales went down further than our estimated forecast, and it's not looking positive for the year ahead."

"Which we could have told you months ago," Owen whispered to himself.

Aidan leant forward, closer to the phone, his voice suddenly sounding very intimate. "So what you're saying, Clive, is that you need our help, just as I said, to get you out of a financial crisis." It wasn't a question, more a statement of fact.

"Yes."

Aidan leant back again, relaxing, trying not to laugh. "I wish I could help you, but, our offices are now officially closed. Did you even think about the time differences when you decided to call, on a Saturday, in what I'm guessing is the last half hour of your financial year? There's nothing I can do to help you now." He punched Owen's arm to shut him up; Owen knew exactly what Aidan was going to do.

The staff members were fascinated. They had no idea where any of this was going, but they carried on listening to Aidan wipe the floor with the American.

"I tell you what, Clive, because it's Christmas and all, scrap the last deal. The thirty/seventy split from sales and marketing doesn't interest me anymore, and I can't rely that your end will keep up to the standard of my staff after this mess up."

He took a puff of his cigarette. "Now, because we're not in the office, and I seriously can't do anything, why don't you get the company heads to call my legal team in the New Year?" He threw a beer mat at Patrick to get him to pay attention. "I think you should be eager to make a start; to begin setting up a new contract that not only saves your arse, but puts JMC in line to open offices in New York where we can watch your progress. It makes sense. We would pretty much own you."

Everyone took a gasp at what Aidan had just put on the table. Then silence fell, as they waited for Clive's response. He was talking with the company heads.

"Don't make me wait any longer, Clive, I've already given you more time than was deserved."

There was a period of silence as he ran the company heads through the newly proposed terms. Megan held Aidan's hand tightly. Everyone was feeling the nerves and tension. Eyes were darting back and forth, and the young members whispered to one another about whether or not Aidan had just made a massive mistake in trusting Norfolk again.

Clive came back onto the phone. "I've discussed the new deal with my clients, Mr. Costello, and–" everyone stopped breathing; everyone except Aidan, "–they agree with the new terms. We will be in contact when your offices open next year."

Aidan and the people around him leapt up in celebration at the news that he'd not only managed to secure the deal, but changed it so JMC would soon be a high-level player in America.

Aidan stayed composed as he signed off. "Very wise. Let's not make this mistake again, shall we? Now, if you don't mind, I have a Christmas party to continue celebrating. Have a wonderful Christmas and New Year. Goodnight." He hung up and hugged Owen, who was laughing hysterically at what he'd just managed to pull off.

"And that's why you're the fucking best, Aidan. Shit, I can't believe you did that!"

Aidan pulled Megan over to him and hugged her as they all celebrated the last big deal of the year.

***

After many drinks, many photos with the boss, and a surprise dance off which had people pulling out some interesting moves, Aidan and Owen sat on the front of the stage, taking a moment to ingest in the scene before them.

"Hell of a night."

"The best yet I'd say, especially after you pulled that last minute deal out the bag," Owen said.

"Yeah, I should negotiate more often with an audience." Aidan nodded. "You're not half as drunk as I hoped you'd be."

"That's because the wife is here, and I highly doubt you'd want to be caught red-handed."

Aidan laughed, nodding in agreement. "Talking of wives, you'll be up there with me when I marry Meg, right?"

"If you're asking me to be your best man, I have two responses for you. First off, what a stupid fucking question. And second, of course, I'd be honoured. I've been storing up memories for my revenge."

"Legend! Can always count on you." He hugged his pal who was more like a brother, and took out a couple of cigars. "End of year celebration?"

Owen looked at him like he was dumb. "Is that not what the party is classed as?"

Aidan smiled, patting his back. "A real celebration. Just two buddies, their two cigars, and an empty room."

"I'll get the drinks."

Chapter 33

The buzzing of the phone vibrating on the bedside table woke Megan, making her stir in the sheets and put her hands over her ears. The thought of answering it was not inviting. She could feel the effects of a mighty hangover even before she moved. Ignoring the phone, she turned over to face her fiancé. She could tell he was still in a deep sleep from the sound of his heavy breathing. She moved across to him and put her arm over his chest. She groaned when her phone rang again.

Whoever you are, ringing me at this bloody hour, it better be important. If Aidan wakes up, I'm going to be more than annoyed.

She turned her head to look at the phone. Squinting, she saw Ben's name on the screen. It continued to vibrate.

She quietly answered it. "Ben? It's early. Can I call you back a bit later?"

"It's ten in the morning."

"Shush, it's early for me after last night."

"Yes, last night. What was I going to ask you about last night? Oh yes, I remember. When, may I ask dear, were you going to tell me that you're dating Aidan Costello?"

"Hang on a minute." She got out of bed and put her pyjamas on. She wasn't about to speak to Ben with nothing on. And she certainly didn't want to wake Aidan. She closed the bedroom door behind her, heading downstairs. "Okay, so you've seen the pictures then?"

"Uh huh! So Megan's been seeing the millionaire CEO of one of one of the top companies in the UK, and somehow found it acceptable to not fill me in on the details? And how did I find out? Martin came into the kitchen this morning, showing me photos of you and Aidan on Google! Tell me, you are safe, right?"

Megan topped up the coffee machine, then opened the patio doors and stepped outside, grabbing a seat on one of the loungers. "Yes, yes, of course I'm safe. I'm sorry, Ben. I wanted to tell you when I came back from London, but we couldn't say anything to anyone at the time."

She sat on one of the loungers. "Only a few people knew."

"Emma and Lucy."

"Emma only found out a few weeks after we got together. And then she told Lucy, but that's beside the point. Only eight people knew up until last night."

"And then you got engaged? Honey, congratulations! I would've kept it secret too you know."

"Really? Really, Ben? I've seen you try to keep secrets, and it doesn't usually end well."

"Hey, I'm better at keeping secrets than you think." He paused. "So, when do we get to meet him?"

"When you two get your arses up to London."

"Or when you eventually get yours back down here?"

Megan was laughing when a large coffee cup appeared in front of her. She looked up to see Aidan standing there in his jogging trousers, wearing his glasses, drinking coffee and handing her a blanket.

"Thank you," she whispered.

He sat down on the lounger with her. Megan pulled him back so he was resting against her and stroked her hand across his chest.

"Is he there? I heard you whispering."

"Yeah. Anyway, how's Martin?" Megan's speech went up an octave as Aidan ran a cold hand up her ankle, making him laugh. "Has he finally moved in?"

"Don't change the subject! Martin's fine, but I'm not calling you about Martin. I want to know everything. What's he like? Is he being good to you? Do I need to worry at all?"

"You don't need to worry, Ben. Everything is fine, really." Megan shook her head to calm the worried look on Aidan's face.

"You've not told him about the past, have you? Do you think you should?"

"Maybe."

"Well, you know what I think. It's a sensible suggestion now that you're a known woman. You two are all over the news and the internet. Jay hasn't been seen for a while, but his sort can pop up anywhere to take advantage of someone else's good fortune." Ben stopped, taking a moment to consider his next words. "What about your parents? Have you at least told Aidan about them?"

"What's there to tell, Ben? I've actually forgotten the last time–"

"Megan!" Ben sighed. "Just let me keep my eye open down here, just in case. And you think about telling him. Will you, for me? So I don't have to worry about you?"

"Okay, I'll think about it. Quit nagging me."

"Good girl, thanks." There was pause on the line, too long to be a sign of anything good. "So tell me, what's he like in bed?"

"Ben!" Megan burst out laughing.

"Actually, don't tell me. He's such a handsome fella that I'll end up having a fantastical affair with him."

"You can't have a fantasy about your friend's fiancé. That is so wrong."

Aidan choked on his coffee.

"Oh God, I've killed him. That's your fault, Benjamin." Megan laughed. "Aidan, honey, you okay? Ben's just ... being friendly."

Aidan coughed, trying to say something, then laughed at that fact that her gay friend was thinking inappropriate things about him.

"Listen, Ben. I'm gonna go, but I'll call you later."

"Okay, give him a kiss for me. Oh, and I hope to see some wedding dress ideas soon. Pinterest?"

"Forget Pinterest. You're coming shopping with me. Who else would I have with me? Bye sweetheart." She hung up the phone. "I'm so sorry, Ben's a bit forward sometimes." She massaged Aidan's back.

He relaxed and sighed under her touch. "I take it the photos have been released?"

Megan nodded. "All over Google apparently."

"You may want to turn the phone off today, then. Might become popular with old friends wanting to take advantage. Funny how they all come out of the woodwork once they know you're successful."

"Ooh, quite full of yourself this morning?"

Aidan turned quickly and pinned her down. Leaning over her, he smiled and looked down at his fiancée. "Yes."

"And I'm successful because I'm marrying you? Because you're such a catch?" she teased sarcastically.

Adjusting his glasses, he thought to himself before responding. "Great. I now have a best friend *and* a fiancée giving me backchat. Think I've made a mistake somewhere."

Megan looked at him. *If I wasn't feeling so hungover from your party last night, I'd be able to think of a decent comeback by now.* The party went to a whole new level after it was announced that Aidan had received a phone call from the Americans; that the deal with the Norfolk was back on. He'd ordered everyone champagne on him to celebrate. No one had objected. There would be many hangovers today.

"Oh no, Miss Ashton is speechless?"

"I'm not speechless, I just, can't think of a decent enough comment to reduce that ego of yours."

Aidan's eyes lit up in amusement. Leaning down, he kissed her in the cool winter air. They should have been freezing, being right next to the Thames, but neither of them cared. Aidan lay back down so he was leaning against her again. She threw the blanket over them to keep warm and rested her cheek on the top of his head.

They lay out on the balcony for another hour, watching London go about its day. The sound of the people below rose up, mixing with the noise of traffic and seagulls. In the distance, they could make out the sound of a Christmas choir, singing festive songs.

Eventually, Aidan sat up. "We should go out, take a walk around Southwark's Christmas market, get some lunch, and have a day exploring. We haven't been able to before. I think that would be nice."

Megan smiled. A day out without having to worry about people seeing them together sounded perfect. "I'd love that."

***

"Aidan, look at these." Megan stopped at a stand selling handmade glass decorations, leaving him wondering where she was, when he found himself walking alone.

"You're one of those shoppers who randomly disappears, aren't you?" he said.

People had to conduct the old-fashioned double take to spot him. It wasn't as easy to spot the famous CEO in a crowd when he wasn't smartly dressed in his suits—but a few people had and asked for a photo.

They walked away from the stall after deciding the products weren't worth the asking price. About five steps later, Megan regretted her choice of footwear for the sixth time since they'd left the apartment. She had chosen to wear her favourite heeled boots, but she kept slipping. Aidan laughed every time she almost went over, and had to catch her more than once.

Aidan caught Megan's waist. "Why do I have this feeling that we'll need to go and find flatter shoes soon?"

"It's okay, I can manage. It's just that the floor is slightly slippery."

"Bollocks! Come on." He stood her upright. Everyone turned to look at where the scream of laughter had come from.

"Where are we going? The apartment's back there."

"Shopping. But more to the point, to get some decent shoes for you."

"Then shouldn't you be carrying me back to the car? People are watching."

"Embarrassed much?" He laughed. "We won't bother with the car. The roads will be full of crazy late-Christmas shoppers. The underground's easier."

"Whoa! Aidan Costello uses the London Underground? Never thought I'd see the day. Does he still know his way around?"

"You can walk for that. I still know my way around, thank you. The question is, can you keep up with a Londoner?" He challenged her, walking away.

"You underestimate my skills when it comes to walking at speed in heels, Costello!" She called back, chasing his quickened pace. People heard her call out his surname and tried to stop him for a photo again, successfully slowing him down.

Megan turned as she passed him. "Hard life being known, isn't it?"

***

After a successful shop, Megan had semi-sensible new shoes and Aidan treated himself to a new dark grey Dolce and Gabbana suit on Bond Street. The tailors always kept his measurements on file, and informed him of the date the new suit would be ready for collection, though they usually hand delivered his suits direct to JMC. Keeping a good relationship with customers was always good for a clothing store, but maintaining a trusted relationship with a CEO made them one of the top stores in the city.

They were in a restaurant now within Covent Garden, after a quick, very busy underground journey from Bond Street. Situated beyond the steady-flowing fountain and various book shelves, they were settled at a cosy table in the corner, away from prying eyes.

Aidan leant back in his chair, feeling satisfied after his meal. "Since we're near the right underground, do you want to see if the girls are around today? We can nip to Hammersmith and be back in time for the drive later."

Megan picked up her drink, thinking. She had to try and find the courage to tell him about her past, like Ben had suggested, but she just couldn't find the words. She needed some breathing space. "Yeah, sure. I'll just nip out and call them. Make sure they are free." She stood.

"I'll meet you out front in a minute," Aidan said. "Going to settle the bill."

Megan turned back. "Sure"

Stepping outside, Megan found a small secluded avenue between the restaurant and an entrance to a church court-yard. Leaning against the brick wall, she glanced to her left, seeing Christmas shoppers walk up and down the main road carrying last-minute gifts.

She unlocked her phone and stared at the screen, trying to build up the confidence to call her best friends. She smiled at the photo of her and Aidan's socks from the first night they spent together. She flicked through her photos, replacing her phone wallpaper with an image from the previous night. A beautiful shot of Aidan as he grinned at her after he announced their engagement. A shot Lucy had captured for her. She shook her head.

Why are you having doubts, Meg? You have to tell him. She frowned, staring into space. *And you have to tell the girls the truth of what happened. Ben knows best.* She began calling them. *Ben knows best. . .*

Lucy answered after the fourth ring. "Meg, how's your hangover? I feel like death."

"It's fine, didn't last too long. Although, I think Aidan was suffering a bit earlier. Are you guys up for a couple of visitors in a bit? We're out shopping. Thought we'd pop over for a coffee or something."

"Emma!" Lucy called, "Meg and Aid are coming over, get Tom to put the coffee on." Megan heard a slight response from Emma in the background. "Em's in the shower. How long are you gonna be?"

"About an hour? Listen, Lucy, I need some advice. Ben called me this morning, and he asked if I'd told Aidan about the past. He thinks I should tell him about my parents and Jay. What do you think?"

Lucy paused for a moment. "I think Ben's right. I mean, you guys are all over the news, it's probably sensible that he knows. You know, just in case."

Megan sighed. "Yeah, I know."

"Are you nervous about telling him?"

"I can't think of how to even begin." Megan stepped out of the avenue, feeling the need to pace to calm herself.

"Tell him when you get here. We'll be able to support you and take over if you find it hard to talk about. Megan, I know you don't want to bring this memory back, but he deserves to know. If anything happens–"

"No, you're right, Lucy. You're right."

Aidan came out of the restaurant. Putting his arm around her shoulders, he kissed the side of her head. "We'll be about an hour. Will Emma be ready by then, or shall we give her a bit longer?"

"Emma is just getting out of the shower now, and we'll have coffee ready for you both," Lucy said.

Megan hung up and turned to face him. "Yeah, they'll be ready."

Aidan's face folded into a temporary knot. "What's wrong, Meg?" Megan had turned white and Aidan had a feeling she was about to open up—about her past; about what had happened to make Emma so concerned about her fully grown best friend.

"Aidan, I need to tell you something when we get to Hammersmith, but it's not going to be easy for me. I imagine Emma or Lucy have already told you that something happened to me in the past, but, even they don't know the full story, and it's about time they learnt the whole truth too."

Aidan placed his hands on her shoulders, then pulled her closer to him. He didn't like the exposed look she wore on her face and with people filling the now busy streets, he did all he could to protect her from any onlookers. "Sweetheart, you don't need to tell me anything if it's too hard to bring up. I'll always support you in any way I can, no matter what it is."

"No, you need to know this. It may never come up, but if it did and it affected us in some way, I would never be able to forgive myself. It's also probably going to upset the girls that I didn't tell them everything. Ben knows. He thinks that I don't know that he knows. I kept quiet so it didn't upset him. It's kind of why he called this morning."

Megan looked distant. Aidan held her as he flagged down a cab. She tried to say something else, but he shook his head. "Not here." He opened the car door for her and gave the driver the address.

They travelled in silence. Megan thought about two things. She was about to tell her future husband about her past. That scared her, but not half as much as the thought of having to tell her two best friends the truth.

She'd lied for way too long. And today, Megan was determined to change that.

Chapter 34

Aidan looked around the small flat Emma and Lucy shared. It was the first time he'd actually visited their home since he had dropped Megan off on the night they'd met, and it felt a little bizarre to be sitting on the same sofa she had texted him from after they'd kissed goodnight.

Tom handed Aidan and Kev a coffee, breaking his focus. They sat together in the living room talking, while Lucy, Emma, and Megan were in the kitchen having a chat.

"Don't know about you guys, but I've probably had four coffees so far today. I've needed the caffeine after the amount we got through last night."

"Surely working in clubs has seen you drunker than that, Kev?" Tom said.

"You'd be surprised. Most nights I stuck to water and Diet Coke."

"I'm sorry, did you just say diet? Dear lord, what the hell did I employ?"

Kev threw a decoration in Aidan's direction to try and stop him from laughing at his choice of soft drink.

***

"I don't think I can do this."

Hugging Megan, Lucy reassured her. "Yes, you can. Based on what you've both been through so far, this is a walk in the park. Nothing from what happened in the past is going to affect you now. Nothing. I promise you."

"Deep breath, Meg, you are doing the right thing," Emma said.

They walked into the living room and took their places on whatever seating remaining. Aidan extended his hand to help Megan sit down beside him. The girls' living room had Christmas decorations scattered everywhere—mainly because Kev had spent all morning being told where to put them. He was grateful for Aidan and Megan's visit; he needed a break from two nagging women.

"How is it that Tom gets out of decorating?" Aidan asked.

"He's our personal barista," Emma said. "And Kev's taller, so can reach places easier."

"And apparently on a diet," Aidan said.

Everyone laughed.

Everyone except Megan, who tried her best to smile. She looked at Emma, who nodded back to signal that whenever she was ready, they'd be there to help. She put her coffee down.

"Okay, let's get this over with." She took a deep breath.

Aidan gave her his hand in support when he saw hers shaking. She looked down at his hand then met his eyes, and knew she had his full support.

Closing her eyes and opening them again, she began.

"As some of you know, a few years back, my parents were going through a tough divorce, and the tension between them was unreal. Life in the Ashton house was just a living nightmare. Once their separation was final, they both moved to different parts of the world so they could start new lives away from one another. Dad moved to Seattle, Mum stayed with friends in Sydney. They never told me the reasons behind the split and I'll probably never know. All I remember was them constantly screaming at one another whenever I'd visit."

Emma and Lucy exchanged a quick glance during the pause, nodding in memory of the time period. Everyone else sat motionless, their eyes focussed entirely on maintaining a gaze. Megan had the room's full attention.

"At first we stayed in contact, updated one another—the usual stuff, you know? But then it slowed down and their level of communication seemed to stop. They'd started such new lives that it was like they had forgotten they had a daughter! I'd call—no answer; email–no response. It was like I was cut out from whatever life they had created for themselves."

"I remember the look on your face every time you tried to contact them," Emma said.

She reached across and took Megan's hand. "Broke my heart to see you that upset, and to not be able to do anything that could help."

"Ben, Emma, and Lucy, they were there for me through it all. But the one person, the one person I thought was going to help me through..." Her voice started to shake, as the emotion of her heartbreak suddenly overwhelmed her. "...wasn't. I mean, Jay had been supportive for a bit, but drinking and drugs became more of a focus in his life."

Megan felt Aidan's hand tighten around hers. "I accepted that maybe it was just a phase. That he'd eventually grow out of it. But it got worse." She looked at the girls, who were trying so hard to be strong for her. "When I needed him to just hold my hand and comfort me when I hadn't heard back from my parents, he did the opposite. It started with shouting: telling me to get over it, that they probably didn't want me as a daughter anymore, to–"

She gagged, choking on the words of her past. Her heart began to race. Rubbing her forehead, she tried to continue. Failing, she turned away to hide her face behind her hand. Lucy sat next to her, putting an arm around her shoulder.

"You're doing really well. We're all here for you, ok?" Lucy lifted her head. "Do you want us to take over?"

Megan shook her head, wanting to tell her story herself. Besides, Lucy didn't know what was coming. She took in a long breath, continuing.

"It escalated. He turned to taking his temper out on me physically. The number of times I said to Em and Lucy that it was only a phase, and that he wouldn't do it again, looking back now, was ridiculous. I don't know why I put up with it. The violence got worse, and one day, I tried to stand up to him. Asked him to stop and finish it for good."

Megan looked at Aidan. She thought he'd be furious, but he looked devastated at the hurt she'd been through. She then looked at Emma and Lucy. "I need to apologise for this next part, I didn't tell you the whole truth and I'm sorry. No one knew. The only people who did were the doctors when they admitted me to the hospital and Ben. I know for a fact that Ben overheard the doctors' discussion of my conditions. Ben kept the secret of what actually happened from everyone, including me—he thought I didn't know that he knew. It's probably the only time he's actually been able to keep something to himself."

"It's okay, Meg, you don't need to apologise for anything." Emma held her spare hand, reassuring her.

"Yeah I do, Em" Megan breathed deeply, before continuing. "When I confronted Jay, wanting to end the relationship, his temper hit a whole new level. There was no response from him, he just looked at me, like ... like I was nothing. That's when he attacked, forcing himself on me. I tried to get away, but he had me trapped. I was vulnerable, and he was going to get what he wanted." Megan was staring straight forward, right at the wall, as if looking back in time.

***

The blood seeped into her eyes as she stared at the wall. It grew fuzzier by the second. Any longer, and Megan was certain she'd have no blood left to give.

"Why do you make me do that?" Jay said, rounding on her. The words brought frothy spit to the edges of his mouth. "I hate having to do that. I wish you'd stop making me. You're a good girl, Megan. You don't deserve such punishment."

"Please, Jay." She held a hand up, hoping the small gesture would stop him. Her tears mixed with the blood that dripped down her cheek. "I'm sorry, I'm sorry."

Jay knelt down beside her, gently taking her hand. "Megan, do you really think apologising is going to make me forgive you?" He gripped her arm harder. "It makes me sad that you think saying sorry will make all this go away." He dismissed her arm like he was throwing out a packet of used cigarettes.

Megan turned away to try and escape, only to let out a deafening scream as Jay's foot came crushing down, breaking her arm.

He grabbed her chin, covering her mouth. His voice turned cold. Cold like hatred. "You have no idea how to even begin apologising to me."

Megan's entire body filled with fear as Jay repositioned himself between her legs. She violently shook her head, begging him not to do it. She screamed into his hand as he forced himself into her, hoping someone would hear her scream and help. She tried all she could to fight him off, despite the pain she was suffering, but Jay's restraints were too strong.

She was trapped, and all she could do was wait for the terribleness to end.

***

Megan's eyes jarred and refocussed. It felt like the blood she'd wiped from them a few years ago was still there. It wasn't as bad though. At least now she could see—think—straight.

Something she hadn't been able to do in many pain-burdened months.

She sat forward, put her hands on her knees, and looked around the room at everyone's face. Individually. Speaking first with her eyes.

"Yes. Jay raped me, and now I'm finally free."

Chapter 35

The Egyptian cotton sheets were like God's touch, the material rubbing against her bare skin, reminding her of her new-found freedom. Megan kept her eyes closed but reached out for Aidan, who, not where he should be, had apparently gotten up.

It was no biggie. She needed her sleep—at least he could respect that.

Respect from men wasn't something she hadn't known during her life. Her father hadn't shown any, Jay was a thousand shades worse, and then every guy who followed them posed as stand-in temps during their out of office hours. But now, all that had changed.

Aidan was different. She realised that the moment she met him. He was kind, gentle, thoughtful, and gave her more love than any man had ever given.

Yesterday, after she had told everyone the truth of what happened to her, he simply pulled her into a close embrace and let her stay hidden against his chest until she felt ready to speak again. That was enough. No extra questions, no cross-examining, just the knowledge that he was there.

Emma and Lucy on the other hand had gone in with the questions. They wanted to know if she went to the police, reported the assault, and also exclaimed what they would do to him if they ever saw him again. They soon quietened their rage when Tom raised a hand, gesturing for them to relax and, as he put it, 'calm their shit'. Megan was grateful for their support.

Once the dark atmosphere had lifted, Aidan had turned the subject to the season that was approaching. Christmas

Day. He had the thought at the JMC party, and he couldn't think of anything more perfect to cheer his fiancée up. Christmas with friends. Tom had been straight on the phone to Owen explaining the plan, and within minutes, things were set in stone. Everyone would travel down to Farnham on Christmas Eve (now only a matter of days away), allowing Aidan and Megan a couple of days to themselves before the festivities began.

Megan smiled. The bright white of the sun—reflecting because of the snow—shone through the large window that looked out over the landscape. She moved so she was in the centre of the bed and put a pillow behind her, sitting up to admire the stunning countryside view.

She felt as though she could have stayed there all day, but forced herself to get up.

Her fiancé was somewhere in the house, and she had him all to herself for the next two weeks—without a single interruption from the pressures of work.

She brushed her teeth, put on a pair of shorts and a vest top, and pulled her slipper boots on. She picked up one of the blankets on her way downstairs, assuming Aidan would be in the kitchen: that was where she usually found him. When she got there, there was no sign of him. She then heard the familiar sound of a woman's laugher coming from the lounge. Mrs. Miller.

Walking in, Megan smiled at the sight she saw. Aidan was sitting beside her on the sofa giving her a big hug. The old lady spotted her. Then Aidan did too. "We've been caught red-handed. How many times have I told you? You need to stop sneaking in." He shook his head.

Mrs. Miller was happy to see Megan grinning at her. "Oh, Megan, my darling." She leapt up, giving her a hug and kissing her cheeks. "Aidan's told me everything, I am so happy for you both, my dear. I knew this day would come as soon as I met you."

"Thank you. I couldn't be marrying a more wonderful and supportive man." She smiled back at Aidan.

"You most certainly couldn't. Well, I should be off. I hope to see the pair of you at the Christmas fete later? Maureen, my hair stylist, said she'd bake some of her famous chocolate and coconut brownies. Oh, they are tasty—you can't just have the one. Goes lovely with a glass of sherry."

"We'll pick you up, Angela."

It was the first time Megan heard Aidan call her by her Christian name.

"My dear boy, that would be lovely." She turned to Megan. "I do like that car! I'll see you both later. I know my way out."

After Mrs. Miller left, Aidan reached out for Megan to join him.

She smiled and happily let him guide her to a spot next to him. Before she even sat back, Aidan had his arms around her, enjoying a morning snuggle.

"Did you sleep well? I didn't want to disturb you."

She nodded. "Yes, just what I needed after yesterday."

He leant back so Megan was lying above him and gave her a good morning kiss that would make her smile for the rest of the day. He held her close, running one hand across her back.

"Thank you for not freaking out when I told you about what hap–"

"Meg," he put his finger on her lips, "you know me better than that. Don't ever think you can't tell me anything. I could tell you were nervous about opening up, but remember, I will support and take care of you the best I can. He's not coming back into your life, sweetheart. But if it'll make you feel more relaxed, I can get security to follow you everywhere. You're safe here."

"Can I just follow you everywhere?"

"Sure, but then I won't be able to make the company any money."

Megan lifted her head up in confusion. "Why?"

"Because you're a massive distraction, remember?"

Megan confidently sat up. Heading for the stairs, she dropped the blanket and began undressing in front of him. "Time to get ready I suppose. I'm just going to shower."

"See? Distracting again!" He jumped up and was on her in seconds. He caught her by the waist in such a quick move that she let out a scream. She was silenced right after as Aidan picked her up and pressed his lips to hers. His strong hands held her in place as she wrapped her legs around him.

"You're wearing too many clothes, Costello."

"Not a problem, just let me get you to the bedroom and that issue will be resolved."

He ran up the stairs and into their room. Gently placing her down on the bed, he removed his clothes and lay above her. The sun lit her face, and for the first time, Aidan noticed the scar in her hairline. He frowned as he moved her hair away, leaning down to kiss where she'd been hurt. She looked up at him, knowing that he'd noticed it, her eyes full of sadness.

"Never again, Megan," he said, moving in to kiss her neck and chest. "There is only one way I want to make you cry out." Aidan moved lower until she felt him between her thighs. Her back arched at the pleasure he was giving her and she couldn't help crying out his name. He kissed her legs and then moved so he was above her once more.

"Aidan," was all she managed to say as he held her hips.

Completely in the moment, Aidan looked down at her with so much love in his eyes, and thrust himself into her. She called out his name again, feeling the warmth build within her. He rolled them so she was above him. And then she convulsed, the decibels growing with each and every thrust.

Breathless and suddenly exhausted, they sat unmoving.

"That's how I want to hear you cry out."

***

They spent most of the day cycling between bedroom activities and decorative festivities—the finest of combinations, Megan had thought. The guys would arrive in a couple of days, so they had to make the most of their time.

Megan watched the lights pass her by as the car picked up speed. It had been a day of lounging, and she was happy to get out of the house for a while. She enjoyed it in the back of the car, it made a nice change. Angela was up front with Aidan. Bless her, she loved the car. Megan would have been a terrible person to call shotgun on an old lady.

Aidan parked in one of the centre's carparks and they all walked to the Christmas fete together, admiring the town's street decorations. Gracefully hung, even in the day with the lights off, the golden decorations gave the town a natural glow. Lace canopies covered the roads, warming the hearts that gazed upon them. Store windows were beautifully decorated in traditional style, mixed with greens, golds, and reds. It was like looking back in time.

People greeted Aidan as they walked around the stands, saying how lovely it was to see him home. From his reaction, Megan could tell they were old friends, figments of simpler times. He'd introduced her to them all, and everyone congratulated their engagement.

Angela wandered off to find Maureen, but said she would meet them shortly for tea in her favourite café. Someone came up behind Aidan and smacked him on the back, making him jump. He smiled when he saw who it was.

"Heck of a way to tell the world, Aid. The wife almost had a heart attack when she saw you both on the TV. Nice retaliation after that shit with the journalists outside JMC, though. Fight fire with flame."

"Been stalking me again?"

"Hard not too, fucking show off!"

Aidan laughed, hugging his oldest friend.

"This lovely lady must be the woman all the newspapers are talking about."

"Meg," Aidan said, pulling her closer. "This is Nick, his wife Lydia, and that little ball of trouble is Sara." He gestured towards them, and then back to her. "Guys, Megan."

Megan nodded. "Ah, Nick. Yes, I've heard about you from Angela. Told me to keep an eye on you two when you're together."

"She's right, it's true. The things they got up to!" Lydia laughed, giving Megan a friendly hug. "It's nice to meet you, Megan."

Nick looked beyond Aidan. "Where is Ang? She with you?"

"Shot off to find Maureen."

"Sounds about right."

Sara, a little behind the conversation, stomped her feet and glared at Aidan. "I'm not trouble, you are trouble."

Aidan laughed, picking Sara up. "And why I am trouble?"

"You said a naughty word on tele."

"And don't repeat it, okay? Learn from my mistake and keep calm and polite in front of the cameras, deal? Angela will tell you off, trust me."

"Okay, Uncle Aidan. Deal." She kissed his cheek as he put her down. "She's growing up too fast, Nick, makes me feel old."

"Not as old as I feel sometimes. Five minutes of peace and quiet would be a miracle!" He shook his head and smiled. "Are you back for Christmas, or is this another one of your flying visits?"

"We're here till New Year. I'm trying to make more of an effort to come down more often."

"About bloody time! Pub tomorrow night? You can pay."

"Cheeky fucker!" Aidan laughed, getting a smack from Lydia for swearing in front of her daughter again.

"Seven? At the usual?"

"Sounds good," Aidan said. "Meg?"

Megan nodded in agreement. "Sounds very good."

"Excellent! I'll message you later to confirm."

Megan let Aidan catch up with Nick ahead of them, choosing to match Lydia's pace as they admired the stands they passed. She smiled, watching Aidan laugh, catching up over the past few months since they last saw one another.

"Nick!" Lydia called him.

Megan turned to find Lydia no longer next to her, but running after Sara.

"Got to run, seems Sara fancies an adventure. She's probably seen something she doesn't need. Just like her mother."

Aidan sniggered. "Don't go getting yourself in trouble, Nick."

"Yeah, some things don't change. Lovely to meet you Megan. See you both tomorrow."

Aidan saluted him goodbye, then held out his hand for Megan. They had half an hour to kill before meeting Angela for lunch. Just enough time to pick up some last minute gifts. Megan stopped to admire a humorous mug that would suit Emma's coffee habit down to the ground. Aidan leant over her shoulder and sniggered when he read the text.

"If you don't get that for her, then I will." He handed the woman a tenner. "Keep the change."

Asking for the mug to be gift wrapped, they thanked the owner and dived deeper into the market. Megan placed Aidan's arm around her shoulders.

"Sara is beyond cute. She certainly knows how to get you off your high horse. Told you off better than Owen could."

"That girl's just got to smile at me and I'll do whatever she wants. She's the only other woman in my life. Her and Angela, of course."

Pulling her into an over-the-top show of affection, he stopped, smelling the aroma of chocolate that filled the air. The memory of visiting the local café, the one that served the delicious beverages, with his mother came flying back. Smiling, he glanced at Megan, who was standing there confused as to what he was doing.

"I think I need to make my fiancée aware of the most amazing hot chocolate she will every taste."

Chapter 36

The wind howled through the nooks and crannies of the building's brickwork, whistling tunes of unity and togetherness. It wasn't an ominous sound, as it usually was. *How could it possibly be ominous in such a beautiful location?*

To Megan, it sounded like home. Pulling on her coat, ready to head out to meet Nick and Lydia, Megan took another look around the barn she now called home.

The tree stood seven foot high and looked like it had been sent direct from Harrods. The barn felt warm, comfortable, and inviting. The glow from the lights, reflected in the snow through the glass walls, made it seem like she had been transported to Santa's personal grotto. Yesterday's fete had given her festive spirit a little push; today it was in full swing.

"Beautiful," Megan whispered.

"I know you are," Aidan slid his arms around her waist, "but what about the tree?"

"Now *that* was corny."

He turned her to face him. "Don't act like you don't love it."

Megan ran her arms up around his neck, placing a kiss on his head.

"If you're not denying it, I'll keep going. I'm full of cheesy lines."

She looked him in the eye and smiled.

"What?"

"Thank you."

"For?"

"For being amazing and supportive." She lifted her head. "You've certainly managed to keep my attention. Even if you were completely full of yourself the night we met."

"Like I said, I wasn't going to end the night without at least getting your name. I will admit though," he gestured to their close proximity with a downward nod of his head, "this is certainly a bonus."

"There you go again. You really are full of cheesy lines tonight."

"Just for you." He picked up his coat. "Ready?"

"Yep."

"Then let's get going." He extended his arm towards the door. "I got a text from Nick a couple minutes ago. He and Lydia are waiting."

***

They climbed out of the car, closing the doors in unison. Aidan opened the building's main door for Megan, and she was welcomed into a warm and cosy pub. A live band was setting up in the corner, and across the room people lined the bar, laughing and smiling with one another. She had to laugh at the amount of people sporting hideous Christmas jumpers and secretly wished she had worn hers too.

"Wonder if Nick's managed to bag the usual spot." Aidan took Megan's hand, battling the crowds in order to push through them. It was like the whole town was here. Aidan spotted Nick and Lydia near the bar. "Nick!"

Nick spun around at the sound of his name. "Hey, hey! You remembered where the pub is. I was sure you'd get lost."

"It's been a while, I know." He pulled Nick into a hug. "But we're here now. We in the usual spot?"

"Naturally." He nodded. "Craig knows that table will always be ours."

"They have a *usual spot*?" Megan asked Lydia, as they made their way across the room.

She nodded. "They were so protective over it that it almost got to the point where people would move when we came in because they knew these two loved the spot. Not that they were being intimidating or anything. This particular table was, and always will be, known as Nick and Aidan's spot."

Nick sat down, sighed in satisfaction, and gestured to the space around them. "And it's the best table in the pub!"

"Which you both got over-attached to when we were in college."

"Which you loved too, Lydia," Aidan said.

She rolled her eyes. "I give up."

"I have to admit, it is a nice spot." Megan looked around. Their table sat on a platform in a corner, with in the main dining area. The bar to their right was decorated with holly and bunting, interwoven with fairy lights, making it glow. Each table had its own small Christmas tree instead of a candle, which gave a festive ambience. "Good view of the whole pub, clear sightlines to the band." Megan sat next to her fiancé. "What the... What are you doing?"

Aidan had picked up a knife from the cutlery pot and began carving the table. "Marking the date."

"Marking the date? Dare I ask?" She smiled at Lydia, completely bewildered.

"Couldn't have waited at least five minutes, Aid?"

"Nope." He leant back to inspect his work. "Every time we come here, we mark the date of the visit."

"It turned into a tradition. Especially after the landlord gave up with trying to get us to stop defacing his table," Nick said. "Craig actually gets upset if we forget to do it now. Take a look."

Megan sat forward, reading the carvings. "Wow. Yeah, this is an extremely unhealthy attraction to a pub."

"Ah, the prodigal sons have return." Craig, the longstanding landlord, approached them. A beaming smile spread across his face when he spotted Aidan finishing off his work. "Nice to have a current date on there. People were starting to think you'd found a new place to drink."

Aidan glanced up at him. "That would be bang out of order, Craig." He finished the carving and then stood up, pulling the landlord into a hug. "It's been too long. How are you? Family well?"

"Good as can be. I'm more interested in meeting the soon-to-be wife, Aidan." He spotted Megan next to Lydia. "And I'm guessing this is she?"

"Certainly is." Aidan reached for Megan's hand. "Meg, let me introduce you to the best landlord in Surrey."

Megan stood up, expecting a handshake. What she didn't expect was to be pulled into a bear hug.

"And extremely loveable," Aidan said.

Placing his arm around Megan's shoulders, Craig turned to Aidan him. "How'd you manage to find one this stunning?"

Aidan held his hand out, which Megan took, stepping into his embrace. "She found me."

She kissed his cheek. "Smooth talker."

"Actually, Aidan, I'm glad I ran into you." Craig perched himself on the edge of the table. "Bought the wife one of those posh new desktops for Christmas, but I have no idea how to begin setting it up. Don't suppose..."

"Need a hand?"

"Would you mind? Wouldn't be until after Boxing Day. We have a strict no-tech rule in the house over Christmas."

"Of course, Craig, never a problem. Might install some free toys for her while I'm at it." Aidan picked up a napkin and scribbled his contact details down. "We're here till New Year. Drop me a line and I'll nip over."

"You're a lifesaver, Aidan, thank you. Next round's on me, okay?"

Nick's ears pricked up. "Gonna hold you to that, mate."

Leaving them be for the night, Craig headed back behind the bar. Once they had ordered food, talk turned to the obviously long friendship Aidan and Nick shared. They went over the past for a long time, telling stories of their wild days back in college.

Dinner was served and they tucked into what Megan could only describe as the most glorious food she had ever tasted. Aidan insisted on footing the entire bill, even after Nick said he was only joking about him paying. Knowing he was about to face a losing battle after they play fought at the bar, Nick gave in. But, he was sure to add a few more beers onto the ever-growing receipt.

Lydia shook her head and giggled as she watched them both acting like teenagers. "I've never known two grown men acting like they're still in college. No one would be able to tell that one's an executive and the other's a doctor." She laughed, taking a sip of wine. "Kids! I'm glad you're here to control the other one now though, Meg."

Megan sank back into the seat, smiling. "You know, I'm sure Clare said something very similar." She leant forward, placing her elbows on the table. "So, Nick's a doctor?"

"Hmm," she finished her drink, waving the glass at Nick, "yeah, one of the head doctors at the local hospital. He loves it. Although, he prefers working in the ambulance."

"More of a thrill." Nick returned with more drinks, Aidan following just behind. "Saved your fiancé's ass more than a couple of times."

"Can I just add that the last time wasn't my fault?" Aidan tried to defend himself, settling down while the band started up.

"Oh yeah? Ice just happened to magically appear in front of you? You tripped on the curb, broke your ankle. You're so accident prone."

Aidan punched Nick's arm.

"And that's the thanks I get. I get to drive your car for that."

"Fuck you do!"

"I drive a bloody ambulance around all day, I think I can handle a Merc."

"Even after three pints? No way." Aidan warned him again. "Never be able to forget when you wrapped your car around that lamp post. You're not doing that to a hundred-and-eighty-thousand pound car."

Megan almost spat her drink out. "Hundred and what? Shit, even I don't wanna drive it again now."

The band began playing one of Lydia's favourite songs. Squealing in excitement, she grabbed Megan's hand. "Come on, Meg, let's leave these two to nag one another. I need a dance partner."

"You're on." They both picked up their drinks and made their way into the growing crowd.

The band's opening number got the entire pub pumped. People cheered and sang along to the popular track, hugging one another and landing more beer on the ground than in their mouths. No wonder it was the most popular pub in town. They knew how to throw a party. Even Craig had given up his post of 'beer lord' and joined the celebrations.

Aidan smiled as he watched his fiancée on the dance floor. "She's one in a million, Nick." He caught Megan smiling back at him. "I feel like the luckiest man alive."

Nick threw his arm over his shoulder. "Happy?"

"Put it this way, when you and Lyd started dating and you told me she was the only woman for you–"

"And you ripped the piss out of me, called me a soft twat?"

Aidan sniggered, remembering. "Well, I can now admit that you had every right to say it. Meg's amazing. Just took me a while to find her."

"Soppy fucker."

"Yep, absolutely." Aidan's phone rang, he answered it. "Turner!"

"Owen!" Nick also shouted down the phone.

"Evening lads, take it we're reliving the college days, are we? Usual pub? Usual spot?"

"Naturally. What's up, precious?"

"So Clare's packed the limo already, and it's like nagging central here, Aid. Tom's hiding, and Kev looks like he may go back to the club to do the Christmas night shifts. They want to know if you need anything before we leave the city tomorrow."

"Shouldn't think so," Aidan said. "Hang on, you're using one of the limos?"

"You're getting slow, Costello, definitely means you've had one too many. Anyway, anything needed? Or can I tell them everything's sorted, like I'm sure it is? Please?"

"Everything is sorted, Owen. Just tell Kev we need help with some last minute decorations. We'll see you tomorrow."

"Get some beers ready, I'm going to need them by the time this lot is sorted. Until tomorrow. Later boys."

Aidan hung up and finished his pint. "Well, I don't know about you, Nick, but I'm gonna give up the spot and go find the wife."

"Right behind you, mate."

Chapter 37

During an early morning run, something dawned on Aidan. Running always cleared his mind, and even though work was closed, he found he made the best decisions for the good of the company while exercising.

Why would a company that's based in the city of all cities manage to get themselves into financial difficulties? Something's not adding up. Wouldn't they approach someone in the US? Why London? Why JMC? They took that last deal far too quickly.

Pressing the remote on his earphones, he called his own voicemail at the office to set a reminder. "First thing you do when you get back, set up a private investigation on Norfolk. Be careful, they could be doing the same to us."

***

Megan was focussed on decorating the Christmas cake she'd baked the night before when he got home. Her hair was tied up with a bandana so it didn't fall in front of her face, and Aidan tried to hide his laughter when he noticed that she'd managed to get icing on her chin.

"Good run?" she asked, accepting a kiss on her cheek and having the icing removed. "Oh, I always manage to get icing everywhere."

Aidan gave her a cheeky look, licking the icing from his thumb.

"Not everywhere like you're thinking. Typical man. One-track mind."

He had another sip of water to cool down. "It was great, just what was needed after last night. Drank way more than I should have." Aidan leant against the work surface behind her, making sure he wasn't in her way. "Any word of when the guys are leaving London?"

"Em just called, they're leaving now. Apparently Tom and Kev woke up feeling a bit rough this morning, hence the big batch of coffee that's ready to go on." Megan pointed behind her towards the coffee machine.

Aidan laughed while finishing the water. "Jesus, Meg. We planning on opening a café?" He tried to pinch some icing from her piping pack, but had his hand slapped away before he could get close. "Meg, that's looking amazing. Can we keep it in a glass case rather than cut it up?"

Megan was creating a traditional Christmas scene, using food colourings as paint and piped icing. "It's nowhere near done yet. Take a photo, but I'm eating it. Shower, go! I'll be here a while yet." She leant on her elbow, watching him walk away. Taking out her phone, she opened her emails. Nothing except the usual spam from stores she had registered with. She opened a new message and began to type.

Hi Mum, how are you? Just doing our prep on the Christmas cake—like we used to when I was younger. It's been so long and I have some exciting news to share. Would be amazing to speak with you. Anyway, it's probably early evening over there in Sydney, but I hope you enjoy the rest of your day. Merry Christmas. Megan Xx

Adding her mobile number like she always did, and typing a similar email to her Dad, she pressed send on both. The likelihood of getting a reply was slim, but she always hoped.

"Meg?" Aidan called, as he came back down downstairs in just joggers.

She locked her phone. "Yes?"

"Have you seen—" He noticed her frown. "What's wrong?"

"Nothing, I'm fine. I was just sending an email to Mum and Dad. Being Christmas, I can only hope and try."

Aidan gave her a questionable look.

"I'm okay, really. Now, what have you lost?"

***

Their friends arrived in Farnham later than expected. The roads were busy with seasonal commuters, heading home to spend Christmas with friends and family. It had been clear that Owen was winding Aidan up about using the limo when they arrived in two cars. Finally, he'd managed to get one over on him. Aidan had shaken his head, smacking his arm in amusement.

Once the well-needed coffee had been served everyone went about their own business. Owen and Kev insisted they help Aidan with the last minute preparations for Christmas lunch. Not hearing no when Aidan told them not to worry and that Angela would be joining them the following day to help. Giving up, he gave them each a job.

Kev was given the task of prepping the sprouts, whereas Owen was asked to hunt out the fine china and the set up the dining table in the conservatory. A job he was sure to excel at. He had a flare for design and due to his mild case of OCD, Aidan knew the table would look like it would be set for royalty by the time he was done. Tom and Clare nipped out to pick up some last minute presents when they realised Nick and Lydia were joining them.

Megan showed Emma and Lucy around the house.

Emma hung up her dress in the wardrobe. "This is where Aidan grew up? It's incredible."

"Well, not in this barn, but the area, yeah. He was telling me about how him and Nick, who you'll meet tomorrow, used to come here as kids. But when it looked like it was going to be knocked down, he bought it outright. It's part of his childhood. Took him two years to get it looking like it does now. It'll always be his real home I think, even though he has the apartment in the city."

"Correction, my dear, you should have said our home," Lucy said, making Megan smile. "So, tell me. Did I see a pool?"

"You did see a pool, but it's not heated at the moment. There is another, though."

"What? You've gotta show us," Emma insisted.

Megan took them downstairs to show them the pool in the basement, along with the mini gym.

"I am so using this while I'm here." Emma ran in to look at the equipment.

"Aid was thinking about getting a lowered hot tub installed in this corner."

"Bet he was," Lucy teased, nudging Megan's side.

***

Evening settled in and everyone was relaxing in the games room after dinner. There was nothing left to do but enjoy each other's company, and appreciate the calm before the craziness of Christmas Day. Work was over for a couple of weeks, and there was no way Aidan or Owen were going to bring it up again. This was the time of year that they could forget about the multi-million pound company and be themselves.

Kev couldn't help himself. He'd found the bar and was mixing cocktails—just to check he hadn't lost his abilities already. Lucy was listening to his instructions on how to make specific drinks, and she was picking it up very quickly.

"You guys should open your own bar," Clare suggested.

"Omigosh, I can see it now. You could name it in some kind of mix up of your names." Emma thought to herself, then held her hands up, visualising. "LU-KEV!"

Lucy almost dropped a glass due to laughing at Emma's suggestion. "Em, that's awful."

"Clearly my expertise does not include advertising."

Megan and Emma were happily testing each drink Kev and Lucy made, giving them both a score out of ten for effort, design, and taste. They were becoming very drunk, very fast.

"Clearly," Kev warned them, "you two need to slow down."

"Hey!" Emma waved a finger at him. "I'm not the one producing the drinks."

Aidan and Tom were playing pool, while Owen watched Kev's bar skills, failing to help. He was coming up with the most hideous mixtures. Kev had permanently banned him from behind the bar after he'd mixed Tia Maria and beer, a drink his friend at university used to swear by.

Owen turned to the pool board. "I think we're going to end up getting a bar at the office, Aid. Having fun, Kev?"

"Would make it nicer than having to deal with whatever new coffee they've brought in. Emma, surely you've noticed a difference?" Aidan commented, just before sinking the black ball to win another game.

"Oh come on, that's three games in a row now." Tom shook his head and drove the butt of the cue into the ground like he was trying to inflict damage.

"Coffee is coffee," Emma finally replied, after finishing a Cosmopolitan. "But I have to admit, it has tasted a bit shit recently."

Kev brought over a cocktail he'd made up and handed it to Aidan. "Drink that, play again. I bet you'll win the next one, Tom."

Aidan took the drink, smelling it first. "Holy shit, Kev, what's in that?"

"I'm not telling until you drink it."

"Kevin?" Megan grabbed the sleeve of his shirt, almost falling off her stool. "Are you about to knock out my fiancé?"

"No, no, just giving Tom a chance to actually win a game." Kev gestured for him to drink it. "Bottoms up, buddy."

Aidan looked at him with raised eyebrows, accepting the challenge. He drank the cocktail, coughing as soon as it hit his chest. "Motherfucker. Shitting hell. You bastard!"

"Strong?" Clare asked, laughing.

"Yeah, what's it got in it?" Aidan was coughing from the burn.

Megan passed him some water, which didn't help at first.

"Vodka mixed with whiskey, martini, gin, and orange peel," Kev said.

"Twat!" Aidan high-fived him. "Okay, Turner. Game on."

"Anyone else want to try it?" Kev asked, getting a resounding *no* from everyone.

Clare stood. "I need to borrow the ladies for a moment. Girl talk—nothing that would be of interest to you lads right now." She gestured for them to follow her. Emma and Megan followed last, after picking up their drinks.

Tom was concentrating on winning the game, but Aidan was still kicking his ass, even after the lethal drink. Tom lined up his shot, pulled back the cue, and slammed it home. The red pinged back and forth in the mouth of the pocket like a rogue pinball, choosing to settle without teetering over the edge. "Shit. How are you still beating me?"

"That was a dramatic exit. I always worry when they run off like that."

"Wouldn't worry about it, Owen," Tom said. "Emma's always doing it, but then she comes back to announce that we need more peanut butter or something. Probably nothing."

***

Clare sat up on the kitchen island, folding one leg over the other whilst she waited for the others to join her. Lucy stood next to her, but Megan and Emma had chosen the bar stools. They felt a little wobbly after the fast exit.

"Everything okay, Clare?" Lucy asked. "You've not touched any of the drinks."

Clare looked at each of them slowly. "Well."

The penny dropped with Megan first. Her eyes lit up. "Omigosh! Are you?"

Emma and Lucy caught on too, and began leaping up and down in sync.

"It's why I nipped into town with Tom earlier. Snuck into a chemist when I had the chance. I was meant to come on the day after the party. When that didn't happen, I thought I'd wait a few more days just in case it was delayed. Nothing."

"Have you done the test yet?" Emma asked. Clare shook her head. "Let's do it now," Lucy suggested.

They all ran upstairs to Megan and Aidan's master bedroom. Megan gestured them all in, closing and locking the door after them. She glanced down and sighed. Subtly, she bent down and picked up Aidan's dirty socks. He had a bad habit of leaving them on the floor. Lucy spotted what she was doing and couldn't help sniggering as she helped close the curtains to give them even more privacy.

Emma looked around the room. "This is a bit swanky. Oh, *ooh*, I'm in my boss's bedroom." She sat down on the bed. "That's so weird!"

Megan joined her. "And this is where you best pal has sex with your boss." She laughed hysterically, pulling Emma down with her as they sprawled out onto the mattress.

"Okay you two, no more cocktails. You've had enough." Lucy turned her attention to Clare, who was standing by the door to the ensuite bathroom. "We'll wait right here. Let us know straight away." She shook her clenched fists like an excited toddler.

"I will do." Nodding, Clare smiled at them all and closed the bathroom door.

All three of them sat on the bed, waiting patiently while Clare did the test. "How's it going in there?" Megan turned to the others. "They need to make those things easier to pee on."

Clare came out, looking nervous but also excited. "Okay, done. We just need to wait for a few moments."

"Relax, deep breaths. At least you're married to the possible future dad. Our friend, Amanda from back home, she ended up having twins with a guy she had just met. He left in a shot after she told him the news."

"Emma, not helping, sweetheart," Megan said. They sat in silence. The wait felt like forever.

"Okay, I think that's long enough." Lucy checked the time. "Do you want us to look with you?"

Clare nodded, and lifted the test to eye level.

***

"If you actually manage to win this one, Tom, I'll give you a grand."

Tom looked at Aidan's poker face, not knowing if he was serious. "Not that I need a thousand pounds, however–"

"Don't, Tom!" Owen warned him, knowing his friend too well. "He may not be talking about money."

Aidan pointed at Owen, shaking his hand in disagreement. "Ignore your brother, Thomas, he doesn't know what he's on about."

Megan, Emma, and Lucy came back down to the games room, looking like they had been up to no good. "Owen? Can Clare borrow you for a moment, please?" He looked confused. Megan waited for his response. "As in, now?"

"Um, yeah of course. Where is she?"

"Kitchen."

"What's going on?" Aidan asked.

Megan smiled at him, closed the door behind Owen, and threw herself down on the sofa. "You'll find out soon enough."

"Okay, Costello, if I win this one, you hand it over in cash."

"Hand what over in cash?" Megan questioned him, looking at Aidan for the answer.

***

"Clare, darling, you okay? Meg said you needed me."

Clare was sitting at the kitchen island, gesturing for Owen to join her. "I'm fine, sweetheart. More than fine, in fact. I have some news."

"What is it?"

She looked into her husband's eyes and smiled. "You're going to be a dad!"

Owen's eyes lit up. He swept her up as she laughed at his excitement He kissed her with all the love in the world. "You're pregnant?" Clare nodded. "This has officially become the best Christmas ever, Clare. I love you so much!"

"I love you too, Owen."

He put her back down. "The girls know?"

"They were there to support me through the test, so yeah. I hope you don't mind?"

"God, no! They're all like family. But I'm telling the lads." Owen burst back into the games room, disturbing the fourth game of pool, preparing to announce their soon-to-be parenthood. Clare followed, and they spoke in unison.

"We're going to be parents!"

Chapter 38

C hristmas Day arrived and the entire house was on alert. Aidan and Megan thought they were the first up, wanting to clean up the remnants of the previous night, but were shocked to find Lucy running around the house like a five-year-old, excited and hyper. Managing to calm her down with a promise that she could open her presents first, they got the kitchen and living area ready for the onslaught of soreheads. The coffee machine was on max and it was bacon butties all round.

By the time everyone was up enjoying their fresh caffeinated beverages, Aidan had already started preparing lunch. Angela was around and hugging everyone, before diving into the kitchen to help. Nick, Lydia and a very excited Sara were the last to arrive, greeting Owen with a man hug first. Owen introduced them to the new recruits of the friendship group, and there was no doubt from the get-go that they would get on like a house on fire.

Lydia was relaxing with the women, having a needed rest—Sara hadn't slept the night before due to her excitement that Santa was on his way. Sitting in the living area of the kitchen, tucking into mince pies on the sofas, they spoke about pregnancy and what Clare was to expect over the next nine months. Emma and Lucy were playing with Sara on the floor, helping her build a princess castle that her Grandparents bought her. Megan was putting the final touches to the cake and had banned anyone from coming near her; even Aidan was warned not to come too close.

Aidan was finally getting a chance to put his secret chef skills to use, throwing orders around to everyone—apart from Angela, who he just couldn't tell what to do. Treating the kitchen like his conference room, he took the lead and made sure everything was done right. The lads were doing as he commanded—they didn't want to see him lose his temper over something that wasn't quite right.

"Aid?" Nick stepped to the other side of the kitchen. "Have you had coffee yet today?"

"Why?"

"Whoa, Nick, you're brave, mate." Owen stood by Nick, waiting for Aidan's response.

Megan looked up from where she worked, trying not to snigger.

"Just asking. Because when you're like this, that usually means no coffee."

Owen tapped Nick's arm. "Some things will never change."

"Watch it, so-called closest friends," Aidan said, without looking up. "And don't forget about all the things I could tell your wives. Choose your next words wisely." He calmly glared at them. "If either of you have nothing to do, though, I would love a coffee. Thanks."

"No one piss off the Costellos, you may not make it through Christmas Day," Owen said. He got a joint look from both Aidan and Megan. "Seriously, approach with caution."

"Owen! Stop swearing!" Angela smacked his arm. "You'll have to get used to piping that in when you have your little one running around."

Megan threw a used icing bag in his direction, which landed perfectly on his forehead.

Kev, Tom, and Nick burst out laughing at the icing that slid down onto his face.

"That's my girl," Aidan said, looking at Owen and smirking.

"Clare, did you see that? There're all ganging up on me."

"See what, darling?" Clare was more interested in what Sara was doing. The icing that coated her husband's face was practically non-existent.

Owen wiped his face. "You're all bunch of twats!"

Over the next half an hour, just under two hours before lunch would be ready, the people who could relax did just that. Sara had the women wrapped around her finger, instructing them how to put her castle together, acting like the boss of the household. Emma and Lucy didn't mind having a five-year-old boss; they both could have eaten her up due to her cuteness.

Lydia was thrilled to have a moment's peace. She hadn't been able to have a grown up conversation with another woman for a while, so was taking full advantage of Clare's company. Usually her conversations consisted of asking Nick what he wanted for dinner, and who was going to put Sara to bed. This was certainly a treat.

The men, still in the kitchen, loved playing chef, and each one of them tried their absolute best to see how far they could push Aidan's temper. A challenge that none of them could complete. Even when Tom decided that 'sprout volley ball' was a grand idea, it still didn't faze Aidan. He didn't even flinch when one of the delightful vegetables landed in the gravy, splashing it all over his white top. He knew Angela would give Tom a clip round the ear from it, and she delivered, causing an outburst of laughter and a concerned look from the women. The Turners were on their way to being kicked out into the snow.

"Okay, I am done." Megan stood away from the cake to double check that it was to her standard.

Aidan came over to look. Holding her waist, he admired her artistic skill. "It's amazing, Megan."

She smiled and whispered to him. "If we ever have kids, I could do a Disney theme one year."

He kissed her neck. "What do you mean, *if?*"

She turned and kissed him at the thought of them one day starting a family of their own. Sara ran over to Aidan. He swept her up so she could look at the cake. Megan melted again at seeing him holding the little girl; he had so much love in his eyes for his friend's daughter.

"Pretty," she said. "Can we have it now?"

"You need to have your main first, sweetheart."

Sara hugged him, and everyone watched the previously nagging CEO melt away in front of their eyes. Owen nudged Kev. "So all I've got to do to calm him down at the office is give him a hug? Why didn't I know about this trick?"

"You'll be going home with a black eye if you're not careful, Owen," Aidan warned him.

"Yeah, leave Uncle Aidan alone," Sara said.

"I'd listen to the woman, Owen, you can't touch me while she's here." Everyone laughed at the fact that Aidan apparently now had a five-year-old bodyguard.

Defeated and feeling like no one was going support him, Owen threw his tea towel down in a huff–much to Nick and Kev's amusement, who were sniggering like children.

Aidan wasn't paying him a single bit of attention. He and Angela were in cooking mode, which meant nothing would break their concentration.

Now that the cake had been created, Megan cleaned her workstation, placing her new baking equipment back in the dedicated cupboard. She wiped down the surface, removing any evidence of the mess she had made, and set the cake down in a safe place, away from prying fingers. She poured herself a red wine and took a well-deserved sip. She took her phone out of her pocket when it announced that she had a new message. She almost spat the wine all over Aidan's white top in shock when she saw why the message was from.

She nudged Aidan's side. "Mum replied."

"Sara," he put her down, "why don't you ask your dad to show you my car? I'll be back in a few minutes, okay?" He threw his keys at Nick. "Go nuts, buddy."

"Yay! Come on, Daddy!" She dragged her dad to the garage.

Aidan escorted Megan to the conservatory that Lucy and Emma had set up, ready for Christmas lunch. They left before anyone noticed they'd disappeared so she could read the email in private. Closing the door behind them, he encouraged her to read.

"Go ahead, Meg, I'm right here."

She read the email to herself first, then began to cry. "Please tell me they're happy tears?"

She smiled, then laughed. "Look." She passed him the phone.

He sat in one of the dining room's wooden chairs and began to read.

DARLING MEGAN, WHAT CAN I SAY? I'VE BEEN A TERRIBLE MOTHER, NOT RESPONDING AS OFTEN AS I SHOULD. I'D BLAME IT ON THE TIME DIFFERENCES BETWEEN BRITAIN AND AUSTRALIA, BUT NO MUM SHOULD DETACH HERSELF FROM HER DAUGHTER AND I'M SORRY. I HOPE YOU WILL FIND IT IN YOUR HEART TO FORGIVE ME. IF NOT, THEN I UNDERSTAND.

"Is she not going to go into why they distanced themselves, then?"

"Right now, I don't care," Megan said. "Keep reading."

I WAS SURPRISED TO SEE SO MANY PICTURES OF YOU ON THE INTERNET WITH SUCH A WELL-KNOWN, HANDSOME MAN BACK IN THE UK. YOU BOTH LOOK SO HAPPY, AND YOU LOOK BEAUTIFUL. I HOPE HE IS TAKING CARE OF YOU THE WAY I SHOULD HAVE OVER THE LAST FEW YEARS. I WOULD LOVE TO SPEAK WITH YOU AND SEE YOUR CAKE. WE DID OURS THIS YEAR TOO: A SCENE FROM THE SNOWMAN, YOUR FAVOURITE CHRISTMAS MOVIE. I MISS YOU, MEGAN, AND I LOVE YOU VERY MUCH.

MERRY CHRISTMAS, MUM XX

Chapter 39

L unch was finally ready. It was served in the conservatory around the large wooden table, set out beautifully for Christmas Day. Owen had outdone himself. Each setting had been wonderfully laid out. He'd taken the time to carefully fold the napkins into the wine glasses, and taken a piece of ivy to hang on the rim. The centrepiece, a mixture of green, red, and gold leaves, sat interwoven around the vegetables and roast potatoes. The lighting was set to a warm tone, making the room feel comfortable and inviting.

Both Aidan and Owen sat at each end of the rectangular table, Clare and Megan at their sides. Emma, Tom, Lucy, and Kev lined one side, opposite the Collins family and Angela. Angela sat between Aidan and Nick, saying it was so she could keep an eye on them. It didn't take long for the first round of bickering to begin.

"Angela, please tell everyone that we behaved when we were younger," Nick begged.

"When you were younger?" Owen asked sarcastically.

"And anyway, it's Aid and Owen you need to keep an eye on now." Nick nudged her. "Isn't that right?"

Angela nodded in agreement. "Hmm, well yes, that is true."

"What? No way!" Owen protested.

"But you boys will never change." She glanced at Aidan, then at Nick. "Poor Lydia had quite the handful, dealing with you two when you were at college."

Lydia laughed. "I don't know how I would have coped without you, Angela."

"I don't know how any of you ladies will cope with these five when I'm gone." Angela held her arms out wide and gestured around the room. "These boys, all in the same room? I'm surprised the place hasn't brunt to the ground."

Megan stroked Aidan's leg under the table in support, sensing his reaction to the subject of people passing. He didn't particularly want to hear about death at this time of year. Christmas always reminded him of when his parents were killed.

Angela looked at him and cottoned on to the expression on his face. She put her hand to her mouth. "Aidan, darling, I'm sorry."

He shook his head in an attempt to force the memory away and touched Angela's hand that was squeezing his arm. "Who's ready for dessert?" he asked.

"I'll help you." Megan followed him to the kitchen.

Kev watched them both leave, waited a second, and then looked around the room. "Um, I don't mean to pry, but is Aid okay? Never seen him act that way before."

Angela sighed. "His parents died this time of year when he was just a child, Kevin. Still hurts him sometimes. I wasn't thinking when I said that. I feel terrible."

"Don't beat yourself up, Angela. He knows you didn't mean anything by it," Nick said. "Probably just wants to take a few moments, you know?"

Angela nodded in agreement. "I guess so."

"He'll be back to swearing at Owen in no time," Clare said.

"Is it pick on Owen day or something?" Owen said, dropping his fork.

"Just getting you ready for parenthood, sweetheart. If he or she is anything like you and your brother, we'll need all the readiness we can get."

Owen shook his head. "Gee. Thank you, Clare."

"Objection," Tom said, supporting his brother.

Everyone laughed at the obvious truth about the Turner brothers while they waited for dessert to be served.

***

In the kitchen, dessert was the last thing on their mind. There was a slight chill in the air—possibly due to the open window, but seeming like it was from something else. Something deeper; more personal. They huddled in the corner, away from the cold, away from the Siamese pain of their past and all the darkness that lurked there.

Megan held Aidan in her arms. "Angela didn't mean to upset you."

"I know." He sighed against her shoulder, allowing her to support him.

This was one the hardest part of the year for Aidan. The memory of receiving the news of his parents' death always came flooding back. His grandmother, Leah, had come into the room after receiving a phone call from the local police department in floods of tears. She not only had to break the news to her husband, Gerald, that their daughter and son-in-law had died in a fatal car crash, but to their six-year-old grandson too.

Aidan had sat in silence as Leah told them what had happened and watched as his grandfather broke down. Gerald stood up, laying a hand on Aidan's shoulder and met his wife's tear-filled eyes. He didn't know what to do or say to comfort his only grandchild, so instead of trying, he simply left the room. Lily called after him, needing his support. When he didn't answer she ran after him, leaving Aidan all alone.

Although he was only a boy at the time, he could still remember the early afternoon sunset that glowed orange in the sky and the sound of the robins, singing their afternoon song. The sound of his grandparents sobbing still haunted him, but he would never make it known.

Megan stroked the back of his neck, knowing that all he wanted right now was for her to hold him. Never had he ever let anyone see this side of him and he never would again. He was meant to be this strong powerful businessman, with skin as hard as concrete; never one to back down from a win. But Megan was eventually going to be his wife and he let his barriers down completely, showing her the fragile man he actually was. She didn't say anything to him regarding the memory he was fighting. She understood that it was harder for him to bring up his parents' death than anything else he had faced.

***

The kitchen door opened and Aidan came through it, smiling like a maniac. He was trying his absolute best to put on a brave face, but Owen and Nick saw straight through it—they knew him too well. They knew he was trying to be strong, so took the lead, steering the conversation to humour and light.

"So, Clare is under the impression that our kid is going to be a handful, Aid, like myself and Tom, apparently. Please tell her we're not that bad."

Aidan sat back down, holding Angela's hand. "You are that bad. The pair of you."

"Ever the CEO and vice to have a dig at one another. Things will never change."

"Don't you start too, Em. We're good as gold." Tom tried to defend himself and his brother again.

"Bollocks!"

"*Kevin!*" Angela would have to put all the guys on the naughty step at this rate. "Sorry, Angela." Kevin looked around. "I may not have known you lot that long, but from the cheek Aid was getting at the bar that night, I'm on Clare's side."

"Thank you, Kev."

"You're welcome."

There was a brief pause, but then, innocence filled the silence. "Mummy, what does bollocks mean?" Sara asked.

Megan came back into the room just in time to hear the innocent voice repeat Kev's profanity, making her almost drop the dessert. Of all the people to be the first to laugh at the sweet little voice asking what bollocks meant, no one expected it to be Angela.

"Go on then, Lyd, what does it mean?" Lucy leant on her elbow, waiting to hear how Lydia was going to answer her daughter, who was staring up at her in fascination.

Lydia gave Kev a look that said he was going to be strung up later, then turned her attention to her daughter. "Sara, you remember when your Uncle Aidan said a naughty word on tele and you told him off?"

"Yes." Sara nodded and wiggled her finger towards her unofficial uncle, reminding him that his bad language had gotten him in trouble. "Naughty Uncle Aidan."

"Well, Kev's language just then was also naughty, so I'm going to need you to tell him off too. Can you do that for me, darling?"

"Yes, mummy." Sara got out of her chair and marched towards Kev, who wasn't a hundred percent sure as to what was about to happen.

Aidan was leaning on the table, trying not to encourage any more bad behaviour with his fit of laughter. The scene had certainly cheered him up, seeing his friend preparing to get told off by a five-year-old.

"Kevin? I think you need to go and stand in the corner for having potty mouth. Naughty Kevin."

Megan hid behind Aidan's shoulder to hide her amusement. "She's so adorable," she whispered.

Kev thought to himself for a moment, then lifted Sara up and whispered something in her ear.

"Yeah! Yeah!" She ran into the living room in a flash, forgetting all about Kevin and his potty-mouth antics.

"Okay, how the fuck did you get out of that?"

"*Aidan*! Honestly, you boys." Angela sighed, still laughing.

"Sorry, Aid, Sara's new name is Elsa, and your living room's about to become a castle made of ice."

Aidan and the other men groaned at the thought of the house being filled with the songs from Frozen.

"Oh, come on you boring farts. It's Christmas." Kev paused, smiling in anticipation of what he knew his next words would cause. "Just let it go."

It took zero point five seconds for the room to explode in song, the vocals belonging to the group's female members, as the house filled with echoed lyrics from the popular Disney movie.

Chapter 40

E veryone had headed off by mid-afternoon on the day after Boxing Day, leaving Megan and Aidan to enjoy the peacefulness of the now quiet house. Clare insisted that she and Owen stop in with both their parents to announce the news that they were going to be grandparents; Emma and Lucy decided to drive to Somerset to introduce the new men in their lives to their families—including Ben and Martin. Once they had visited everyone they needed to, the New Year celebrations would begin.

Megan reached for a towel as she stepped out of the shower. Using it to dry her hair first, she wrapped it around herself and opened the door to the wardrobe. She admired her clothes and ran her hands across them, trying to decide which dress she should wear to the evening's festivities. She stopped. She slid her hand between her favourite jeans and one of her many new leather jackets to reveal a long emerald green sequinned dress.

"Huh."

During their shop the day after the JMC party, Megan had seen the dress in a window in Covent Garden. She fell in love, but felt she had no need for it. Obviously Aidan had thought otherwise and had secretly bought it for her. She hung the dress up, sitting on the bed to admire it. It was then that she spotted something on the tag. Standing up, she inspected it closer and felt herself fill with emotion. Attached was a note with Aidan's handwriting on it.

HAVEN'T A NEED FOR IT? BOLLOCKS! LOVE YOU, AID Xx

She sniffed, wiping a tear away. "He remembered."

They'd been enjoying a lazy afternoon, that was until they were startled by Nick, bursting through their front door demanding that they join him and Lydia for New Year's Eve. It was a charity night in aid of the local hospital where he worked. They had planned to have a quiet night in, celebrating at home over a few bottles of wine and ordering take out, but couldn't resist Nick's pleading face. And now here they were, a few hours later, almost ready to go. Megan spun around in her new sequinned gown, loving how it caught the light. She watched Aidan walk in and pull on his black Armani jacket, once again looking powerful and in charge. She wrapped her arms around his waist.

"Thank you."

Aidan stroked a piece of hair back that she had missed and kissed her forehead. "You're welcome."

They caught a taxi into town after deciding it wasn't wise for either of them to drive.

The taxi drove down the gravel drive, stopping by the entrance of the red brick building. Lights shone up the building, making it look both inviting and eerie. Like a medieval royal family was seconds away from demanding that they join their court.

Aidan held his hand out to help her out the car, which she happily took. "It does feel weird not getting out the limo dressed like this."

"Sounds like someone's gotten used to her new lifestyle."

"What? Oh my, I've turned posh, haven't I?" Megan threw a hand over her eyes in embarrassment.

Thanking the taxi driver, they decided to wait for Nick and Lydia before making their grand entrance. They didn't have to wait long. Nick and Lydia were moments behind them, looking flustered already, trying to catch them up.

"Are we late?" Lydia panicked. "I feel like we were running late."

"We've just got here ourselves." Megan hugged her.

"We couldn't get Sara to settle at my parents' house, she really wanted to come with us. Said it wasn't fair that we get to spend the night with you and she doesn't."

"Tell her she can come to a JMC event next year and be a special guest of honour."

"You want a five-year-old running around and being demanding?" Nick said, more sarcastically than he expected to be.

"If Sara was there, that would make two of them."

"Two?" Megan began, then twigged. "Oh, Owen."

"And that's one of the many reasons I'm marrying her."

They entered the castle, were greeted by the doormen, and made their way to the main bar where Aidan insisted on starting a tab for the night. Since they were dressed up to the nines, Megan decided that beer wasn't the most glamourous choice of drink. She was wearing Dolce, she and Lydia would stick to Prosecco. Never had she seen Aidan pull a disgusted face over a drink choice, showing his wealth and status so publically, but at the mere mention of Prosecco, he turned to the barman and demanded his best champagne for the evening, and to keep it flowing.

It looked like the whole town had turned up for the party, including the town's Mayor and his wife. They rushed over to Aidan when they saw him, to say how lovely it was to see him back home and that they would be honoured if he'd say a few words—since Aidan was the town's most successful resident.

"Really, I'm here to enjoy the evening with my fiancée and friends. I'm not working tonight."

"Aidan, you're an inspiration to the youth of Farnham." The mayor complimented him. "A speech from you at this time of year could do wonders for the students."

"Are you trying to persuade me by using education?"

"Come on, Aid! Doesn't have to be too long." Nick tried to encourage him. "Look at Mayor Harper's face, you'd make his year."

Aidan looked at Megan and could tell that she was thinking the same as Nick. She raised her eyebrows at him in a dare, giving him a secret message. *Do it, and I'll reward you later.*

"Okay, but just a short one."

"Great." Mayor Harper dragged him up to the stage.

"Own the room, baby!" Megan shouted at him, knowing that after the speech he gave at the JMC Christmas conference—which was made up on the spot—this would be a walk in the park.

"Ladies and Gents," the Mayor began. The crowd quieted. "Thank you for coming out tonight and for helping to support the hospital's charity for improvements by buying your ticket to this New Year's Eve party." Everyone cheered and clapped for one another. "I was going to give a little speech about our town, but that was before I ran into someone unexpected, who has a little more experience doing this sort of thing than I. I've just managed to persuade him to say a few words. If there is anyone this town should feel proud to call one of their own, it's our very own CEO, Aidan Costello."

Taking his cue, Aidan walked up onto to the stage, back in boss mode. Megan could tell he had his barriers back up from the way he was holding himself and shaking the Mayor's extended hand. The crowd sounded their approval of the guest speaker.

"Thanks, that was a little more than I deserved."

Mayor Harper shook his head, laughing in denial.

"You know, usually I have some idea what to say at these things, but when you are put on the spot like this, it takes some digging for inspiration to hit. But don't worry, I'll get there. What's more amusing—and those three down there will like this—is that trying to find the right words to say to you all is more nerve-wrecking than giving my end of year JMC speech! Don't repeat that to Owen, Megan."

Everyone laughed, feeling like they were connecting with him on a down-to-earth level.

Aidan looked around the room, feeling the pressure of the last minute speech disappearing. Megan smiled at him, and as he looked back at the woman he loved, he had no trouble finding the right words to say to his hometown. This wasn't the JMC party and he certainly wasn't in his conference rooms, so he was going to make the most of feeling at home. He was going to be Aidan—nothing more and nothing less.

"Living in the heart of the city is great, being blessed to be able to afford a place in the city is even better, but it doesn't match the feeling of coming back home, here, where I grew up, being greeted by each and every one of you. This town has always felt, to me, like a community filled with warmth and friendly people, ready to make you feel welcomed from whatever walk of life you come. Like when Meg and I attended the Christmas Fete this year. Feel I need to apologise for not coming down as often as I should. Sorry, Nick!"

Nick yelled his acceptance back at him.

"But you welcomed her into the town with open arms, no questions asked. That meant a lot, thank you. Megan said to me that evening that she felt more at home here than back in her own hometown. Another great example of how amazing you guys are is your dedication to a needed cause."

Aidan raised his arm to point at the picture of the town's hospital. "How many of you, here right now, have had to visit the hospital for anything? I know I have, many times! No need to shout out why, just a show of hands will do."

Near enough the whole room raised a hand to his question, including Aidan himself.

"So pretty much everyone. You're all here to show your support of the hard work the medical staff provides. I think that means you all deserve a round of applause yourselves." Aidan started the applause off, quickly followed by the Mayor and then everyone else in attendance. "How much has been raised for the hospital so far?" Aidan asked, when the roar died down a little.

"Well, tickets were twenty pounds each, and we sold around two hundred–"

"So near four grand then?"

The Mayor nodded in agreement.

Aidan turned to look at Megan before continuing. "Hmm, and let's say the charity wanted to make a big change to the hospital to make a difference to everyone's lives, how much more do you think they'd need?"

"Oh, I don't know–"

"Fifty grand do it for now?" Aidan held his hand out.

People cheered and cried in emotion, as Mayor Harper pulled Aidan in to thank him for such a generous donation. "I-I ... don't know what to say. This is unbelievable! Thank you."

"Don't thank me. When Meg and I start a family, I'd like to make sure our kids are in the best hands here," Aidan said quietly to him, before turning his attention back to the crowd to wish them all a fantastic night.

Jumping down from the stage, he made his way back over to Megan through the crowds as they expressed their thanks.

Wiping tears away from her eyes, she hugged his arm. "How do you manage to reduce me to tears like that? I thought the conference speech was emotional."

Nick threw his arms around him. "Dude, you didn't have to do that."

"Well, I did." He laughed. "Think of it as... supporting your career."

The evening's entertainment continued, including auctions for experience days to help raise money, and soon the DJ was playing a mixture of classic tracks. Aidan watched Megan dance with Lydia as people approached him, wanting to talk and ask if they could have a photo with him. Turning his attention back to his fiancée, he found it hard to concentrate on what people were saying to him.

She gestured him over when she felt his gaze, and he happily joined her on the dance floor, excusing himself from the growing crowd around him.

"Excuse me, my fiancée needs me." He smiled at Megan, knowing she'd appreciate the sarcasm. He wrapped his arms around her waist. "Thank you."

"Being nagged?"

"More like not leaving him alone, Meg," Nick said. He was beside them, dancing with Lydia.

"And they say I don't have an off switch?" Aidan lifted her up, kissing her in the middle of the dance floor. "It's worse than being in London."

"Aidan? I haven't seen you in years! Loved your speech, very touching." A woman approached him, not giving a damn that he was trying to have a private moment. "Samantha! Uh, hi, how have you been?"

"Good as can be." She laughed. "Married with a teenager. How about you? This must be Megan?"

"That's right." Megan greeted her, feeling Aidan's awkwardness towards this woman who she imagined was an old friend.

"Wow, teenager... way to make us feel old."

"Yeah, hasn't given me the best chance to leave the town. But he's at Uni now, so I'm enjoying the freedom while he's in the city. So what are you up to?"

Aidan gave her a look that answered her question without the need for words.

"Oh, silly me, busy with JMC?"

Aidan nodded. "Among other things."

"It would be nice to meet up, maybe, for coffee or something while you're both back? Or perhaps when we come to the city to visit Marc at Uni? It has been too long."

"Oh, um, yeah."

"You know, Marc actually just began studying Advance Computing at King's College this year. It would be great to be able to introduce you to him. He really looks up to you, being from Farnham and all. That's not far from Canary Wharf, right?"

Megan stepped in, getting a feeling that Aidan wasn't sure how to dismiss the directness of her question. "Aidan's pretty tied down with his work right now, but I'm sure if Marc asked, Aid could, I don't know, drop him an email with a supportive message?"

Aidan squeezed her waist in thanks, smiling at Samantha at the same time.

"That would mean the world to him."

"Samantha?" her husband called from the bar.

"Excuse me, duty calls. Lovely to see you. Nick, Lydia."

"Samantha." Nick waved awkwardly.

Aidan sighed. "Didn't think she'd ever leave."

"You were with her for two years, right? Or was it three?"

"Thanks, Nick Really, thanks." Aidan smacked his arm.

"So that's why she seemed like she was about to pounce on you," Megan said.

He turned, grabbing her arm without looking back. "Outside, now."

***

The air outside was full of frost—the type of air that means numb toes and pink faces. Aidan was feeling more than exposed after being harassed to give a speech, but that surprise visit from his ex tipped him over the edge. It was nice to breathe in the cool air; to enjoy it with no one but his darling fiancée.

Megan broke the silence. "Are we hiding from everyone out here, or just your ex?"

Aidan filled their glasses with more champagne. "Both, but it's also a nice way to end the year. Alone, where no one can annoy us." He passed her the glass. "I feel like that won't be the last we see of Samantha. Remind me to upgrade security at JMC."

Megan turned to face him, slipping a hand under his jacket. "Do you want me to make a scene so she won't come back?"

"Why do I have a sneaking suspicion that you want to call it a night?"

She shrugged. "Maybe spending the last hour of the year at home—alone—would be nicer than having to deal with everyone wanting to speak with you, or wanting a photo."

Aidan pulled her into him again, dialling the number of the taxi firm that had dropped them off a few hours ago. "Best say goodnight to Nick and Lydia, though... Yeah hi, taxi as soon as you can from Farnham Castle, please? Excellent, thanks." He hung up. "Ten minutes. Come on."

Picking up the bottle of champagne, Aidan escorted Megan back into the castle to bid goodnight to their friends. The gathering had grown, with late arrivals filling the dance floor. Aidan carefully placed a hand on each of the backs that were stopping them from getting to their destination. He did it in a way that the dancer didn't turn around and cause them more delay by wanting a photo with him. Or another longer than expected chat about JMC.

Megan, holding his hand tight, spotted Nick and Lydia near the back of the dance floor, catching up with another friend.

"You're going? Now? Dude! Is this because of your ex?" A now more-than-tipsy Nick asked, hugging him.

"No!"

"Babe," Lydia removed her husband from around Aidan's shoulders, "if they want to go, let them go."

Aidan paid the bill at the bar, then turned to Lydia to give her more than enough cash for the remainder of the evening, even though she protested. "Come by the house on the second so we can see Sara before heading back to the city," he said.

Nick nodded. "Sure. I'll call you."

***

The roads were virtually empty by the time the taxi picked them up. The only sign of civilisation was the occasional drunk group of friends cheering and chanting songs—like they were reliving their younger years—at the top of their lungs. They were home within minutes. Aidan paid the driver, handing over more cash than expected, and wished him an incredible New Year. The driver couldn't believe his luck, and the great end to his year.

Megan was already in the kitchen opening up a couple of beers when Aidan joined her, after closing and locking the front door. He watched her for a moment, then grabbed her hand and dragged her out to the back garden.

Turning on the lights which illuminated the pool and gazebo, he turned to face her, loving the glow of the lights on her face.

"If that was hot right now, I'd jump in."

Megan looked down at the pool. "How cold is it?" She looked back at him with mischief in her eyes.

"You're not, not in that dress."

"Fine." She placed her beer down and slipped out of the dress and jumped in, wearing nothing but her underwear, and not giving a damn that it was cold.

Aidan burst out laughing.

"Mr. Costello, you're needed in the water."

He took a long sip of beer. Removing his Armani suit, he joined her to spend the last few moments of the year in the pool together. "Fuck, this is freezing. If you're thinking what I'm thinking, there's not a chance in hell. Not when it's this cold."

"Hot shower after, then?" Megan suggested, laughing, swimming up to him as the bells of the local church sang for the New Year.

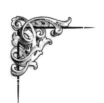

Chapter 41

Aidan had only been reading through their findings for five minutes, but already he shook his head and picked up the phone to call his legal department. "Si, cut any ties that have been made with Norfolk." He hung up before Simon Reynolds, his head lawyer, had a chance to ask why. "Bastards! I knew something was up."

Clive hadn't told Aidan the truth about Norfolk. They hadn't been in financial difficulties—they were hitting their targets—but instead thought they would see how long they could string JMC along; see if they were a possible target to take advantage of.

How wrong they had been; they were about to hear all about the discovery of their dishonesty from a more-than-annoyed CEO.

Aidan looked at Owen as he dialled the number. "Don't even think about hugging me."

Emma had to try hard to hold her laugh in. "I'll give you guys a moment. Coffee?"

"Please! I'll try and keep him as calm as I can."

Emma left the room just as she heard Aidan's temper hit the roof. Her phone sounded a text from Owen when she got to the lift.

GIVE IT ABOUT HALF AN HOUR, THIS MAY TAKE A WHILE! MAKE AID'S EXTRA STRONG.

***

Megan entered the JMC building after catching the underground to Canary Wharf. She had left the apartment more than an hour ago, stopping by their favourite coffee house in Borough Market to pick up a treat for Aidan. She couldn't face the fact that he was at work, getting more and more stressed, so knew the stop off would be worth it. The tube journey was only around ten minutes from the market so the drink was sure to be the perfect temperature by the time she got to JMC.

Andrew, Aidan's head of security, was at the door when she arrived. He opened the door, wishing her a good afternoon.

"Hi, Andy." Walking up to the reception desk, she smiled. "Afternoon, Patrick. Is he upstairs?"

"Hey, Meg. Yeah, should be. Do you want me to call?"

"It's ok. He's expecting me."

The doors opened to reveal Owen rubbing his head. He looked over to see who was getting out the lift and was relieved when he saw Megan. "I've never been happier to see you, Meg. You're probably the only one who can sort his temper out right now. He's this close," Owen held his hand up, his thumb and index finger millimeters apart, "to getting on a plane to New York."

"Where is he?"

Owen pointed towards Aidan's office.

She opened the door and looked around the room before she spotted him. He was spread out on the sofa with his feet up, trying his absolute best to calm down. Putting the two cups of coffee down on his desk, she dropped her bag. She took her jacket off and swung the door shut with her foot.

"Oh, what now?" Aidan's voice was just shy of booming.

Megan could hear the anger in his voice—she'd felt it before he even spoke.

Kneeling down, she leant over him and moved his arm. He blinked rapidly a couple of times as the light hit them, and then froze when he saw her face.

"Now, that is no way to speak to your fiancée."

Aidan lifted his head. She saw the stress of the day in his eyes before he pulled her into a crushing embrace.

"Now, tell me, how will flying to America help this situation?"

He groaned.

"That's not an answer, Aidan."

"Which one of them told you?"

"Both of them, and they are equally worried about you." She let her eyes soften a little. "Sweetheart, I'm so sorry."

"No need to be sorry, Meg. They'll never get near us again—legal will make sure of that. I'm just fucked off with myself that I didn't spot it sooner."

Megan stroked the side of his head which instantly helped him relax. Satisfied she'd managed to calm him down a bit, she stood up to fetch his coffee.

He gratefully accepted.

Sitting next to him, she stroked his arm. "Okay, tell me all about it."

Aidan opened up quicker than she expected, telling her about what the security firm had found out about Norfolk. Once he'd shared everything with her and showed her the investigation notes, he leant his head on her shoulder and sighed.

"Got much on this afternoon?" she asked.

"No idea."

"Maybe we can get an earlier dinner, catch a movie?"

Aidan stood up to check the daily schedule on his desktop computer. "Lois?" "Yeah," she said through the intercom.

"Hold everything until tomorrow."

"What about the interview with the magazine this afternoon?"

"They can wait. If they really want it, they'll reschedule. Email the new time when you have it, thanks." He picked up Megan's coat and bag. "Come on."

"Another one? What's this interview for?"

"Just a magazine that wants to focus on JMC, and where we're going as a company this year. Nothing exciting."

Leaving the office, Megan caught Owens eye, and winked to signal to him that all was ok again.

"Thank you," He mouthed back.

***

Sitting on the floor with his back against the sofa, now dressed in just joggers, Aidan was enjoying the shoulder rub Megan had promised him on the drive home. He felt like he could fall asleep, but the sensation didn't last long.

His eyes flew wide open when Megan screamed in excitement.

"Holy shitting hell!" he said, sighing loudly.

"Ben and Martin are coming up!"

She called Ben and put her mobile on speaker phone so she could continue rubbing Aidan's shoulders. She felt him ease up again.

"Afternoon, stranger," Ben said, answering after the first ring.

"Ben! I'm so excited that you guys can come up."

"Us too, Meg. It's been what, six months?"

"Hardly, more like three."

"Still ... long enough. We've missed you, Meg. Are you ever coming back down to visit? Em, Lucy, and their chaps managed it. What's your excuse?"

"I know, I know. We'll get down eventually—maybe when Aid's not so busy." Aidan nodded in agreement. They should visit her home town when they got the time.

"I'll hold you to that promise, sweetheart. Your old room's still empty, so you can both stay here."

"Thanks."

"So, regarding finding you the perfect dress."

"I'm not speaking about designs now, Ben, Aidan's here."

"Hi Ben," Aidan greeted him, sounding more sleepy than he intended.

"Hello to you, too. Has Meg drugged you?"

"Benjamin!" Megan laughed.

"It's ok," Aidan reassured him, "been a bit of a stressful day."

"Megan? Are you taking care of your tired fiancé? Actually, forget that. I'm sure you are. We'll be up the day after tomorrow, if that suits?"

"Absolutely. Call me when you're close, we can meet you at the station and go on from there."

"Of course. I can't wait to see you. Love you, Meg."

"Love you, Ben." Megan hung up, and looked down at Aidan who was looking back up at her, his head resting on the sofa cushion.

"What does Martin teach?"

"Something close to your line of work." Megan leant down and kissed his head. "Now, regarding your stress levels. Are you feeling more relaxed, or do you need some more attention?"

"I always need more of your attention, Meg."

"Well, you have me for life, so you can have all the attention you want."

"Fantastic!" Aidan pushed her back on the sofa as she let out a scream of laughter.

Chapter 42

"Thanks, Lois. I told you they'd change with no issues. I'll be back in the office later this afternoon, but I'll be available on my mobile all day. Cheers." Aidan hung up.

Lois had, as promised, contacted him with the time change for the interview the following day, which had been rescheduled for after lunch. He'd not long hung up, when the phone rang again.

"Yeah... hey Simon."

Megan ran downstairs, thinking she was making them late for the appointment Aidan had organised with the garage. Seeing him on the phone, again, she picked up her bag and his suit jacket and waited for him to finish the call. Even though he was about to spend the majority of the day out of the office, it didn't mean he wasn't working. He would answer every phone call, respond to every email, and check in with Owen when he could, despite running around the city.

"Yeah, hang on, hang on." Aidan covered the mouth piece. "Meg, let's head out while I chat, this could take a while."

Megan nodded, grabbing his car keys and locking the door behind them as he carried on the conversation with his head of legal.

Once in the car, Aidan connected his phone to the media console so he could carry on the conversation with Simon as they drove to Stratford. "Tell them that under no circumstances are they to try and make contact with JMC again, Simon. I'm not going to explain it to them more than once."

"Aidan, they're saying they feel hard done by."

"Who's saying that?"

"Clive, the lawyer that dealt with the original contract. He called as soon as I broke ties, like you asked, and demanded to speak with you to explain."

"Explain what? Why they were trying to fuck us over, or that they're sorry they got caught?"

"Beats me, he only wants to speak to you."

"He'll have a long wait before I even think about picking up the phone to him, Simon. Once again, email back and tell them there is not a chance in hell they're getting anywhere near us, or me!"

"Certainly, Aidan. Can I add a couple of legal threats in there to give them a scare?"

"Sure, go ahead. Be sure to copy me into the email." Aidan hung up. "Sorry baby, that took a little longer than expected."

"They're still trying to make amends with you?"

Aidan pulled into the Mercedes garage he always used, and could already see the salesman waiting for them. "Trying and failing."

They exited the car. Aidan slammed the door with force. Clearly he was still carrying a lot of tension.

When Aidan suggested they go car shopping for her, she imagined the dealership would be as pristine as JMC. Clean, white, sparkling tiled floors. That certainly wasn't what she was seeing. The garage, home to thousands of pounds worth of horse power, looked like it could do with a lick of paint. And someone had to have a word with the manager about the weeds that creeped through the paving slabs.

Aidan caught her pulling a disgusted face, and couldn't help laughing. "It's not about the look of the place, Megan. It's how good the service is." He smiled at the man who approached them. "And our loyal salesman."

The salesman in question approached them. There was a wide grin on his face as he held his hand out.

"Mr. Costello, how nice to see you again."

Aidan shook his hand. "Nice to see me? Or nice to see my cash, Terry?"

Terry laughed. "Well, you know. Always a pleasure to fit you out with a new car." Aidan smiled and gestured towards her. "Terry, my fiancée, Megan."

"Ah, so this is the beauty they keep snapping you with. Good morning, my dear." He shook her outstretched hand. "Come, let's get this going, shall we?" He opened the entrance for them. "Please, after you."

Aidan let Megan go ahead of him. "Still black, Aidan?"

"Sorry?"

"Black coffee is it still?"

"Oh yeah, sorry. Meg? Latte?"

Megan nodded. Taking a seat on the sofas, she admired the beautiful cars around her.

Terry told them he would be back shortly with their coffees.

Megan couldn't help but notice the smiles and head tilts towards them from the sales team. She glanced back to Terry who was chatting with a colleague at the in dealership cafe.

He waved, holding up a pack of biscuits, which Aidan gave a thumbs up too.

"He seems to know you well."

"I always come to see Terry when it's time for a new car. He's the best."

Terry returned with the drinks, taking a seat on the sofa. "So, what can we do for you this time?" Terry began, slouching back, knowing full well that there would be a sale at the end of Aidan's visit.

***

The paint glowed beneath the showroom lights, looking more and more like a heartbeat with each step Megan took. The cars in here were so full of life, so full of energy and personality. She still couldn't believe her eyes. Terry stepped up beside her, nodding along. But it was Aidan she caught sight of. He was over in the corner on his phone, shaking his head disappointedly.

"Megan, I do believe that from your fiancé's shake of the head there, we're looking at the wrong cars."

She set off walking. Approaching Aidan, she pulled the phone away to see who was calling, to make sure she wasn't about to interrupt an important call. She smiled when she saw Owen's name. "Owen, Aidan will call you back in just a second."

"Huh?" Owen managed to say before she hung up.

Aidan stared at her in disbelief at what she had just done. He was speechless for once.

"What's with the disapproving looks, Aid?"

"I'm about to get told off aren't I?" he asked.

Megan nodded.

"Okay, but what's the point in looking at the used cars when Terry already knows that I'll end up ordering a new one?"

"He does have a point, Megan."

"Then why didn't you say that to start with? We could've saved so much time." Megan gasped when the penny dropped. "Omigosh. Are you both time wasting?"

Terry and Aidan exchanged a look, but Aidan answered. "I do have a lot to do Meg, and doing it here, rather than while we're driving around the city, makes life so much easier." He picked up another fresh coffee. "Plus, these are better than filling up on Starbucks."

Megan placed a hand on her hip and faced the salesman. "Terry? Are you in on this too?"

Terry didn't know where to look. He ran a hand through his hair. "Well, you know"

"Terry! You're as bad as Aidan and Owen put together!"

"Take that as a compliment, Terry. I would."

Laughter filled the Mercedes garage. "Okay, let's stop mucking around and get the car you want ordered." He smiled. "Usual extras is it, Aidan?"

"Absolutely, Terry. Need to be across town soon anyway."

***

Once Megan's new white convertible had been designed and the order put in place, Terry slid the documents over for Aidan to sign. After giving them a good checking over, he did just that. Nothing got past him. He dealt with new contracts and deals every day.

"If that's it, Terry," Aidan said, passing them back, "when should we expect your call?"

"Two to three weeks."

"Call my office in that case. Easier to get hold of me."

"Certainly, thanks again, Aidan."

"Don't thank me, you know that. We'll see you in a few weeks."

Megan smiled at Terry, waving goodbye to the other members of staff, who probably wished they were a CEO's favourite salesman so they could reap rewards of the commission.

"I'm not sure I'm going to be able to sleep through excitement. Thank you, sweetie."

"If you're not going to sleep, perhaps we should use the spare time for other activities."

"You're awful sometimes, you know that, right?" Megan said, as they got in his Mercedes.

"Hey, I'm buying you a car... think I deserve a little credit."

Chapter 43

M egan paid for an hour of parking and walked around the corner to climb the steps of the grand building in the heart of the city. She thought about the last time she was here. It felt like a life time ago, not a few months ago. She looked up at the entrance and smiled.

Approaching the escalator, she joined the busy crowd of travellers to see when the southwest train would be in. Platform three, and it was on time for once.

"Megan?" She heard the voice from across the train station.

"Ben!" She ran towards him, hugging him when he opened his arms to her. "Oh my God, I've missed you so much."

"Do you two always have to shout at each other?" Martin asked once he'd caught Ben up, rubbing his ear.

Megan hugged him. "Good to see you, Martin. Has my Ben been behaving?"

"What do you think?" Ben answered for him.

Megan had arranged for them to come up to London to shop for wedding dresses, as planned. Martin wasn't the shopping type, but he couldn't resist the trip when Megan told them they would be staying with her and Aidan. He was an IT tutor in the local college. The education system dictated that they used JMC's software on their computers, so the chance to personally meet the CEO of the company who provided the equipment for his students was exciting to say the least. Although he was busy with the New Year's teaching schedules, they'd managed to sneak a few days in to accept the invitation.

"Where's the main man?"

"At the office, Ben. I said we'd spin by to meet him at JMC before heading back to the apartment later."

"You drove? In what?"

Megan smiled, picturing Aidan's black Merc with its private plates. "Come and see."

***

With the music playing at full volume in the car, Ben rolled the back window down and gasped at what he saw. There it was, the JMC building in all its glory.

Megan stopped the car by the front and let them stare at it in amazement. She turned the volume down and smiled when she saw Martin's bewildered face. Slowly, he took his phone out his bag and snapped a picture.

With the sun beginning to set, its golden glow reflected in the glass panels, making the building even more impressive. Tom had certainly outdone himself when he designed it. Even in the rain and gloomy weather, it still managed to look stunning.

Sending Aidan a message to let him know she'd parked up outside, they all got out to look around the area. Megan decided not to drive the car down to the garage; they weren't planning on being there long.

"This is incredible, never thought I'd ever see the JMC building with my own two eyes," Martin said more to himself, taking another photo for his students.

"Is it weird," Ben up looked at the building, "that I'm feeling nervous now that I'm here?"

Megan frowned. "Why?"

"Well, we're about to meet not only my best friend's fiancé, but a famous, well-known, powerful businessman. Who wouldn't be nervous?"

Megan shook her head. "You have no need to be worried, Ben. Aidan is just like everyone else. Besides, you've already spoken to him on the phone. He may have the big career title, but he's more down to earth than you'd expect." Megan looked into the ground floor of the building. "So suck it up, because he's in the reception now."

Aidan came out the front of the building after having a quick discussion with Patrick.

Megan's heartrate increased, seeing him in her favourite tailor-made, black Dolce and Gabbana suit. He looked like a movie star who had just stepped on to the red carpet to greet his adoring fans. His fans being his future wife and her close friends.

"My goodness." Ben admired him. "Would you take a look at that view."

"Hun, I am right here you know. But I will admit, you've done well there, Meg," Martin said. "The guy responsible for all the equipment we use at the college." He felt a little star-struck. "Dear Lord."

Aidan spotted his fiancée and sent her a smile that charmed all three of them. She threw his keys and he caught them mid-air. He looked down at his feet as he walked and ran a hand through his hair, roughing it up now he was out of the office. Ben sighed, not even hiding the fact that he was checking him out in front of his boyfriend. Aidan noticed the attention he was getting, but was more interested in scooping Megan up in his arms.

Megan kissed him. "Hey, how's your day been?"

"Not bad, nothing exciting to report." He snapped his fingers, starting to laugh. "Except some office banter. Jimmy sent an email to Patrick earlier, asking him out for a drink. And not in a heterosexual way."

"Hasn't Patrick got a girlfriend?"

"Yeah, but that's not the worst part. He managed to send it to everyone. Poor guy's humiliated."

"Oh poor Jimmy. I'll drop him a message later asking if he's ok"

Aidan turned his attention to the two men who were standing aside, not knowing what to do. "So, this is the famous Ben I keep hearing about? Nice to finally meet you, Ben."

"Hi, Aidan."

Aidan shook his hand before turning to shake Martin's. "Martin?"

Martin nodded, slightly nervous at meeting such a big role model for his students.

"How exactly do you keep these two in line? I've heard some crazy stories from Emma and Lucy."

"I've been trying to figure out that same question for years." Martin was unable to hide his smile. "It's an honour to meet you."

"The feeling is mutual," Aidan said. "Right, let's get out of here before the media have a field day. Damn vultures are crawling all over the place.

Chapter 44

"Are you sure no one will mind?" Martin asked for probably the fourth time, standing at the foot of JMC, looking up.

After the initial greetings, and feeling like the lads were going to be as close as he and Nick, Aidan had offered Martin an exclusive tour of his building.

Since the reason for their visit was for Ben to help Megan hunt out the perfect wedding dress, Martin jumped on the opportunity. He wasn't much of a shopper like his boyfriend was. His students' minds were sure to blow when he told them where he had spent the past couple of days.

"Martin, I own the whole building," he held the door open for him, "so, yes, I'm sure no one will mind. Think of it as a fieldtrip to gather knowledge to take back to your students; you'll be the most popular tutor on campus."

"Morning, Mr. Costello." Patrick greeted them.

Aidan smirked at him. "Patrick."

"Don't." He confidently warned his boss. "Just don't."

"Wasn't going to mention a thing." Aidan leant on the front desk. "Tell your girlfriend?"

Patrick signed. "Yes, she thought it was hilarious. And everyone's been asking if I'm going to take up the offer."

"Well... are you?"

Patrick gave him a look that could kill.

"Can definitely tell you studied law. Anyway Pat, I need you to get me one of those passes for the building. We've got a special guest today, so set it up for all-access please?"

Patrick did as his boss asked, and handed him the security pass.

"Thank you. On a different note, how's it going spending some days in legal?"

"Brilliant. Simon's included me on the latest contract signings, and should be getting my review done in a couple weeks."

"Great news, I'll make sure I'm there. Email the date and time."

They rode the lift to the top floor. Aidan set a couple of rules, mainly not to wonder down to legal, since they were still fixing the issue with the New York office. The lift pinged and the doors parted.

"Morning."

"Morning, Aidan," Lois said, looking up from her computer screen.

"Someone's chirpy today—usually a good sign that deals will go ahead," Owen said.

"Martin, this is Owen—Tom's brother, who I believe Megan said you met at Christmas?"

"Nice to meet you, Martin." Owen shook his hand. "Hope my brother was on his best behaviour?"

"Pretty sure your brother and Kev were more shocked into silence seeing the amount the girls and Ben drank, to be honest."

"Tom? Silent?" Owen laughed. "Never thought I'd see the day."

Aidan nodded towards Lois. "And Lois, my PA, and mother to us all."

"Hello Martin." Lois shook his hand.

"Martin's an IT tutor for a college that we provide the software for. Since Meg and Ben are shopping today, I've offered him a tour."

"It's an absolute honour to just be in the building, let alone the top floor. Really, I can't tell you how excited the students will be."

"Get a selfie in Aid's office chair, they'll love that," Owen said.

Aidan and Martin's eyes lit up at the thought of it.

"Oh God! You're going do it, aren't you?"

**

Megan was trying on a dress behind a velvet curtain in one of the wedding dress shops that had been shortlisted by Ben. The boutique had closed their doors to anyone else after receiving the news that Aidan Costello's fiancée was visiting them to try on wedding dresses.

"So tell me again... your mum actually emailed you back over Christmas?"

"Yeah, and it's like we've not had that massive gap, you know? We've just carried on like before the divorce. Not heard from Dad yet, though. I left my number on the email, so the ball's in his court now." She pushed hard against the tight fabric but the dress wouldn't budge. "Oh God, Ben? I'm scared I'm going to rip this. I don't think this dress is the one. Oh no, there we go!"

"And you've been in contact ever since? Have you told Em and Lucy?"

"Em and Lucy have had a brief rundown, but nothing as in depth as what I'm telling you. Aidan and I thought it best to keep the majority of it between us for now."

Megan came out of the dressing room smirking, trying not to laugh at the dress they'd thought looked stunning on the hanger.

"Oh, baby girl. That's, umm, pretty ... might be a bit big, though?" Ben held his arms wide in a meringue gesture. Megan couldn't contain her laughter.

"So, something a little sleeker?" The saleslady asked.

"Yes, I think so. I can't imagine Aidan being able to keep a straight face if I walked to him in this. As beautiful as it is."

"Do you have anything that doesn't scream typical bridal dress maybe? Something classy with a vintage twist, perhaps?" Ben asked. "We have some Anna Campbell in?"

"Perfect! If we could try some of hers please? Thank you."

Megan went back into the dressing room to await the arrival of the next dress. She heard Ben's voice through the curtain.

"Darling? Are you going to try and contact your Dad again before you get married? You know, to have someone to give you away."

"I don't think so, Ben. He's not responded to my attempts to contact him in the last few years. Besides, I was hoping that maybe someone else would walk me down the aisle?" Megan hinted, coming out in a vintage laced dress, wearing a beaming smile.

Ben stared at her, smiling also. "Megan, it's beautiful. You look gorgeous. Aidan will love it." He stood and turned her around to hold her hair up, which showed off her neck line.

The saleslady sniffed. "Stunning, simply stunning. Not many ladies can pull these dresses off, but it's like it's been made for you. And believe me, I don't say that to many brides."

Megan smiled and raised her shoulders. "I think I've found my wedding dress. And a lot quicker than I thought I would, too." She hugged her friend. "Ben?"

"Yes, sweetheart."

"Will you give me away please? You've been there for me for a long time now. I can't imagine anyone more perfect for the job."

"Megan, sweetie, I'd be honoured, thank you." He hugged her. "Does this mean I get to give Aidan the father-to-future husband chat?"

They both laughed. Megan nodded.

"Fabulous! Right, accessories and shoes!"

***

After Megan and Ben had finalised the order on her wedding dress and hit a few more high street shops, Megan messaged Aidan saying they would meet for dinner in Bank rather than coming all way over to JMC. They found a barbeque smokehouse near London Bridge, requesting a table for four near the back of the restaurant, and waited for Aidan and Martin to join them. The pair arrived at five-thirty, laughing and chatting like long-lost friends catching up over the years gone by.

Megan sent a text to Emma, Lucy, and Clare saying that she and Ben had found the dress and that the plans were—if you didn't count setting a date and finding a venue—going well. Every time she thought about the fact that she would soon be Mrs. Megan Victoria Costello, she beamed with excitement.

"I always worry when she smiles like that after texting the girls," Aidan said. "So how'd it go? Find anything?"

"That's for Megan, myself, and the ladies to know." Ben nudged her, beaming a smile.

"That's a yes, then."

Megan put her phone away. "Ben has made me swear not to say anything, so ask all you want, darling, I'm not saying a word. How was your trip around JMC, Martin? Did Aidan and Owen behave themselves?"

Aidan gave her an innocent look.

"Oh please, don't try looking innocent."

Martin began telling them about his day, and how he managed to sort out an IT glitch while he was there, which Aidan was extremely grateful for.

"Guy knows his stuff." He looked at Martin. "Wish half of IT were as knowledgeable as you. Why aren't you in a consultancy job, making big bucks?"

Ben looked at his boyfriend, nodding, also wondering why.

"The students really," Martin said. "They make my day interesting."

"Can't say fairer than that. Tell you what, because you helped out today, why don't you tell the college principle that the CEO has granted access for your students to have an educational day out? Bring them up to Canary Wharf to see how it's done in the real world."

"That would be incredible. Thank you." Martin looked at Megan. "Megan, you're marrying a good one here."

Aidan took her hand under the table and gave it a squeeze.

"You'll be okay with about twenty-odd students running around the building?"

Aidan nodded, smiling at Ben. "Yeah, it'll stress Owen out."

"See, they are always at it, misbehaving." Megan pointed to her fiancé. "Just wait until you see what they are like when they're with Tom and Kev."

Martin looked surprised. "They seemed like wonderfully charming guys when they came down."

"Probably on best behaviour to meet Emma and Lucy's parents." Aidan laughed.

"Tom and charming doesn't sound right. Kev, I can see it. But Tom? No way!"

"I'm not sure myself and the other ladies will cope with all six of y—"

"Don't forget Nick, sweetheart," Aidan reminded her.

"Oh for the love of... *seven* of you, all together."

Chapter 45

That afternoon, Aidan sat watching a movie with his feet up on the coffee table, while Megan spoke with her mum via Skype in the office. They'd spoken quite a few times now, and even Aidan had been involved in a couple of the chats. Diane Ashton was a sweet, caring, loving woman, and it was clear that Megan was her world.

Why she hadn't stayed in contact with her daughter, neither Megan nor Aidan could tell. He'd do anything to have one more conversation with his mother. Megan had told her mum stories of how she and Aidan met, the engagement, and how she would love it if Diane could fly back from Australia to be there for the wedding. He was happy they were growing stronger again, but to him, it was a reminder of what she had been through during the darker times of her life.

Megan's mobile started ringing on the coffee table.

"Meg? Your mobile's ringing, shall I get it?" he yelled in the direction of the office.

He heard a faint response shouting back.

"Hello?" Aidan said, still watching the movie.

"Oh? Have I got the wrong number?" a male voice said from the other end. It had the slightest hint of an American accent. "I do apologise, I was trying to reach Mega—"

"This is Megan Ashton's phone, but she's busy at the minute. Can I help?"

"Oh okay, good. And you are?"

"Her fiancé." Aidan looked at the screen, wondering who he was speaking with.

"Aidan?"

"Yep."

The man on the other end sounded nervous. "I'm, umm, Marcus, Megan's Father." He paused for a long moment. "I believe she's been trying to reach me?"

Aidan was seeing red. *Believe she's been trying to reach you. Believe? Yeah, she's been trying to reach you! What dad doesn't try and mend a relationship with his only daughter? At least her mum's giving it a good shot.*

Instead he took a deep breath; this was his future father-in-law after all. "Yes, she has. For quite a while now, if I understand. But like I said, she's currently busy on a Skype call. Would you like me to leave her a message?"

"If it's not too much trouble?"

Not too much trouble? Not too much... I'd love to get my hands on you right now.

"If you would be so kind as to let her know I called, and that I'll try her again later, I'd be most grateful."

Aidan tried to sound friendly, but was struggling to contain his anger. "Hmm. Anything else?"

"Umm, how is she? Is she happy?"

"Happy as she'll ever be."

"Good, good. Please can you tell her also that I'm sorry? Sorry for what we did, sorry for the lies, the fighting, and covering up the truth."

That's more like it, but hang on... lies? What lies?

"I'll make sure Megan gets the message as soon as she's free."

"Thank you."

Rubbing his eyes and running his hand through his already misplaced hair, Aidan hung up. Something didn't feel right. It was the same feeling he'd gotten when he figured out that the Norfolk Computers were pulling a fast one. He stood and went to Megan.

He needed to hold her. She was the only one who could instantly calm him down. Kneeling down beside her, he wrapped his arms around her waist, and greeted the light-haired, brown-eyed woman on the screen.

"Hi, Diane."

Megan looked down at Aidan and could tell something was bothering him. "Hi Aidan, stressful day?"

America to Australia—it was like he'd just flown around the globe. "No, no, just a bit exhausted. How's life? All good?"

"Can't complain. Making amends with my daughter; happy to see she's being well taken care of... things are looking up. Are you sure you're okay? Because Megan's giving you such a look."

Aidan met the stare of Megan's green eyes and could see that Diane was telling the truth. He didn't want to tell either of them who he had just spoken with on the phone. He couldn't imagine it going down very well.

"Mum, I'm gonna go, see if I can figure out whatever it is that's eating him up. I'll call you in a couple of days, ok?"

"Of course, sweetheart. Take care of each other, won't you? Love you."

She hung up and turned to face Aidan. "What's wrong?"

Aidan stood and turned. He pointed to where her phone was. "Just had a nice chat with your dad."

"What? From no responses to hearing from the both of them? Aidan, this is great!"

She shot off in the direction of her mobile to check that it wasn't a joke. Searching her call history, she hovered over the American number.

"Megan," Aidan took her hand before she pressed the call button, "believe me, please, when I say that something doesn't feel right. He said something about covering up the truth?"

Megan frowned. "I'm sure it's just to do with the break up, it'll be fine."

Aidan wasn't convinced. He had a growing feeling that she was about to be hurt, and nothing on God's earth would stop him from hunting down the person who broke her heart.

Megan smiled at him. She hit call and held the phone to her ear.

"Hello?"

"Dad."

"Megan! My God, it's good to hear your voice. Your fiancé passed on my message? Congratulations, by the way. He said you were on another call?"

"Yes, Aidan said you'd called, I was talking with Mum, in Australia." Marcus sighed at the mention of his ex-wife.

"Dad, I've tried for so long to get in contact with you. Are you even in Seattle still?"

"We moved to New Jersey, about a year ago."

"We?" Megan looked at Aidan with a concerned look in her eyes. He moved to stand next to her in an instant. She turned on the speakerphone so they could hear, and leant on her hands as she asked a question she wasn't sure she wanted the answer to. "Who's we?"

Marcus took a long breath. "That's one of the reasons I called you, Megan. You need to know what happened and why we distanced ourselves from you."

"What is it that you need to tell me, Dad? Why have you waited this long? I thought I'd done something to hurt you both."

"No, no. You didn't do anything, Megan. It was us. We're to blame. Well me, actually. It feels wrong not telling you this face to face. What's your Skype? That'll have to do."

Megan gave him her details and ended the call. She turned to the flat screen TV, booting up Skype on there. "I'm nervous, Aid, I have a sinking feeling. You may have been right about something feeling weird."

Aidan held her and kissed her forehead. "I'm right here for you, baby."

The call came in. Megan took a deep breath and answered it. Aidan moved aside so he was just out of shot. Known as the smart businessman in the media, he didn't think it was wise to meet her father in jogging trousers, a t-shirt, and messy hair.

"Megan, goodness, you look more beautiful than I remember. Are you alone?" Megan's dad looked old and tired, like he'd been without sleep for at least a month. His white hair was getting thin and his green eyes looked like they were turning grey. Age wasn't on his side.

"Aidan's with me and he's not going anywhere. What is it you need to tell me? You're making me nervous."

"You've been speaking with Diane?"

"Yes, with Mum. She's doing well, by the way. Why do you ask?"

Marcus looked to the side, as if someone was with him.

"Dad, seriously! What's going on?" Megan was starting to feel agitated because of his stalling.

"I've got someone here with me who wants to meet you, Megan."

He gestured for whoever it was to come into view. Megan stared at the woman sitting next to him.

"What is this? Who is she?"

"My darling girl, this is Katherine, my wife."

"You remarried!" Megan screamed. She turned away from the camera, catching Aidan's eye. "And you're telling me this now? Did it slip your mind to mention this to your daughter? Oh yeah, sorry, being in contact wasn't at the top of your priorities."

"Megan, please, there's more."

"More?"

Marcus took Katherine's hand and gave it a reassuring squeeze. The world fell silent all at once, awaiting the return of his voice.

"She's your mother, Megan. Katherine is your biological mother."

Chapter 46

Ignoring the message for the fourth time, Megan put her phone back on the table and continued to admire the view of the island from the poolside. Aidan had called a friend, who owned a private villa in Rhodes, to see if it would be possible to spend a week there. He had connections and friends in high places, so he could usually guarantee that they'd do him a favour here and there.

Getting to the Greek island didn't seem to be a problem either. Aidan hadn't thought to mention that JMC had its own private jet, and the look he'd gotten from Megan when she saw it was priceless.

"To be honest, I don't even know why we have it. I always fly BA."

During the flight, they'd spoken about the moment they first saw each other at the bar, laughed at Aidan's drink requests, and how they really should go back to visit the food market. They'd also spoken on how they both felt a connection like never before and how they now couldn't wait to become husband and wife. And now, here they were, basking in the endless sun.

"Maybe we should fly to Vegas and get married now?" Aidan suggested, pouring them some drinks.

"Very tempting. Would you like to call Angela and tell her that?"

"Good point."

"Do you ever get bored of this?" Megan asked, looking around. She pointed at the crystal clear waters of the private pool, leading to the crisp white building behind her, standing tall and proud. The drapes from each window gently swaying like they were waving at the sea, also as clear as the pool. Finally her finger landed on where she lay. A large, extremely soft, lounger. Big enough for them both to lay upon and soak up the Greek sun.

"God, no! Worked my ass off to get where I am and I intend to take full advantage of the perks. With you by my side, of course." Aidan cheekily winked at her.

"I was hoping you'd say that." Megan pulled her hat over her eyes to block out the glare of the sun. She loved the hot weather, but the brightness was making her squint.

She hadn't been able to focus since the call from her Father and the news that the mother who had brought her up wasn't her mother at all. She felt more abandoned that ever. Her real mother was American, an American who she looked exactly like. She couldn't deny it. Even Aidan's reaction told her that. He'd looked as confused and furious as she had.

Fighting back more tears, she threw her hat on the floor, downed her drink, and covered her eyes once more with her arm. The emotion was getting the better of her again and she gave up and let the tears fall.

Why had her father kept this from her all these years? Did Diane even want to try and tell her she wasn't her mother, and how could either of them live with themselves, knowing what they had secretly put her through?

She had so many questions, but the thought of having to speak to any of them was not appealing.

HI. WE NEEDED A BREAK FROM LONDON. WILL BE BACK IN A WEEK. HOPE WORK'S NOT TOO STRESSFUL WITH OWEN IN CONTROL. LISTEN, ME, YOU, AND LUCY NEED TO CHAT WHEN WE'RE BACK. SAY HI TO TOM AND EVERYONE FOR US. M x

She put her phone down and let her eyes focus on the thing that mattered most. He was in the water now, splashing around with all the carelessness of a sugar-coated two-year-old. Damn, she really loved that man. He was everything she'd ever needed. With him, there was no stress about family and friends and work, there was just this moment, right here and right now, the way all breaths should be. And as Megan inhaled and exhaled, she leapt into the air, ran, and jumped. She felt the cold water on her skin and the warmth of his touch. She was free from the demons.

As free as a bird.

Chapter 47

The rain hammered against the office window. London was seeing its fair share of bad weather, putting everyone in a bad mood. Emma stared out the window, watching the drops of rain slide down. She bit her lip. The heat of her nerves consumed her body. And it wasn't the weather making her feel that way.

She was worried about Megan. Worried about what could have happened to make them perform a disappearing act. She spun around and sat in one of the chairs opposite Tom's desk. They were in his building today for a change. She leant her elbows on his desk, watching him read.

"So?"

Tom sat his phone down. He pursed his lips and shrugged. "So, what? They're having a nice time ... there's nothing to worry about."

Emma shook her head, stood up, and walked over to the window again. "I don't think you understand. Megan's message doesn't sound like her usual text voice, they disappeared without warning, and then there's that comment that we need to chat? She's been in contact with her mum, Tom." She sighed and rubbed her temples. "Something's happened. Something to do with what happened in the past."

"Don't you think you're overreacting?" Tom said, walking up behind her and massaging her shoulders.

She dialled Lucy's number. "No, I don't. I need to ring Lucy." Emma suddenly looked worried. She didn't say anything more, just looked at him in a state of near panic.

Lucy answered. "Hey, Em, what's up?"

"Lucy, it's about Megan. I think I know why they ran off so fast." There was a brief moment of silence.

"Surely it's not to do wit–"

"That's what I'm thinking," Emma said, cutting her off. "I think she might know about Katherine."

Lucy almost dropped her phone. "That's impossible. She can't know about Katherine."

"She can. But for our sake, let's just hope she doesn't know everything."

THE END(?)

Acknowledgments

There are far too many people I want to thank to list them all here, but they know who they are. The one notable exception is the person I owe the biggest amount of gratitude.

A special thank you goes to Geraint J. Coll.

HubbyG...

...you are not only my partner, my friend, my confidante, and my photographer, you are my rock. This journey would not have been possible, if not for your strength and support.

About the Author

WHAT WOULD YOU say if we told you Amy C. Beckinsale began writing One Night Forever (originally named 'Book') on her phone? Well, that is exactly how her writing career began.

After a discussion about their futures in the shop where they worked, one of Amy's friends mentioned she could see Amy writing a screenplay one day. Thinking nothing of it, Amy carried on her day, only to find herself randomly typing on her phone, about how the day was dragging on and how she found herself in a career she really didn't want to be in.

Lo and behold, she had the opening sequence of the story you have just read.

Finding she had stumbled upon something special, Amy began exploring, developing and building a world that had been stuck inside of her. She was creating the story and characters she now couldn't live without.

A third of the novel—the very first drafts—are still on her phone to this very day.

Amy has a love for acting, enjoys movies, and has an extreme addiction to Armani and Adam Ant, but not necessarily in that order.

ONE NIGHT FOREVER is Amy's debut novel, and is the first book of what is actually a trilogy; the rest of the story will be available soon.

FIND AMY ONLINE

www.amycbeckinsale.com

WWW.RHETASKEWPUBLISHING.COM